A Song Called Home

A Song Called Home

SARA ZARR

BALZER + BRAY

An Imprint of HarperCollins*Publishers*

Balzer + Bray is an imprint of HarperCollins Publishers.

A Song Called Home
Copyright © 2022 by Sara Zarr
All rights reserved. Printed in Lithuania.
No part of this book may be used or reproduced in any manner whatsoever without
written permission except in the case of brief quotations embodied in critical articles
and reviews. For information address HarperCollins Children's Books, a division of
HarperCollins Publishers, 195 Broadway, New York, NY 10007.
www.harpercollinschildrens.com

ISBN 978-0-06-304492-0

Typography by Joel Tippie
21 22 23 24 25   SB   10 9 8 7 6 5 4 3 2 1
❖
First Edition

For my mother and my sister, with love,
and in memory of Ed

PART I

We

1

IT RAINED ON THE SATURDAY they were supposed to move, a hard rain that filled the city gutters with leaves from trees in faraway neighborhoods. It blew against the windows with a ferocity that sounded more like a million tiny pebbles than raindrops. Telephone lines swayed and pigeons tumbled past on tilted wings, wherever the wind took them, as if they'd given up trying to actually fly.

"It's raining cats and dogs," Steve kept saying. "Cats and dogs. Literal cats and dogs, huh, Lulu?"

He wanted to call Lou *Lulu*. He wanted her to call him *Dad*.

"Not *literal* cats and dogs," she said.

"You know what I mean." Steve handed her a box labeled *GARAGE*. It seemed like every box Lou helped stack by the door of the apartment was labeled *GARAGE*, waiting to be loaded into Steve's pickup truck and driven the sixteen miles to his house in the suburbs. To his *GARAGE*, to be exact. Their lives before Steve, going into storage.

"We'll have to wait for the rain to stop before we can load," he continued. "Then I have a tarp I could put over everything, but I doubt it would do much good. This is some serious rain."

Lou set the box on top of two others. Just under the tucked-in top flap, the leathery cover and gold trim of Mom's photo album peeked out. The special one, with pictures of Mom and Dad when they were young.

"You're pretty strong, Lulu," Steve said, poking at her bicep.

She pressed the box flap down. "I know. In PE, I did the flexed-arm hang for nineteen seconds."

She moved away from Steve and headed back to the room she shared with Casey.

Lou was Louisa but had been Lou since she was little. Only Casey called her Lulu and only Mom called her Belle and only her dad got called Dad.

Casey was up in the top bunk, on her phone. She'd bought it with money she earned last summer, watching a baby while the parents were at work. She was very responsible and attentive for a fifteen-year-old, the parents said.

Or, she used to be. Now all she did was text and call her boyfriend, Daniel.

She'd fixed up the top bunk to be almost a whole room of her own, with a blanket hanging from the ceiling, like a curtain, for privacy, and a power strip bolted onto the railing so she could charge her phone at night, and a little orange safe with a combination lock for stuff she didn't want Lou to touch or borrow or steal.

Lou stepped onto the bottom bunk and gripped the frame of the top, and pulled the privacy blanket aside. Casey was curled around her pillows with her phone close to her face.

"Steve says we can't move our stuff until the rain stops," Lou said.

"Good."

"Yeah, good." That was Daniel, his voice spilling over out of Casey's phone. He must have heard what Lou said.

Casey spoke back to him in Spanish. Daniel had moved to the city from Peru a few years ago and now Casey could speak Spanish almost as well as her Spanish teacher, or so she claimed.

When Lou got to high school, she was going to take Spanish, too. Then she and Casey could have private conversations when Mom and Steve were being nosy. Steve, still there when Lou got to high school. That was difficult to wrap her mind around, but Mom really was going to marry him and they really were moving.

"Lulu," Casey said. "Can you, like . . ." She waved Lou away with one hand.

Lou let the blanket fall, then jumped down and went back out to the living room.

Mom was helping Steve now, looking at the stacks and checking things off a paper she'd been carrying in her hand all day. Did she even know her special album was headed to *GARAGE*?

"She still on the phone with Daniel?" Steve asked Lou.

"I don't know." She wouldn't be his spy.

When Mom had told Lou and Casey that Steve wanted to adopt them—after the wedding, of course—Lou's stomach had churned. How could Mom tell them something like that while spooning out mac and cheese, the same way she would if she was telling them about her day at work?

"Adoption is for orphans," Lou had said. Kids without parents, like in some of her favorite books. *Anne of Green Gables*. *The Silver Crown*. *Orphan Island*. Lou and Casey *had* parents. They had two parents and their dad's last name.

They also had their own apartment, and schools and teachers they liked. Lou had a best friend, Beth, and also a group of friends who did things together like trick-or-treating, who always invited one another to birthday parties, who knew Lou was scared of ladybugs and spiders but not moths, who knew she was the best in their class at reading aloud, who didn't care that she usually had dirt under her fingernails and went to church every Sunday.

Casey, too, had friends and a boyfriend and summer jobs.

"Actually," Mom had said, "adoption isn't *only* for orphans."

"Mom. Don't."

That was Casey, and when Casey said those words they had the power to stop Mom right in her tracks. It didn't work when Lou tried it.

Anyway, the point was that their lives had been *their* lives. Dad had left over two years ago now, and Mom and Lou and Casey were finally getting used to life without him in the apartment. No more walking on eggshells. No more peeking around corners, trying not to walk through a room where Dad might be drunk. No more guessing when he'd get home and what he'd be like when he did. No more wondering how long he'd be able to keep his job this time, or if he'd remember things like your birthday or your baptism or if it was a Saturday or a Tuesday.

He didn't live with them anymore, and he still drank. But also, he was still Dad. She didn't need a new one. She just wanted the one she had to be different.

Now they had to change everything, including houses, towns, friends, and then also schools next year. It was February; in the fall, Lou would have to start sixth grade in a totally new place with all-new people. And Casey would start eleventh grade the same way.

Steve already had furniture and dishes and everything a

house needed. Which was why so many boxes were marked *GARAGE*. "Until we decide what to do with it," he'd said.

We. Who was the "we" he was talking about?

Before Steve, *we* was Lou and Casey and Mom. Even before the divorce, that was true. *We* hadn't included Dad for a long time.

Now it seemed like *we* was Steve and Mom, while Lou and Casey had suddenly become a separate *us*. And Casey didn't even much seem to want to be part of it anymore.

"She's on the phone with him all the time," Steve said now, still annoyed about Daniel. He finished writing on a box with his special black marker and turned to Mom. "Maybe we should set some limits."

There was the new *we* again.

"She pays her own phone bill," Mom said. "And it's going to be her first heartbreak. Sixteen miles is the end of the world for them."

He laughed. "They're still going to see each other every day at school!"

"For now." She squeezed his arm and smiled. "Don't you remember your first crush?"

"No. You're the only girl I ever loved," he teased, and then they kissed.

Lou turned away. Steve's black marker sat on top of the boxes. She picked it up and slipped it into the pocket of her purple fleece vest. Then, while they were still kissing and hugging, she pulled the flap back on the top box, slipped the photo album out, and took it to her room before they could see.

In bed that night, after Steve was gone and Mom had tucked her in, Lou found herself talking to God. There were prayers, and then there were *prayers*. One kind of prayer was what she felt she was supposed to do: thanking God for the day, asking for forgiveness for what she did wrong, praying for help for other people. The kind you did in church was like that, saying the Lord's Prayer or praying along with Pastor Richards when he collected requests.

Then there was this kind, which happened only once in a while when Lou had a lot to say from her heart, not because thought she was supposed to.

She told God how she felt about Steve and about him and mom getting married. She asked God to maybe stop it somehow, or at least make it so they wouldn't have to move. Then, like in every kind of prayer she prayed, she asked God to make Dad stop drinking and keep Dad safe and make him . . . "Just make him better and happy."

"Shut up, Lulu," came a sleepy voice from above her.

Not God. Casey.

"I'm praying."

"Yeah, I know. Do it in your head."

And make Casey nicer, like she used to be, she added—silently. *Amen.*

2

THE RAIN CONTINUED FOR DAYS, lashing at the windows and leaving huge puddles in the alleyway. The boxes stayed stacked by the door.

Lou's jacket got soaked on her walks to and from school, and was still damp in the mornings even when she hung it right by the radiator at night.

The delay in moving gave Lou time to stow away more things in the tote bag she'd been keeping in the back of her closet. It now held: Mom's special photo album, the book of nursery rhymes Mom used to read to Lou, Casey's old stuffed lamb (Lou rescued it from the throwaway pile), and Dad's Neil Young coffee mug—which Lou'd found in a stack of dishes meant to be donated. It was stamped with a black-and-white photograph of a man with dark shaggy hair, playing guitar. Dad's favorite musician.

Twice now since taking the photo album, Lou had sat in the closet to look through it. It was full of pictures taken with real cameras and developed on real film, then stuck on adhesive pages of the album. A sheet of clear plastic went on top. The edges of the stiff album pages were getting yellowy and some of the pictures had gotten unstuck, overlapping each other, hiding a head here or a leg there.

Lou had three favorite pictures in the album. The current ranking was:

1. Dad really young, in hiking boots and a plaid shirt, standing on top of a hill somewhere woodsy. He had his hands on his hips and he looked over and past the camera, sort of to the side. There was a small guitar—a backpacking guitar, he'd told her once—slung over his shoulder, and an old metal canteen hooked on to his belt. It was from before he'd even met Mom. He was handsome, with dark hair and eyes that flashed like Casey's.

2. Mom in high school. Her hair dyed black, her face in pale pale pale makeup but with dark dark dark eyes. Bright red lips. Glaring at the camera even though Lou got the feeling that, right then, she liked having her picture taken.

3. Mom and Dad at their wedding reception in 1998, standing by a four-tiered white cake. Mom looked

down at the cake, concentrating on making an even cut with the knife she held in her hand. Dad looked right at Mom like she was the best thing in the world.

One of their wedding presents was a digital camera, and there weren't many pictures in the album after that. They were all on a computer somewhere and they never remembered to look.

Mom started to worry that they wouldn't have time to finish the move and clean the apartment out the way they were supposed to, and the landlord would charge them for another month. Whenever Mom worried about money—which was a lot—it was like part of her was away on another planet. She would say "Mm-hmm" and "Huh" when Lou told her about her day, but then she wouldn't remember anything about it.

"I'm sorry, Belle," she said the next Sunday when they were doing dishes. Casey was at Daniel's and Steve had gone home to his own house. He never spent the night. "I guess I wasn't listening. What did you say?"

"I said Beth wants to know if I can sleep over tomorrow."

"Monday?" Mom said, swirling a soapy plate under the hot water. "A school night?"

"We'll go to bed at school-night time," Lou promised.

"That's fine, I guess. With so much of your stuff in boxes anyway, it might even be easier for you to be at Beth's."

They finished washing and drying, and then Lou said, "I'm going to call Beth and tell her."

"Tell her what?"

Exasperated, Lou said, "That I can sleep over tomorrow!"

Mom pretended to hit her head with the palm of her hand. "Right!"

When Mom tucked her in that night, Casey still wasn't home. Lou didn't like it when she wasn't right there above her, the frame squeaking whenever she rolled over, the glow of her phone showing through her blankets.

At Steve's house, they were going to have their own rooms.

Mom sat on the edge of the bed and said, "Tell me two things?"

Sometimes they did this at bedtime—told each other two things on their minds, or about their days. Lou wasn't in the mood tonight, though, because she really only had one thing on her mind: "I don't want Steve to adopt me. I don't want his last name."

"I know, Belle. What made you think of that right now?"

"I'm always thinking about it."

Mom lay down next to Lou in her bunk. "You don't have to change your name or be adopted or any of it. Steve just wants you to know that he would. If you want to. And you can think about it as much as you want and even change your mind."

"I won't. I already have a dad."

Mom was quiet. Then she said in a low voice, "I know. Second thing?"

"I don't want Steve to call me Lulu. Or Belle."

There was another pause, like Mom had been hoping Lou would have moved on to a new topic for thing number two. "He's so used to hearing it from us. It's what comes out."

"I *know*, but . . ." She clamped her mouth shut. Mom should understand without a whole explanation. A name was everything. What people called you was who you felt like.

"I'm sure he's not trying to upset you, Belle."

"He can call me Louisa." The name on her birth certificate. It didn't mean anything to her.

"I'll tell him."

The way Two Things worked was that Lou was supposed to ask Mom about *her* two things. She didn't want to. Everything was about Mom lately. Mom's wedding, Mom's worries, packing for Mom's move. Yes, they were all moving—they had no choice—but it felt like *Mom's*. Lou nestled close to her now, to her warmth and her quiet voice and her smell. Except Mom smelled different. A new perfume, probably from Steve. Or a new shampoo or lotion. A new something. Lou turned her nose to clear that new smell.

A year ago, Steve was just a guy at church with blond-silver hair and a beard. He drove all the way from the suburbs to San Francisco just for church, and wore cowboy boots. No one else they knew wore cowboy boots. One time, before Mom told them she was dating Steve, Casey made fun of his belt buckle while they were walking home from church. "It's the size of a dinner plate."

"Casey," Mom had said. But then she added, laughing, "Maybe the size of a *lunch* plate."

"Does Dad have our new address yet?" Lou asked now, shy to say the word "Dad" to Mom, or to ask questions about him, because of the way Mom's body and voice tensed up and her eyes flicked to the side. But Lou needed to know.

"Well," Mom said, sounding careful. "I'm not sure, Belle, that we're going to give it to him just yet."

We. The Steve and Mom *we.*

Lou tried to form her thoughts, but they wouldn't take a shape.

"Remember . . . remember how sometimes, even after the divorce, Dad wouldn't leave when I asked him to?" Mom continued, pulling Lou in tight. "How sometimes, when he was drinking a lot, we didn't feel safe?"

She didn't like to remember those times, and Mom didn't like to talk about them. When Mom told Dad that she was marrying Steve, he'd walked up and down their block all night long, drunk, shouting and crying. Someone called the police. Mom had to go out onto the sidewalk and explain what happened and even though she didn't think Dad was going to try to get in, could they do something

~15~

about him, please? Lou and Casey had stood by their bedroom window, peeking out from behind the closed curtain, listening, sure Mom and Dad wouldn't look up at them there in the dark of their room.

"So it might be better for us to keep Steve's address private for a while," Mom said. "Until we've all gotten adjusted."

"But what if he needs us?" Lou asked. "How can he write to us? How can he find us?" Her eleventh birthday was coming up. He sometimes forgot birthdays until a week or two or more later, and what if he didn't remember until they'd already moved? He might have a card to send, or maybe even a present.

"He has Casey's phone number. And you can call him from her phone like you do sometimes. Or use email. That's how I send him things."

"Does he answer you?"

"Well, no."

"He doesn't like email. He doesn't answer his phone."

She felt Mom sigh: a big breath in, a big breath out. "I know, Belle. Later on, we'll give him the new address. After the wedding and after we're all moved in and settled down and we're all used to our new life."

A new *we*, a new *our*, a new life. A new life Lou never asked for and didn't want.

Mom laid her hand on Lou's head and murmured a bedtime prayer, while Lou imagined Dad coming to the apartment and finding it empty. Forgetting that they'd moved, that they'd gone to live with Steve. Calling her name. *Lou? Loula?* Lost and looking and looking and not finding her, not finding Casey, not finding home.

3

AFTER SCHOOL, LOU AND BETH waited inside the main doors, sheltered from the rain. It wasn't coming down as hard as it had been, but it was steady. No breaks. Though Beth's house was within walking distance, her mom was going to pick them up.

"I hate getting wet," Beth said from under the hood of her raincoat.

Lou pictured the piles of boxes by the apartment door. "We can't really move to Steve's until it stops raining."

Beth looked at her, then pulled her hood back and took a few steps outside of the doors. "Actually, I love getting wet!" she shouted, face up to the rain.

Lou joined her and said, "Me too!"

They watched the rain bounce off the sidewalks and

the street. There was no sign of Mrs. Tsai, and soon they both stepped back under the shelter. "Will the wedding be called off if it keeps raining?"

"No," Lou said. She added *unfortunately* in her head.

"How far is it to your new house, again?"

"Steve's house. I think like half an hour."

"That's not too far," Beth said.

It wasn't true and they both knew it. Not when it was a different town, a different school district, different streets, different buses, different everything. It could be ten minutes away or ten hours. No matter what, Lou couldn't go to the same school as Beth next year, or someday, the same high school.

"Maybe we'll go to the same college," Lou said gloomily.

Mrs. Tsai's blue car glided to the curb. Beth pulled her hood back up and they dashed through the rain, jumping over puddles as they went.

There were always good things and bad things about being at Beth's house.

Good things: Mrs. Tsai sometimes let them fry prawn crackers and wonton skins right at the table in an electric skillet. Beth had a trundle bed. Beth's orange tabby, Rex, would sit on Lou's chest in the early mornings and meow softly in her face. Lou liked the warm weight, the purr in Rex's voice, the feeling that she could give him something he wanted—a chin scratch or a handful of dry food dropped into the plastic bowl in the kitchen.

Bad things: Beth's little brother, Alan, was very, very annoying. And her dad, Mr. Tsai, could be serious and quiet, and Lou couldn't tell whether he liked her or not. Fathers in general made her uneasy.

Dinner for Beth and Lou and Alan that night was delivery pizza. Celebrations for the Lunar New Year were last week and Mrs. Tsai said, "I'm tired of cooking. I never want to cook again!" She and Mr. Tsai were going out to dinner. On their way out, Mrs. Tsai said something to Beth in Mandarin.

When they'd left, Alan looked at Lou. "She said be good and you better not be mean to me. And no hitting, *Beth*."

Beth scoffed. "She said *you* better be good, or else."

Alan took a bite of pizza and purposely let strings of cheese hang out of his mouth while he wiggled his head back and forth.

"Stop it." Beth's cheeks were already getting darker with irritation. When it came to Alan, her temper was very short.

"That's gross," Lou said, scrunching her nose.

"What?" he asked. "What's gross?" Cheese stretched from his mouth all the way to the table, and stuck to his face in white, greasy strips.

"You're invisible and I can't see you," Beth said. She turned to Lou. "What if you moved in with us? Or told school that you moved in with us? And used our address so you could stay at school next year?"

Lou was having trouble pretending Alan was invisible. He'd put a slice of pepperoni over each of his eyes. She worried he was going to burn himself or get spices in his eyeballs and it would be her fault somehow for not saying anything. "Alan, don't. That's dangerous."

He stretched out his arms as if he were a zombie, cheese hanging and red circles over his eyes.

"I'm telling," Beth said. Then she added something in Mandarin. Alan took the pepperoni off and gathered the strings of cheese and put it all in his mouth.

"That won't work," Lou said.

"Huh?"

"Pretending I live here, I mean." Mom and Steve had gone around and around with what to do about school and now the whole thing was settled. Mom would give them rides on her way to work for the rest of the school year. Steve, who worked an earlier shift, would pick them up in the afternoon. Then, in the fall, they'd start at their new schools in the suburbs. It was all decided. The rain would eventually stop, and the boxes would go to Steve's, and the wedding would happen, and she would move. Dad would be left somewhere behind without the new address and Lou and Beth would see each other less and less.

"I know," Beth said. "It was just a wish."

Alan had stopped eating. He was rubbing his right eye and couldn't open it.

Beth shook her head, exasperated. "Lou *told* you that would happen."

"Here," Lou said, sliding Alan's glass of ice water closer to him. "Hold this on your eye."

After dinner, in Beth's room, they did each other's hair. First Lou sat cross-legged on the trundle bed, Beth perched above her, practicing French braids on Lou.

"I wish I had your hair," Beth said. "It, like, stays." Lou's hair was a little curly, a little wavy, a little coarse. Beth could make it do almost anything.

"I wish I had *your* hair," Lou said. Beth's was always shiny and smooth, her bangs lying perfectly flat. Never a weird cowlick. Never frizzing after they'd walked home on a foggy day. Lou liked to comb it out and arrange it into a silky curtain on Beth's shoulders.

They switched places, and Lou sat on Beth's bed while Beth was on the trundle.

"What if . . ." Beth said. "What if we could trade bodies and then you could stay at our school next year?"

"But then you'd have to be at Steve's."

Beth looked over her shoulder. "I'd do that for you. So you could be where you want to be half the time."

"I would only want to be here if you were here, too, though."

Beth faced away from her again and Lou combed her hair, then pulled it back into a shiny ponytail. Beth sniffled. Her shoulders began to shake.

Lou felt like crying, too, but wouldn't. Whenever she cried in front of Dad, he'd say, "Don't *cry*, Lou. Don't *cry*."

"Don't *cry*, Beth," Lou said now, in his exact tone.

That made Beth cry harder. "I can't help it!"

"Stop," Lou said. She pushed Beth's shoulder a little, even though she knew it was mean. A sob stuck in her own throat while Beth tried to suppress hers and crawled over to the box of tissues on the bookshelf.

Lou could see now that Beth's ponytail was crooked. She had on the pajama bottoms with foxes on them, and her favorite green sweatshirt. The fox pants and green top were so familiar and comforting, and maybe it was strange to think about missing your best friend's pajamas, but Lou knew she would.

"Sorry," Lou said. "You can cry if you want."

With delicate fingers, Beth swiped a tissue under her nose. "No." She fixed her fierce eyes on Lou, and showed how she could keep them dry.

Lou kept waking up that night, checking for the sound of rain against the window and then falling back asleep. The third time she woke up, the sound had stopped and it didn't start again.

It was still dark out when Rex jumped softly onto Lou's chest. She rubbed under his chin until he stretched his neck out and closed his eyes, purring ferociously. "I have to get up," she whispered to him, then moved around until he sprung off her with a chirp of displeasure.

The bathroom was between Beth and Alan's rooms; they each had their own door to it. Lou locked both. She looked out the bathroom window. Under the closest streetlight, she could see that the ground was drying in patches.

Soon the sun would be up. Soon everything would be in Steve's truck.

After she washed her hands, she opened all the drawers in the vanity. She didn't need anything. She was just nosy and had a habit of looking. Like always, in the top drawer on Beth's side were hair ties, combs, half-used tiny tubes of toothpaste, lip balms. Lou picked out one that came in an orange ball-shaped case. It smelled fruity and said *Mango* on the label on the bottom.

The drawer on Alan's side tended to be more varied. There could be combs, half-eaten candy, more toothpaste samples, tiny toy cars, random socks, and linty action figures. This time there was a whole messy layer of small red envelopes.

They contained money, she knew, from Lunar New Year. Mrs. Tsai gave Lou one every year with five dollars in it for good luck. The envelope from this year was already packed up with her desk stuff. Eventually, she'd spend it on candy.

Imagine being Alan, though. Imagine getting piles of red envelopes and then just stuffing them in a bathroom drawer.

If each had five dollars and there were dozens, he could have hundreds of dollars. Imagine being an eight-year-old—*Alan*, with his pepperoni eyes—with hundreds of dollars.

She took one of his envelopes and tucked it in the waistband of her pajamas. She needed extra luck and Alan didn't. With the envelope in her waistband and the lip balm closed into her fist, she went back into Beth's room, where she quickly crammed both into the side zip pocket of her schoolbag. Then she got back into the trundle bed and hoped Rex would come find her one more time.

Breakfast was quiet and rushed. Mr. Tsai was already on his way to work. Mrs. Tsai drank coffee and tried to smooth down Alan's bedhead while he groggily shoveled cereal into his mouth.

"Don't eat so fast," Beth scolded. "It's disgusting."

Alan ate faster; Lou slowed down her own chewing.

Mrs. Tsai glanced toward the kitchen window and said, "You girls can walk to school. It looks like we're finally getting a beautiful day."

4

MOM WORKED A HALF DAY and Steve took a whole day off to load up the boxes, then they all drove to his house after school. Mom made Lou ride with Steve in his truck, while she and Casey followed behind in Mom's car to make sure nothing fell out. Lou sat as close to the passenger door as she could get, staring out at the ocean along the Great Highway, flat under a steely sky.

Thinking of Dad, she'd put on the R.E.M. band shirt that he'd given her two Christmases ago.

"Good band," Steve had said when they'd gotten in the truck. "I didn't know kids still knew about them."

"They don't. My dad gave me this."

That got him to change the subject.

"I bet you're excited about having your own room,"

Steve said. She felt him glance at her. "You must get sick of hearing Casey talk lovey-dovey to her boyfriend on the phone all night."

"I don't mind. I like Daniel."

They passed the back of the zoo and made a right turn, officially leaving the city. She watched Mom's car in the side mirror, wondered what they were talking about, what Casey was thinking.

"Your room is smaller than Casey's, but it has a nice big closet," Steve was saying, as if she hadn't already seen it a bunch of times. "I think once you get used to it, you'll be happy to have your own space. You're almost eleven! Too old for bunk beds and all that. You'll see how it is."

"I like the bunk bed."

Did Steve even know about the history of the bunk bed? Had Mom told him? For the longest time, Lou and Casey had slept on mattresses on the floor because they couldn't afford frames. Then one of Dad's friends, who knew carpentry and had extra wood, had helped Dad build the bunk bed. They cut the wood. They used screws and bolts and dowels to make it sturdy. Dad painted it glossy purple. It wasn't just any old bunk bed.

"Come on, Lulu—sorry, Louisa," he said. "Don't you think you're going to like *anything* at my house? The back patio? Not having to go to the laundromat when you need something clean to wear? The big TV room? You know I love that TV room."

She'd never *had* a back patio or a front yard or a lawn or anything else like that, so she didn't miss them and didn't know whether she'd like them or not. She didn't care that much about TV. It *would* be nice to have the washer and dryer right in the house, but she'd walk her dirty clothes to coin-operated laundromats the rest of her life if it meant not having to move.

On her own block, she knew which squares of the sidewalk were smooth enough for roller-skating. She knew which houses to avoid because the people in them didn't like kids hanging around. She could walk to Beth's house and the library and the store when Mom needed an ingredient for dinner or she wanted to buy a candy bar.

Lou had been to Steve's house; Mom and Casey and Lou spent a few Saturdays there over the holidays. It was the house Steve grew up in and he lived there with his mom before she died, and he didn't even know what it was like to have to leave your home forever.

The house still felt old-ladyish, with pea-green carpet and doilies everywhere. Worst of all it wasn't in the city. The sidewalks on Steve's block were one-fourth the width of city sidewalks. You could barely walk anywhere without people looking at you like you should be in a car.

"And there's that nice big stereo in the TV room, too, I bet you'll like that." Steve was still trying to convince her.

"Does it have a record player?" Lou asked.

"No, but I've got one from my old system somewhere. I

haven't fired it up in a long time, though. It needs a new needle. Why?"

"I just wondered." The tote bag from Lou's closet now held a dozen vinyl records that Dad left behind when he moved. He'd taken his stereo and most of his records, but these had been forgotten on a different shelf in the apartment. Lou took them before Mom could add them to the giveaway pile.

"Well anyway," Steve continued, "*I'm* happy you're moving in. I'm excited and blessed to have you girls in my life and to get to know you, and I'm looking forward to a time when we're all just getting along and it feels natural. You know?" She didn't answer, so he went on. "I know this part is bumpy but you can maybe be a *little* optimistic? For your mom? It's hard for her to enjoy all this when she knows you two aren't happy."

"I know" was all Lou could say. It was hard for her to enjoy it, too, knowing that Mom *was* so happy.

When Mom first told Lou and Casey that she was going to marry Steve and they'd be moving, Lou had written a letter outlining all the reasons this was a bad idea. Steve wasn't like them. He was kind of old; older than Mom at least. He didn't like the city. He never just sat still and read a book. He complained about weather and Mom *used* to always say that complaining about weather was silly. "It's like complaining about being alive."

When Lou gave the letter to Mom, somewhere deep

inside she believed it would work, that if she used the right words, she had the power to stop all this from happening. She'd even prayed about it, because Pastor Richards said that if you came to God with sincere faith, God would give you the desires of your heart.

But either Lou didn't have sincere faith or Pastor Richards had lied or God was punishing her, because Mom sort of laughed at the letter and said, "Oh, honey," and now Lou was in a truck taking the exit to Steve's house.

She reached into the pocket of her fleece vest. Felt the marker she'd taken from Steve, Beth's round ball of mango lip balm, and Alan's small red envelope.

Lou stood in her assigned room. The smaller one with the big closets.

The walls were orange. The carpet was pea-green like the rest of the house, and was mashed down in the outlines of the filing cabinets and desk that used to be there when it was Steve's home office. It smelled like dirty feet.

She went out the door of her room, turned right, and walked to the end of the hall to find the door of Casey's room closed. They'd never lived with a door between them like this. She knocked.

"Come in."

Casey's room was nearly twice the size of Lou's, with light blue walls and carpet. It had a queen bed and a white dresser with a mirror over it. Lace curtains.

"I hate it," Casey said. "It's so . . . frilly." She was standing in front of the mirror, twisting her hair—darker and curlier than Lou's—into a knot at the base of her neck. "His mother died in here."

"Steve said that? I thought she died in a hospital."

"I don't know. I just hate it."

Lou sat on the edge of the bed. It was all really happening. "I don't want this," she said. *Don't cry.* Her hands went to fists. It wasn't fair how Mom could decide to do this to them. Just *decide.*

"I don't want it either, but guess what, it doesn't matter what you want or what I want. We have literally no say." Casey dropped her hands to her sides and looked at Lou in the mirror. "We're going to live here. In this cold, moldy house with Steve and his dumb polo shirts and belt buckles, and we're going to be stuck here until we're done with high school."

Lou wanted to bury her face in the blankets and rage and sob and cry. But they didn't do that in their family. She stayed perched right on the very edge of the mattress.

"Mom said not to give Dad this address," she said. "That's not fair either."

Casey turned to her and narrowed her eyes. "Really, Lulu? You want *Dad* dropping by?"

Lou could imagine what she was thinking about. The pounding on the door. The neighbors across the courtyard peering through their curtains, asking later if everything was okay. The sound of Dad's wailing in the street. Mom putting her hands over Lou's ears as they stayed close on the bunk.

But also: Him reading to them. Building their bed. Cooking her favorite meal—roast chicken and his special buttered noodles with herbs. Playing his Neil Young records at full volume and going with them to the schoolyard to shoot baskets. The ways he was Dad between drinking and between stays in rehabs and between all the times he got fired.

Those between times never lasted very long, though.

"He needs to know where we are."

"No, he doesn't, Lou. I'm sorry, but that's the truth."

Whose side was Casey on? She was against Steve but also against Dad. Against Mom. Against what Lou wanted, at least as far as Dad was concerned. "All you care about is Daniel."

Casey shrugged. "So?"

So I want you to care about me.

Mom and Casey and Lou would drive back to the apartment tonight after dinner. They would sleep there, go to school in the morning, bring another load of stuff after school like they'd done today. A few more days like that before dismantling the bunk bed and bringing the last few things. Lou's birthday was on Friday. And then Saturday, the wedding.

* * *

With Casey in the top bunk talking low to Daniel, Lou emptied the pockets of her fleece vest onto the lower bunk. The marker, the lip balm, the red envelope, and now an acorn carved out of wood that she'd found on a shelf in Steve's living room.

She opened the lip balm and smoothed it on, the scent of mango strong. The acorn was solid and heavier than a real acorn, and felt good in her hand. She set it down and picked up the envelope so she could loosen the seal and get the money out. She planned to spend the whole five dollars on as much of the cheapest candy she could buy at the corner store tomorrow.

Only, when she got it open, it wasn't a five-dollar bill.

It was a fifty-dollar bill.

A zap of heat shot from her stomach to the tips of her fingers. She'd taken *fifty* dollars from Alan. Stolen it. She pushed it back into the envelope and pressed the seal down again. She should throw it away. Burn it. Hide it.

Her fleece vest had a hidden zipper pocket on the inside where she kept her apartment key. She put the envelope and everything else she'd stolen in it, zipped the pocket closed, and tried to put the money out of her mind.

5

TURNING ELEVEN IS A BIG deal.

Mom kept saying it, Steve kept saying it. "It's a big deal!" Even Casey got in on the whole thing, leaving "11" everywhere all week: on the fridge whiteboard, with two fingers streaked through the fog on the mirror when Lou got out of the bath, even writing the number inside Lou's school copy of *Where the Red Fern Grows*, which she and Beth were reading for a school project.

But the real big deal was the wedding. Though it would be small and not all that fancy—people from their church and a few friends, no wedding dresses or tuxedos, no bridal party—it was still the biggest thing in their lives right now. Bigger than birthdays.

A small part of Lou worried that when Friday came,

Mom wouldn't remember. And an even smaller part of her *hoped* that she wouldn't. That her birthday would not even happen. That time would somehow stop.

Time, however, did not stop. Friday morning came and Mom got into the bottom bunk with her, early, and whispered, "Happy birthday, Belle. I'm so proud of you."

"Why?" Lou asked, slipping her arm around Mom's warm, soft waist.

"Well, I'm proud of you because you're smart, and you're kind. You're a good girl. You love God."

Was she really a good girl? Did she love God enough? She wasn't sure. She knew all the answers in Sunday school; she knew the right things to say. She understood what she was *supposed* to think and believe, but that wasn't the same thing as thinking and believing those things. And Mom wouldn't say she was a good girl if she knew she'd stolen fifty dollars from Alan, even if it was mostly an accident. And the lip balm, the marker, the acorn.

"Tomorrow is our last morning here," Mom continued. "On Sunday we'll wake up in Steve's house. A new family."

Lou rolled over, away from Mom. She didn't need to be reminded.

Maybe Dad would call today, either on the house phone or on Casey's phone, to wish her a happy birthday. And then he'd say, *Lou, my Loula-Belle, I've got it all figured out. You haven't heard from me in so long because I've been working on fixing things. I quit drinking. I got a good job and an apartment in your school district and you can live with me half the time and not change schools and . . .*

No, even better would be: *I got a job and I can take over the apartment after the wedding. You'll live with me half the time and we'll keep your room. We'll keep your bunk bed.*

Mom smoothed her hair back, "Give it a chance. It will get better with time."

"No it won't."

"Oh, Belle," Mom sighed. "Come on." She kissed Lou on the temple. "I'm going to make you cinnamon toast and bacon. I didn't pack the big pan yet because I knew I wanted to use it on this special day."

The bunk above them squeaked. "Save some for me," Casey said sleepily.

Mom and Casey had conspired to get Lou a new jacket for her birthday. Denim with a wooly lined collar, perfect for the year-round coastal chill and fog. It fit over her fleece vest so she could wear both if she wanted. It had pockets for her hands and inside pockets and a button pocket on the chest.

"I love it."

"You thought we were going to forget," Casey joked, taking a bite of her bacon. "We've been planning this since Christmas. I've been saving a little of every babysitting job."

"Really?"

"I mean, yeah."

That made Lou feel special. And she really did love the jacket. She loved the cinnamon toast and bacon, and her mother's striped robe, and how Casey's eyes looked the mornings after she was too lazy to take her makeup off before bed. Smudged and wild, like the old picture of Mom.

At school, Beth surprised Lou by bringing cupcakes for the class. Lou could tell Beth had made them herself: white cake mix and pink frosting with silver candy balls sprinkled on top a little messily. Their teacher, Ms. Tom, insisted they wait until after lunch to eat them, and they were worth the wait.

Beth also gave her a homemade coupon book for sleep-overs at Beth's, and a promise from Mrs. Tsai that she'd drive Beth to Steve's to visit Lou at least once a month when they were going to separate schools. "We just have to plan ahead so she can put it on her calendar," Beth said.

Once a month. From almost every day to not even every week. She could barely imagine it.

They were sitting in the school library now, supposedly doing language arts worksheets. Lou had to leave soon to help take another load of stuff to the house.

"Did you explain to your parents about the wedding?" Lou asked. "Like not to dress up too much and it will be really Christian-y and the reception is just a potluck?"

"Yeah. My cousin goes to a church like that. We're used to it."

Beth's parents grew up Buddhist but now they didn't really do anything religious. Lou felt embarrassed sometimes at how churchy Mom could get, even though Beth never said anything about it, and even though she knew she shouldn't be. Being embarrassed about Jesus was what the disciple Peter did that time the rooster crowed three times, her Sunday school teacher said. A betrayal.

"I don't want to be at the wedding," Lou blurted. "I don't want to move. I wish . . ." *Don't cry.*

Beth grabbed her hand. "I know." Her chin quivered and Lou willed her to not cry, either. "At least you get to stay through this school year. Let's not think about after that."

Steve took them out to dinner. It was a combination Lou's-birthday-and-wedding-eve dinner at Giorgio's, which had always been Casey and Lou's favorite place except not tonight because Casey hadn't been allowed to invite Daniel, and also because Giorgio's was where they used to go with *Dad*. Why couldn't Steve have picked some place they didn't care about?

They got a pitcher of root beer. Steve poured everyone a cup and held his up for a toast.

"To Ann and her awesome girls," he said. "For brightening my life. I gave up a long time ago on ever finding true love. Then I spent a decade taking care of my mother. I just never thought . . ."

He looked down and cleared his throat, pressed his lips

together. Steve was a *crier?* Lou shifted her gaze to Casey, who was stone-faced.

"Anyway, I'm happy." He leaned over and kissed Mom and they all touched their glasses together like they were supposed to. "And of course, to Lulu—sorry, Louisa—on her birthday!" They clinked again.

Their pizzas came. During dinner, Casey kept looking down, obviously texting under the table. The third or fourth time she did it, Mom said, "Casey."

Casey sighed. "I don't know why Daniel couldn't come tonight."

"Because this night is for family," Mom said.

Casey pointed at Steve. "He's not family."

"Hey," Steve protested.

"Maybe if we'd known you for more than five minutes . . ."

"Casey!" Mom said again.

Steve reached a hand to Mom's arm. "It's okay."

When he spoke, he sounded like someone whose feelings had been hurt but was trying act like they weren't.

"I know it was fast," Steve said to Casey. "When it's right, it's right, and you just know. God's timing is perfect. Might not make any sense to us, but we're only human."

Steve had proposed on their third date. Mom and Steve and Pastor Richards all thought it was a great idea, that they were too old for a long engagement and there was no time to waste.

That was the part of it they'd been talking about for the

last few months. The love, the timing, how it was all God's plan. The part they didn't talk about so much was that Mom had trouble paying the rent and buying groceries, even though their rent was so much lower than it could be because Mom had been in that apartment for over twenty years, even before she married Dad. And Dad couldn't pay the child support he was supposed to. Mom worked hard but San Francisco was so expensive and she was only one person. And then Steve came along, and not only did he love Mom, he also had a house that was paid for and a job and health insurance.

Their money problems felt like something everyone knew—Pastor Richards, everyone at church, Lou's friends. They'd had bags of hand-me-down clothes appear at their front door and sometimes one of Mom's friends would take them grocery shopping "just because."

Mom and Steve were really in love, probably, and maybe it really was God's plan. But God's timing was also good in that Mom marrying Steve meant them being saved from unpaid bills.

Casey reached for the last piece of sausage and mushroom pizza.

Steve said, "Were you going to ask if anyone else wanted that?"

Lou looked at Mom. Casey loved pizza the most, and sausage and mushroom was her favorite. They both knew that. Mom avoided her eyes.

"Do you want it, Steve?" Casey asked, sticky sweet.

"Maybe. But, I'm going to let you have it."

It felt like he was being nice, maybe, or maybe Lou missed something. All she knew was Casey didn't like it. She stood up and put her phone in her jacket pocket, took the piece of pizza and a couple of paper napkins, and turned to walk out.

"Where do you think you're going?" Steve asked.

"Home."

"I don't think so. This isn't about you. It's Lou's birthday."

"*Louisa,*" Lou said.

"Steve," Mom said, placing her hand over his. "Let her go."

Casey turned around and said, "You want to come, Lulu?"

Without even checking Mom's face again, Lou stood up and took her birthday jacket off the back of the chair, and followed Casey out.

6

THE EVENING WAS FEBRUARY-DARK, AND the air still carried the feeling of the rain from earlier in the week. Lou slid into her new jacket to ward off the chill and damp.

She had to walk fast to keep up with Casey, who zigzagged into the darkest parts of the block as if running away from Mom and Steve. It reminded her of one time before Dad left—more than one time—when he was drunk and yelling in the apartment. Not really at Mom and not at Lou and Casey. Just yelling at nothing. Also making big noises as he ran into furniture, fell on the hardwood floor while Casey and Lou stayed in their room until Casey said, "Let's go," and took Lou down the stairs and out the door and around the block.

Was there really anything to run from now? Steve hadn't

yelled. He and Mom were just sitting there.

Casey had her phone to her ear, talking partly in English and partly in Spanish, crying a little. She kept her back to Lou, almost like she'd forgotten she was even there.

They were over thirty blocks from their apartment. They had either a long walk in the dark ahead or a bus ride. They zagged and zigged, and Casey got more calm as she talked to Daniel. She said goodbye and stopped walking. She turned around, and Lou knew she hadn't been forgotten.

"Sorry to ruin your birthday, Lulu."

"You didn't."

Casey held the phone out. "You want to call Dad?"

Lou put her hands deep in the pockets of her new jacket. "He never answers."

"You can leave him a message. Tell him he should have remembered your birthday."

She shook her head. That's not how it was supposed to work.

"Fine, I'll do it." Casey tapped her phone a few times, then put it to her ear again; Lou held her breath and watched. Someone answered and Casey looked confused. "Who's this? . . . I'm looking for Patrick Emerson. . . . Since when? . . . Oh. Well can you give him a message? That he forgot his daughter's birthday. Thanks."

She lowered her phone.

"Who was it?" Lou asked, thrilled at Casey's bravery.

"No idea. A stranger. Dad sold his phone or his phone

number or he's, like, *renting* out his phone and number? Or someone's holding it for him or some stupid thing. It's so Dad."

They got to a bus shelter.

Lou watched Casey stare into her phone. Her dark hair frizzed around her face and the chill had put a pinkish-red into her cheeks, made her eyes sharp and bright. Lou loved Casey's looks. Sometimes Casey stood in front of their bedroom mirror and detailed everything she didn't like about herself. She would squeeze the skin on her upper arms and make a face, or wear two sports bras to try to mash her chest down. Lou loved not only how Casey looked but also how she wasn't afraid of people and how she walked in wide steps, daring the world to stop her, loved the rasp in her voice and the dozen ways she wore her blue scarf.

"Stop staring at me." Casey stood up and leaned into the street, watching for the bus. "Mom keeps texting," she said, glancing at her phone again. "If we tell her where we are, they'll pick us up. Do you want them to pick us up? It's your birthday."

"No." Getting a ride from Steve felt like giving up. He maybe didn't deserve to be walked out on, though. Lou bit her lip. "But tell them we're okay."

The fifty dollars was still zipped into Lou's fleece, which was under her denim jacket. If they spent it on getting home, they wouldn't need Steve and they wouldn't have to wait for a bus or walk in the cold, *and* they could even beat Steve and Mom back to the apartment.

"What if you called a cab?" Lou asked.

"And pay how?" Casey didn't have anything like Uber on her phone because she didn't have any bank cards or accounts and Mom didn't think she should.

"I have some money."

Casey laughed. "You don't know how much a cab costs, do you."

"I have fifty dollars."

Casey laughed again, then got serious. "Wait. Really?"

Lou showed her the money.

"Where'd you get that?"

"Mrs. Tsai." Maybe it was true. Maybe it had come from Mrs. Tsai before it went to Alan. "Don't tell Mom," she added, expanding on the lie. "I know she doesn't like it when people feel sorry for us but I think Beth's mom does. Feel sorry for us."

"I don't like it either," Casey said. "But fifty bucks is fifty bucks."

From the back of the cab, Casey texted Mom and told her they were on a bus. Mom wrote back that she and Steve were going to go to a coffee shop to talk and then he'd just drop her off later and not come in. *He's sorry, though*, Mom wrote. *And I hope you are, too. We're glad you're safe.*

Then Casey started sniffling and facing the window

and lifting her sleeve to wipe her eyes every ten seconds. "Sorry," she mumbled. Dad had used his *Don't cry* on her, too, Lou knew.

The ride cost twenty-seven dollars, including a tip. The driver was not happy about getting a fifty-dollar bill. He gave Casey the change, then Casey gave some back to him and handed the rest to Lou. Their apartment had a gate and then a courtyard and then twelve units—three floors, four apartments on each floor. Theirs was on the second. Casey opened the gate and they trudged, cold and tired, up the stairs.

There was something leaning against their door.

"What's that?" Casey asked.

"I don't know." They got closer. It was a guitar case.

Lou reached for it; Casey pulled her hand back and said, "Don't."

"But it's for me. Look." There was small index card tucked under the handle of the case. All it said was:

LOUISA EMERSON

"Weird." Casey looked around the apartment courtyard, as if expecting someone to appear from the shadows. "Get the door."

Lou retrieved her apartment key from her special inside pocket and let them in. Casey handed Lou the card with her name on it, carried the case to their room, and laid it out on the lower bunk. Before Lou could say she wanted to do it herself, Casey flipped up the brass clasps and opened the lid.

Lou laughed.

"What's so funny?"

"I don't know. It's a guitar."

Lou had half expected there to be something else inside, like maybe old clothes or books or something. City life could be strange. You'd go out in the morning and find a pile of dolls on the sidewalk, or someone would put a TV on the curb with a sign that said *FREE* or ring apartment doorbells until someone buzzed the gate open and announce they'd found a bike with one wheel missing and did you know whose it was?

But this really did have her name on it and it really was a guitar. A nice one, too, not something from the trash, discarded. It had all its strings. It didn't smell like smoke or beer.

Casey started to lift it out of the case; Lou said, "No, I want to."

"Be careful."

She lifted it partway out. The wood was light in the front, darker in the back.

"Did you buy yourself a guitar with your riches?" Casey teased.

"No." Lying on the green velvet lining of the case was an envelope. Lou passed the guitar to Casey and picked up the envelope; she removed the card that was inside. Balloons on the front and *Happy Birthday* inside. But no other note, no signature.

"I guess it's from Dad?" Casey said.

"I don't know."

"Did you *ask* for a guitar?"

"No."

"Like, *ever?*"

She shook her head. She hadn't even talked to Dad since Christmas Eve, when he'd taken Lou and Casey downtown to ice-skate. That was a good night. He was sober and had money to buy them hot chocolate on top of the skate rentals and everything, and though the night was a little foggy they could see the lights of the Bay Bridge shining through. He rode the bus with them back to the apartment and hugged them goodbye. Lou felt hope that night. Like God was really doing something, finally, about Dad and his drinking, and maybe it was a new beginning.

Then he called Casey's phone on New Year's Day, drunk. He told her she was a traitor without explaining why. Casey hung up on him and didn't answer when he kept calling back. Ten times, twenty times. Thirty-two times total, before he stopped. That was a bad day.

Now, Casey strummed the guitar strings lightly and looked at Lou. "It has to be him, though. Right? Like, who else would it be?"

"It's not his handwriting," Lou said, looking at the *LOUISA EMERSON* card that had been under the handle. "Wouldn't he put Loula or Lulu on it?"

"He probably didn't deliver it himself. That's probably

just a delivery company or something. They would probably use your full name." She strummed again. "This is actually in tune, I think."

She handed the guitar back to Lou, who could barely wrap her arms around it. It immediately slipped down to her knees.

"Sit down," Casey said. "Put it in your lap."

Holding it while sitting was easier. Lou had small hands, though, and it all seemed made for someone a lot bigger. She strummed a little. Touched the silver-colored pegs. Tapped the wood in different spots and listened to the hollow sound.

Casey started to sing softly, jokingly, the "Happy Birthday" song.

Lou strummed along tunelessly until they were both laughing.

They fell quiet when they heard the apartment door open.

Mom came straight to their room. "Girls, we need to talk about what—where did you get that?"

"Someone left it at the door," Casey said. "For Lou. It's from Dad."

Lou handed Mom both the cards. The one with her name on it, and the blank birthday card from inside. Mom turned them over in her hand, looking for some kind of explanation.

"It came like this? No other notes or anything?"

"Doesn't it seem like something Dad would do?" Casey asked. "Some stranger answered his phone earlier tonight. He probably swapped it for this because he felt guilty. I don't know."

"It does seem a little like . . . his way of doing things." Mom handed the cards back to Lou. "Do you want to keep it, honey? We can ask him to return it if you don't think you'll use it. We can get you something you really want."

"No." Lou hugged the guitar tighter against her lap. "I want it. I can learn to play." She could learn to play like Neil Young or like R.E.M. or U2 or Bob Dylan or any of the other records from Dad's collection.

"There are probably videos and stuff she can watch online," Casey said to Mom. "At least to get the basics."

"It looks awfully big for you, Belle."

"I'm still growing."

Mom gave a tired laugh. She tucked a piece of her brown-gray hair behind her ear. "True." She looked at Casey and sighed. "About tonight. I wish you hadn't—"

"I know," Casey said quickly. "I'm sorry."

"It was such a silly thing. A slice of pizza."

"I know," Casey said again. She pressed her hands over her ears. "I know I know I know. I'm sorry I'm sorry."

"You'll tell Steve that?"

Casey nodded. Mom's eyes got soft as she stood there, watching them. "I love you two. As much as ever. A lot of things will be changing, but not that."

For the third time that night, Casey cried. She dropped her hands from her ears and let Mom hug her. Lou watched as she clutched on to Mom's sweater with big sobs, like a little girl. Lou wanted to just cry that way. She wrapped her own arms around the guitar instead.

PART II

The Wedding

1

Lou woke up in the night.

The apartment was normal-quiet: the faint sound of a neighbor's TV, an occasional car driving by, the pinging of the radiator. She could see well enough to get out of bed without turning on a light; it never got totally dark in the city. A body-like shadowy shape leaning against the wall startled her until she remembered what it was: the guitar case.

She walked over the braided rug—one of the last things left to pack—until her feet hit the cold wood of the hallway. It was another several steps to the one board by the hall closet that always squeaked. In that closet, they'd had coats, old clothes ready to give away, Mom and Dad's college papers and pictures, and the emergency kit in case of an earthquake. It was all gone to Steve's now, except for two packs of ramen and a gallon of water alone in the dusty corner.

Lou turned, placed one foot carefully in front of the other, trying to stay in a straight line down the hall to the living room. It was empty of furniture, empty of boxes. Only the big maroon-and-beige rug remained; they were going to leave it behind for whoever lived there next.

How could someone else live here?

The apartment had been Mom's since the end of college. She'd lived there with a roommate after that, and then Dad, and then Casey, and then Lou.

"It's *ours*," Lou whispered to herself fiercely.

But even as she heard her voice bounce around the empty room, she knew it already wasn't true. In one week it went from home for her and Casey's whole life to just another apartment for rent.

Don't cry.

Lou walked over to the bay window where they put the Christmas tree every year. Behind her, French doors led from the living room to Mom's room. It was actually supposed to be a dining room but they hadn't used it as a dining room since Lou was born and the apartment's one bedroom became hers and Casey's. Mom was asleep now behind those doors, a sliver of the bed visible between the green flowered curtains Mom used for privacy. That bed was going to go onto the curb with a *FREE* sign soon.

Lou ached all over. It hurt so, so much.

She crept into the kitchen and shivered in the now-empty space where the yellow table used to be. Another thing Dad had fixed up and painted. He liked cheerful colors. The purple bunk bed, the yellow table, the red coatrack that was also in Steve's garage. The yellow table had been where Mom made meatballs for spaghetti, where Dad served Lou's favorite roasted chicken, where Mom cut out biscuits with a water glass from a sheet of dough.

Don't cry.

"What are you doing?"

Startled, Lou turned. Casey stood in the kitchen door with her arms folded across her chest, hunched against the chilly room where the radiator heat didn't reach.

"Nothing," Lou said. "Just . . ." Wasn't it obvious? "Just saying goodbye."

8

THEY GOT TO THE CHURCH early and the first thing that happened was that Pastor Richards said, "You must be so excited!" And then the second thing was that Sharl Yang, who was helping put out programs, said, "It's the soon-to-be-Cook sisters!" meaning Lou and Casey. Cook was Steve's last name.

"Nope," Casey said with an edge in her voice. "We're staying Emersons." She took Lou's arm. "Let's go outside and wait for Daniel."

They had on dresses. Lou's Easter dress from last year still fit and she still liked it, a simple flowered T-shirt dress that she wore with a cardigan. Casey had waited until the last minute to find something at Goodwill. It was light blue with a flared skirt and a little bow at the waist. She tugged at the bow now. "I hate this stupid thing."

"I think you look pretty," Lou said.

"It's not me."

Daniel appeared from around the corner and Casey went running to meet him, the soles of her good sandals clacking on the sidewalk. Daniel had a dress shirt and tie on.

Lou went back inside, hoping Beth would get there soon so she'd have someone to run to, too.

The church—its dark wooden pews and stained glass and squeaky floors—was almost an extension of the apartment in the way that it felt like home to Lou. For as far back as she could remember, she'd been coming here with Mom and Casey. Every Sunday morning, and once in a while, other days, too.

Dad wasn't a part of that, didn't come with them except to Casey's baptism when she was nine and then Lou's, and sometimes on holidays. He didn't believe in church, or in God, really. Mom believed in all of it, and brought Lou and Casey up to believe. That was part of what made them the *we* that they'd been, and kept Dad on the outside of it. Pastor Richards and others, including Lou herself, had prayed out loud in this room for Dad to stop drinking and to be able to keep jobs and to believe in Jesus.

When you prayed and prayed and prayed for help and nothing changed, did you just give up? Maybe that was something adults knew. When to keep trying, and when to give up and move on. Like Mom was doing.

Some of Mom's church friends had decorated the small sanctuary with candles and colorful flowers. Light filtered in through the stained glass, and the pews glowed from a recent polish.

"It looks nice, huh?"

Steve had come in and now stood a few feet away from her. He had on new-looking jeans with sharp creases, his cowboy boots, a shirt and tie and jacket. No giant belt buckle today.

"Mm-hmm."

He kept talking and Lou tried to listen, but she felt herself drifting away. It was a thing that happened sometimes, a feeling like part of her was going inside a silent, cozy bubble while another part of her still walked and talked and smiled and nodded. She could make anything she didn't want to listen to stay outside the bubble, muted and blurry, while she stayed safe *in*side it.

She didn't need it that much anymore. But that morning, during her bath, thinking about leaving the apartment forever and Beth and school and everything changing, she went into it. She didn't come out until Casey knocked on the door and said, "Hurry up! Other people live here."

What pulled her out now was Mom's arm around her shoulders. "How you doing, Belle?"

"Fine."

Mom looked beautiful and happy in a cream-colored dress with her dark hair down around her shoulders. She might have been even happier if some of her other family could have come, but all of them were back in Kansas and Ohio. Some of them hadn't talked to Mom in years; others had sent cards. None of them could afford to fly across the country to celebrate a second marriage, she said. On Steve's side, his father had died long before his mother. He had one brother, Mom told her once, but Lou hadn't heard anything about him coming to the wedding.

So Lou and Casey were the family.

"Beth and Alan and their parents just got here, if you want to go say hi."

Lou immediately peeled out of Mom's arms and went over to where the Tsais were sliding into a back pew. Beth had on a pink dress and denim jacket. They hugged and told each other they looked pretty.

Alan said, "Congratulations," like it was something he'd been told to say.

"Thanks." Had he noticed the fifty dollars missing from his drawer?

Casey and Daniel came back in. Daniel offered Lou a stick of cinnamon gum.

"She can't be chewing gum while she's sitting up there in the front row," Casey said, giving him a playful nudge.

He shrugged and gave it to Lou anyway. "Put it in your pocket for later. It's a present."

Casey rolled her eyes and clung to him. She always acted a little funny around him compared to how she was when it was just her and Lou. "Let's go sit down before anyone else tries to congratulate us," she said.

If it was someone else's wedding, Lou probably would have loved it.

Barbara Pearson, who played the piano every Sunday, played the hymn "All Things Bright and Beautiful" while Mom walked down the aisle, escorted by Pastor Richards. Steve stood up front, watching Mom and glancing at Lou and Casey in the front pew, and back to Mom, and Lou felt she was in a dream, that this could not really be happening.

She went deep inside the bubble.

The rest of the ceremony was a muted blur. Like trying to see outside through a rain-streaked window. In moments, the window cleared and the wedding came into focus: Pastor Richards laughing as he went from being Mom's escort to the person performing the wedding, saying some words about love. Mom and Steve facing each other and exchanging vows, then Steve facing Lou and Casey to say something that Lou didn't hear. The wedding guests laughed. A ring. A kiss. She'd missed them saying "I do."

It all came back into focus when a woman Lou hadn't ever seen before at church or anywhere else replaced Barbara at the piano, and a man stood next to it with a guitar, and they sang a duet.

Light—tinted slightly pink by the stained glass—fell right onto the woman's face. She had short, light hair and creamy skin. Full lips and a singing voice deeper than Mom's. The man looked Asian or maybe even Latin, like Daniel. Muscular. The edge of a tattoo peeked out from his rolled-up shirt cuff as he strummed.

They sang in harmony one of the prettiest songs Lou had ever heard. Slow and sweet but also a little bit sad. It expressed something Lou was feeling but couldn't say. For those few minutes, the wedding wasn't muted or blurry. It was clear and warm and Lou didn't feel alone anymore.

Near the end, the woman at the piano caught Lou's eye and smiled before looking back down at her hands.

"Who are they?" Lou whispered to Casey.

9

THEY WERE MARCUS AND SHANNON Merritt-Mendoza. Between the wedding and reception, they came over to Lou and Casey and Daniel and introduced themselves while people were mingling and hugging around them.

"We're Steve's neighbors," Shannon said. "We've been hearing a lot about you guys from Steve and your mom. We're excited you're coming to the block."

They knew Mom? Lou looked to Casey to see what to think. Could they be trusted? They were friends of Steve's, after all. Casey looked uncertain, and her hand went to Daniel's again, as if for protection.

Then Marcus said the thing no one had said to them all day: "It must be hard for you two. So many changes." He said it right to Lou and had a listening expression on his face, eyebrows up, head tilted.

"Yeah," she answered, and noticed Casey let go of Daniel's hand. "It is kind of hard."

"We don't want to move," Casey said bluntly.

We. The new *we* of only the two of them.

"I don't blame you," Marcus said.

"Pacifica takes a little getting used to," Shannon added. "We moved out there about four years ago and we still miss living right in the city."

"You lived in the city?" Casey asked. "Where?"

"West Portal most recently. Before that, Glen Park. Before that . . ." She looked to Marcus. "Where we were before Glen Park, babe?"

"Ninth and Irving!" He said it like, *How could you forget?*

"I love that neighborhood," Casey said.

Lou watched them talk. Casey was so grown up, speaking as if she was the same age as them. When did Casey ever go to Irving Street? It was all the way on other side of the park.

Shannon looked down at her and smiled. "There's good stuff in the 'burbs, too."

Casey laughed through her nose. "Like what?" She weaved her fingers through Daniel's again.

Then Steve was standing there, interrupting them with a clap on Marcus's shoulder.

"Hey," Marcus said, turning to Steve. "Congratulations, man. So happy for you." They shook hands and slapped each other's shoulders some more.

"The music was beautiful. Perfect. Thank you so much."

"Our pleasure."

"Did you ask them about babysitting yet?" Steve asked.

Babysitting? Lou thought. She and Casey were way too old for a babysitter!

Shannon leaned toward Lou and Casey. "We have three kids. Small ones. Steve said you guys might be available to make a little money here and there, but no pressure. Personally, I hated babysitting when I was your age, so I get it if you don't want to."

"I don't hate it," Casey said. And she especially didn't hate making money, Lou knew.

"How about you?" Shannon asked Lou.

Oh, they wanted *her* to babysit? "I haven't done that much of it. . . ." She helped in the church nursery sometimes. She could change diapers and hold a crying baby, play make-believe games with toddlers.

Marcus said, "We were thinking of both of you together. With three kids, as many hands as possible is the name of the game."

"*Any*way," Shannon said, "don't worry about it right now. We didn't come talk to you just to rope you into watching our kids. I wasn't even going to ask until you're all moved in and settled."

But Steve opened his big mouth, Lou thought. *He interrupts. He barges in. He helps himself to your conversations and your life.*

Speaking of Steve's big mouth, he now cupped his hands

around it and yelled at everyone that it was time to go down to the basement and "get your grub on." Lou caught Casey's eye and they snickered.

"We'll see you down there," Marcus said, and he took Shannon's hand.

After that, there were only a few people left in the sanctuary. Pastor Richards was picking up programs that had been left behind. Sharl Yang had loops of microphone cords hanging over her shoulder while Daniel helped her put the sound equipment away. Mom had already gone downstairs.

Steve stepped between Lou and Casey and put his arms around them, squeezed them both to his sides. "Casey. Louisa. I'm so happy right now," he said in a low voice. "I feel like I've been waiting my whole life to have a real family."

Lou checked Casey's face. It was steely, but Lou felt a little hitch in her feelings. Steve sounded honest right then, like he was saying something true and personal. He'd had a mom and a dad and a brother, but they weren't here now and maybe there was something about them that hadn't ever felt like a real family.

"Come on, Lou," Casey said. "Let's get some food." She grabbed Lou's arm and pulled her away, picking up her messenger bag from where she'd left it in a back pew. When they were going down the carpeted stairs, she said, "I'm going to change into jeans and stuff. Then I want to eat, then I want to get out of here. Me and Daniel are going to go hang out in the park. Want to come?"

"How are you going to get to Steve's later?"

"We'll be back in time to get a ride. You know how receptions are. They'll be here for hours."

Lou didn't have clothes to change into, and sometimes when Casey invited her to do stuff with her and Daniel it was only to be nice. What they really wanted was to be alone, and Lou would find herself sitting on a swing or hanging from the monkey bars with no one to talk to or play with while Casey and Daniel huddled close on a bench, kissing and whispering and in a world Lou wasn't a part of, their own *we*.

"I'll probably stay here."

Casey stopped on the stairs and scrunched her nose. "Really?"

"Yeah?" Was it the wrong choice?

"Okay," Casey said with a shrug. "Up to you." She trotted the rest of the way down the stairs and disappeared into the restroom.

Lou continued, cautiously, into the fellowship hall. Music played on wireless speakers someone had brought, and wedding guests were lined up in front of chafing dishes and bowls and casseroles. Mom's friends—the same ones who had decorated the sanctuary—had also made all the food. There was glazed ham, cheesy potatoes, macaroni salad, green salad, white rolls. Also a platter of lumpia and fried rice, and Beth's family had brought a pink box of

Chinese almond cookies. Instead of a towering layer cake, there was a white sheet cake from the Safeway bakery.

"Things are a little different for a second wedding," Mom had said last month, when she was going over her plans. "I want it to feel more like a church potluck than a wedding."

It did feel like that, and even though Lou hated the whole idea of the wedding and what it meant, at least there was the comfort of the church fellowship hall and the folding tables, the spread of familiar food and the same paper napkins they used every Sunday at coffee hour.

She looked around for Beth and couldn't find her or any of the Tsais. She looked again, slower this time, making sure to see each person at every small, round table. They weren't there.

"Ooh, who made lumpia?" Casey asked, hovering over the table next to Lou in her jeans and a lime-green sweater—her current favorite thrift-shop find—and her blue scarf twisted around her neck. She took two lumpia and scooped rice next to them, and rounded out her meal with macaroni salad and a roll balanced on top.

Lou was slower to decide which food in what order and how much to put on her plate. Church potlucks were comforting but also tricky because not everyone is a good cook. And she didn't like too many things touching. She only liked potatoes if they weren't undercooked. She only liked macaroni salad if it didn't have anything weird like olives or bell peppers. She only liked green salad if there was ranch. After examining everything carefully, she took lumpia, rice, ham, and two almond cookies and arranged it all so each thing had its own quadrant.

She scanned the room one more time for Beth.

An arm waved her over; it was Shannon Merritt-Mendoza's. She sat at a table with only Marcus. Lou walked with her plate. "Hi again," Shannon said, pulling out a chair. "We don't really know anyone here except Steve. And now you! Want to sit with us? If you need to be with your family, that's okay, but you looked kind of lost over there."

Lou sat, glanced over her shoulder. "I was looking for my friend Beth, but I think she left."

"Give me your honest review of the lumpia," Marcus said. "It's my mom's recipe and I haven't made it in years." His sleeves were rolled up now and she could see his tattoos: a cross with a snake around it on one arm, and an arrow wrapped in roses on the other.

"Is your mom Filipino?" she asked him.

He laughed. "Yeah, she is. So's my dad."

She felt herself blush, like she'd asked a stupid question and he and Shannon would probably joke about it later. "Sorry," she muttered down at her plate.

"Oh, hey," he said, tilting his head so he could see her face. "I wasn't laughing at you. I like that you're double-checking my lumpia cred."

"Go ahead," Shannon said, "try it."

She bit into the crisp fried roll, and the savory filling hit her senses with layers of spices and vegetables and meat.

"It's good," she said before she'd chewed it all, then covered her mouth and said "Sorry" for talking with her mouth full, and then "Sorry" again because she did it again!

"Don't worry," Shannon said. "Manners are just loose suggestions. They've mostly gone out the window at our house."

They ate for a while, and Shannon talked a bit about her kids, who were being watched by grandparents today. As she did, Lou studied her mouth. She had on red lipstick. It wasn't shiny and it stayed perfectly in place while she talked and ate. Mom sometimes got lipstick on her teeth or outside the lines and seemed like she could never pick quite the right color.

Shannon raised her eyebrows and Lou felt suddenly shy, aware she'd been staring and that Shannon knew it, too. She made her eyes go anywhere else. Marcus's guitar leaned against one of the other chairs at their table.

"I play guitar," she blurted.

"Oh yeah?" Marcus said. "We should jam some time."

"Well . . . I mean, I *have* a guitar. I just got it for my birthday. I don't know how to play yet."

"Marcus can teach you some chords," Shannon said. She looked at Marcus and he said, "Absolutely." He finished chewing and wiped his mouth to say more, when Lou saw, over his shoulder, an uninvited wedding guest walk into the fellowship hall.

Dad.

10

LOU ONLY NEEDED ONE FAST glance at him to know Dad was drunk.

"Drunk." She hated that word but also hated all the nicer ways to say it that Mom used: *not sober, tipsy, had been drinking, wasn't himself, not in his right mind, feeling sick.*

Drunk was drunk was drunk.

Dad used that word, but he said it like, *I'm a drunk.* Not *I'm drunk* but *I'm a drunk.* Saying: It's *who* I am. Saying: It's *what* I am. Saying it like it was *all* he was.

He hovered in the doorway of the fellowship hall, loose-kneed, swaying slightly. Shannon followed Lou's eyes and turned around, saw Dad, looked back at Lou. She leaned toward Marcus and whispered something in his ear. Lou couldn't hear it because she was back in her bubble, catching sounds here and there, while people blurred and unblurred.

Marcus unblurred. He got up. He walked purposefully toward Dad. One part of Lou wanted to find Mom, go to her, see if she had seen yet. Keep her from seeing. But she couldn't take her eyes off Marcus as he shook Dad's hand and at the same time put his other hand on Dad's shoulder to steer him back out. The way Marcus did it looked friendly but also firm.

But Dad was firm, too. He glanced back over his shoulder, pushed Marcus's arm off of him. And he said in a loud voice: "Where are my girls? I just want to see my *girls*."

"Sweetie? Do you want me to get your mom?" Shannon's voice came from the blurry edges.

Others had noticed what was happening. Some people at church had met Dad before, or "encountered" him, as Mom would put it. On the street, around the church, at Lou's baptism when he showed up, exactly like this, swaying and loose and shouting. Lou hoped Beth and her family really had left.

Shannon didn't have to get Mom, because Mom and Steve were already on the move toward Dad and Marcus, and Lou wondered if she should go over there, too. It was *her* family it was happening to. It was *her* who Dad had come for.

She stood.

"You don't have to—" Shannon started to say, then

stopped. Which felt like a kind of permission to go.

Lou kept her eyes fixed on Dad so that he couldn't slip away, so that Mom and Steve couldn't make him disappear even though it seemed like that's what everyone wished would happen.

She got closer. Their voices got louder. Dad didn't like to be told what to do, pushed around, called out. The rule in their house was always: only Dad could be angry at Dad. It wasn't a rule that was ever said, but Lou knew it. It was unspoken, like so many of the rules that Lou and Casey and Mom had learned and created and followed.

Steve was in Dad's face. Marcus and Mom were trying to get Steve away from him.

"Dad," Lou said. "I'm here."

At the sound of her voice, he turned and his eyes focused. "Lou, my Loula. M'Lou." He pulled her into a rough hug, messing up the careful hairstyle Casey had done for her. He smelled vodka-sour and unwashed. She clung to him anyway.

"I love you so much, my Loula," he said. "You have no idea. No idea." His voice got softer but higher, started to break apart, his words in pieces. The *Don't cry* Dad was only there when he was sober. When he was drunk, he cried more than anyone.

Crying was one thing he *only* did when he was drunk.

Saying *I love you* was another.

Hugging her like he meant it was another.

Love only came this way or not at all. It made Lou wonder sometimes: Was his drunk self his true self, and love his true feeling, or was the sober person who couldn't say I love you and forbid her to cry the real Dad?

Lou slipped back into the bubble, where her senses seemed to turn off and time and space were like slime. Dad had been holding her and now he wasn't. Steve and Mom had been right there and now Mom was gone and it was Steve and Marcus talking.

After seconds or minutes, her mind un-slimed. She turned the corner into the hall and found Dad and Mom, and Dad was crying even more, saying, "I'm sorry, I'm such a screwup, I'm so sorry, please please, give me another chance, I want to be with you. I want to be with my girls."

Mom said, "Patrick, this is my wedding."

Dad said, "No."

Mom said, "Yes."

Dad said, "Why?"

Mom said, "This is my wedding. You need to leave."

Dad said, "I want my girls."

Mom said, "Patrick, you need to leave now."

Dad said, "Where's Casey?"

Mom said, "I don't know. I thought she was here."

Dad said, "Where's Casey?"

Mom said, "Please leave now."

Dad said, "What if . . . what if I . . . what if I could . . . what if . . ."

Mom said, "Patrick. Come on."

She took Dad's hand in a tender way and he followed her toward the stairs that led to the main door out. It was so strange, seeing them hold hands. Lou hadn't seen that in a long, long time, and now it was happening but not like it was supposed to.

Lou crept behind them. She wanted to thank him for the guitar, ask him—why a guitar? What did he want her to do with it? If she knew that, knew what he wanted, maybe she could do it and make something change. Make it so he wasn't so sad, make it so he wouldn't want to drink.

She kept watching their clasped hands, Dad following along like a child being led. If she spoke now, she knew they would let go and she didn't want them to let go.

Out on the sidewalk, Mom asked him, "Do you have a way to get home? Do you have a place to go to?"

Dad said, "I don't know."

Mom said, "Where are you going now? Do you want me to get you a cab?"

Dad said, "I don't know."

They faced each other, and Mom took his other hand. She said something in a quiet voice, too quiet for Lou to hear, though she heard the word "love" and she heard the word "help" and she heard the word "daughters."

Then Mom let go of Dad's hands.

And he walked down the street, away from Mom, away from the church, the wedding, and Lou. His steps zigzagged and she could hear him still crying but he never turned around.

Mom did. When she saw Lou standing there, her mouth opened and she rushed over. "Oh, Belle." She knelt down in her dress and gathered Lou into a hug. "My sweet girl."

A wedding day was supposed to be happy—everyone knew that. But Lou's stomach was upset from swallowing tears, and her chest ached with sadness, and even her arms hurt, her hands, her fingertips. She dug them into Mom's back.

"I know," Mom said. "Today is hard."

Lou pulled back. "Even for you?"

"Yes." Mom bent her head to look into Lou's eyes. "Life is complicated sometimes."

"All the time."

Mom smiled a little. "I want it to be not so complicated for you. I want to make things better." She got serious again. "Marrying Steve, moving, that's all part of that. Making things better, in the long run. But at first . . ." She tucked a piece of Lou's hair behind her ear. "At first, it's going to hurt. And I'm sorry for that." She hugged Lou close again, then stood up and brushed off her dress. "Is my mascara still okay?"

"Yeah. You look pretty."

"Do you know where Casey is?"

Before Lou could say, Steve came out of the church and walked slowly over. His blue jacket looked brighter in the outside light and the gray strands of hair in his light curls seemed to multiply.

He glanced down the street and put his arm around Mom. "Everything okay?"

Mom nodded. "I'm sorry, honey. I had no idea he'd show up like that."

"How did he even know?"

"I told him." Mom said it like: *Of course.*

"I thought—"

Mom put her hand on his arm and he stopped. "I want to find Casey."

Lou told them that Casey and Daniel had gone to the park but they'd be back in plenty of time to ride home to Steve's house. She tried to make her voice light and easy, not a big deal.

Inside, though, Lou couldn't believe that Casey had missed Dad showing up. That on this day, of all days, Casey had left.

PART III

Steve's House

11

THAT EVENING, AFTER THE WEDDING, they ate leftover ham and macaroni salad and cake. Steve did the dishes while Mom did some more unpacking and Casey went in her room and closed the door. Lou went into her own room but didn't feel like putting the rest of her clothes and things away.

There was a window right over her bed and she opened it a couple of inches to let in the cool air. She did like how the curtains stirred. She could imagine it would be a good reading spot, under that window. If she piled all her pillows up, like this . . .

"Hey, Louisa."

She turned; Steve stood in her doorway.

"Can I show you something?" he asked.

"Okay."

He motioned her out and led her to the front room. "I dug out the record player. Found a replacement needle in one of the kitchen drawers. My mom was kind of notorious for saving things forever."

The record player sat in a space on the shelf that he must have cleared out for it. Lou didn't remember what was in that particular spot before, but it was the same shelf where she'd found the wooden acorn.

"Do you have a record you want to play?" he asked. "I figured you must, since you asked."

She nodded. "I don't really know how to work it, though."

"It's easy. I'll show you."

She went back to her room, pulled the tote bag from under what was now her bed, and picked out one of the Neil Young albums that Dad had left behind. When she handed it to Steve, he flipped it over a couple of times and glanced at her.

"You like this?"

Did she? Dad liked it. "Mm-hmm."

"I don't think your mom was even born yet when this came out."

Lou didn't know what to say. She didn't want to tell Steve all about her dad's music and his Neil Young mug and how sometimes he would lie on the floor with his head between the stereo speakers, listening to these records.

He slid the vinyl disc out of the cover and put it on the

turntable. "Here's the power button," he said, pointing. "You flip this lever depending if you've got a thirty-three or a forty-five. The little ones are forty-fives. You have any of those?"

"I don't think so."

They left it on thirty-three.

"The way this one works is once the record is spinning, you just lift the arm and put the needle right where you want it." He demonstrated. "Carefully. Not too hard, see?"

He set the needle down at the beginning. The song was familiar to Lou.

"All I've got for the speakers are these little cheapies," Steve said, pointing at small plastic boxes next to the turntable. "I don't have the right cords to connect this to the big stereo in the family room. I used to have some big old speakers when I was in high school. My dad did *not* like that."

She tried to listen to only the guitar part in the song. Could she ever learn to play this on her guitar? Or any song?

Steve hummed along with the record. Lou thrust out her hand to turn the power off. Neil Young's voice got slower and deeper until the spinning finally stopped. She didn't want to hear Steve hum to Dad's records.

She held the album cover to her chest.

"I can see what records I have down in the garage, if you want. Probably some good guitar stuff to check out, if that's what you're interested in."

"That's okay."

"But . . . you like the guitar?"

"Yes," she said quickly, feeling defensive, in case he was trying to imply anything about Dad and his gift. They stood there like that for too long, until Lou swallowed and said, "Thanks for showing me the record player."

"Sure." He put the tips of his fingers in his pockets. He still had on his wedding jeans. "Well, I know it's been a long day. If you get cold in the night, you can bump the thermostat up a couple of degrees. Just holler out if you need something you can't find. Tomorrow we'll have the whole day to get settled and I'll show you a bunch of other stuff."

They were going to skip church, something they hardly ever did, and spend the day finishing the unpacking and all. Mom and Steve joked that staying home from church tomorrow was going to be their whole honeymoon.

Lou put the record away and stood outside Casey's door. The idea of knocking made her mad. Casey had left her at the wedding reception, barely talked the rest of the day, and now had her door closed. Didn't Casey want to come to *her* and say good night?

Impatient and hurt, she gave in and knocked anyway.

"What?"

"Can I come in?"

"I guess."

Never mind, Lou wanted to say. *Forget it.*

She opened the door. Casey was lying back on the bed, holding her phone above her like she was taking a selfie.

"The signal here sucks," she said.

"Dad came to the wedding."

"I *know*. Mom told me."

"Oh." If she knew so much, how come she didn't talk about it? "Have you tried calling him?"

"Not since your birthday." She rolled onto her stomach and tried a different pose.

"Can we call him now?"

"No."

"Why not?"

"He was already wasted this morning at the wedding," Casey muttered. "How do you think he's going to be right now? Anyway, who knows if he got his phone back." She glanced up. "Why do you even want to talk to him, Lulu?"

Lou had to think. Given how hard it was to talk to Dad, and how he never said what she wanted him to, why *did* she? "I just want to see if he's okay."

Finally, Casey put her phone down. "He's *not* okay. We know that already. Can you even remember the last time he was okay?"

"Christmas Eve." It wasn't that long ago; of course she could remember.

Casey's eyes changed, from the hard and bright stare she had so much of the time to something softer, and Lou wondered if she was remembering the hot chocolate, the lights of the bridge. "You're right," she said, nodding. "That wasn't bad."

With a sigh, Casey turned her phone faceup on the bed, hit Dad's number, and put it on speaker. A woman's voice answered with, "The number you have dialed is not in service."

Casey gestured to the phone and gave Lou an *I told you so* look, followed by an apologetic one. Then said, "Don't look so brokenhearted. It'll come back on when he pays his bill."

Maybe by then Lou will have learned something to play on her guitar.

She turned to leave; Casey stopped her by asking, "What were you talking to Steve about? In the living room just now?"

Had she heard the music? Lou shrugged. "He said we can turn the heat up if we get cold in the night."

Casey made a scoffing noise and picked her phone back up.

"I guess I'll go to bed now," Lou said. "Doesn't it . . . It feels weird not to be sleeping in the same room."

"You'll probably like it once you get used to it." Casey glanced up. "Are you scared? If you freak out, you can sleep with me. Just don't touch me with your icy feet and don't wake me up in the morning. I want to sleep in."

It wasn't that she was scared, and she didn't want Casey

to think it was that. It was that it was all new. It seemed like they should say something about what was being lost. But maybe Casey didn't care.

"I'm going to stay in my room."

"Up to you," Casey said. "Either way."

Lou waited another few seconds to give Casey a chance to say yeah, it *did* feel weird and they *should* spend this first night together. Mom just got married. They just moved away from where they'd lived their whole lives.

Starting now, they had to call this place home.

At church, for every big occasion and religious holiday, there was always a ceremony, a prayer, a song. Baptisms and graduations, Christmas and Palm Sunday and Easter, funerals, marriages. Mom and Steve had their wedding. *They* got their special ceremony and prayer and song. There should be one for moving, too, for everything Lou and Casey were going through.

"Good *night*, Lulu," Casey said, her voice impatient.

"Night, Casey."

12

STEVE'S HOUSE HAD A LIVING room and dining room in the front when you walked in. The dining room had a big table but it was covered with stacks of papers and mail, a toaster Steve had taken apart to fix, and his toolbox. They ate meals at the kitchen table. A hallway off the front led to Casey's room and Lou's room and a bathroom. The windows had frilly curtains, and Steve's mom's framed cross-stitch projects hung on the walls. There was a big bleach stain on the carpet in front of the hall closet.

Through the kitchen and down two stairs was what Steve called "my former man cave, future family room." That's where there the big TV and stereo were, and a recliner and an old couch covered in worn, cracked leather. They'd hung out in this room before on visits to Steve's, and Lou knew that couch would be a good place for reading when the TV wasn't on. There was also a fireplace, and Lou liked that, too. It made her think of a scene in the book *Heidi*, where Heidi and Grandfather toasted bread and cheese over the fire.

"I can even teach you girls how to build a fire," Steve said as they stood there the next morning. "If you want."

Lou looked at Casey, excited, but Casey only shrugged.

In one corner of the family room, a door led to stairs that went up to Steve's room and another bathroom. It was the only room they hadn't seen before, but today they got to go up.

"You should have seen it before," Steve said. "Your mom has already worked wonders."

"All I did was buy more hangers so you could actually put your clothes away!"

Steve and Mom laughed. Lou went around the room and peered out the window that overlooked the backyard. Mom had put pictures of Lou and Casey on the dresser. Lou caught a glimpse of Mom's familiar skirts and shirts in the closet next to Steve's clothes. Casey hung back with her arms folded, mad because Mom had suggested she leave her phone in her room until the time they would normally be getting back from church.

"I still want to hang some new curtains," Mom said. "And we need a bookshelf in here."

Steve put his arm around her. "I'm afraid I've never been much of a reader."

It was hard for Lou to imagine anyone Steve's age not needing even a small bookshelf in his room.

Mom looked as happy as she had yesterday, and comfortable in the house. Lou still felt like a guest, and had doubts that she'd ever be able to be *Lou* here. Like there was something of herself that got left behind in the apartment, along with the abandoned packs of ramen and old jug of water.

"Can I go back down?" Casey asked.

"Yes," Mom said, "but no phone yet."

"Seriously?"

Steve opened his mouth, then closed it again without speaking.

After lunch, Steve asked Lou and Casey if they wanted to walk over to the Merritt-Mendozas' house and say hi to Marcus and Shannon. "You can meet the kids. See about that babysitting opportunity."

And guitar lessons, Lou thought, hoping Marcus would remember.

Casey looked at Mom. "I have more stuff to put away, and all this homework I didn't get to do yesterday." Which meant she didn't want to go, because if she did she wouldn't be mentioning anything about homework.

"That's fine; you don't have to go."

"I want to," Lou said.

"Since Casey would be the main babysitter," Mom said,

"maybe we should wait until she's available?"

"We'll just go say hi. Lou can see where they live and we'll get some fresh air," Steve said.

Lou checked Casey.

"Go ahead," she said. "I don't care."

It was sunny out, like yesterday. "What a day," Steve said.

"Beautiful," Mom agreed.

Lou preferred fog, or at least a few clouds in the sky.

As they walked, Steve pointed at the houses they passed. His best friend in high school had lived there. His childhood sweetheart lived here. The block bully had been three houses down but moved away when Steve was in seventh grade. This house had just been remodeled; that house had a kitchen fire two years ago.

When his parents bought their house, it was brand-new and no one else had ever lived in it. The church where he was baptized was around the corner.

"How come you're at our church in the city if you have one right here?"

"Oh, I haven't been to *that* church since I was a kid."

"How come?" Lou repeated.

"After I was thirteen or fourteen, I didn't go to any church. Not until about five years ago when I decided I wanted some spiritual meaning in my life again. I tried all kinds of different churches for a few years before I found one where I felt at home." He took Mom's hand. "Little did I know I'd also meet the love of my life."

"God's timing," Mom said.

Lou didn't know you could just stop going to church when you were thirteen or fourteen if you wanted. She wondered if Casey would stop if she could. But she couldn't imagine Mom being okay with that.

"Anyway, the city's really not so far away when you're a grown-up with a car. Especially compared to driving over to Oakland for work every day!"

He pointed to a house set a little ways off the street. It seemed bigger and maybe older than the other houses. The front yard was all a jumble of different kinds of plants Lou didn't know the names of, because she'd never had a yard. "Here's Marcus and Shannon's place."

A dog started barking inside and pretty soon Shannon opened the door and smiled. The dog—black with curly fur—ran at them. Lou froze. She was a little scared of dogs that weren't on leashes.

"Bossy!" Shannon said. "Get back here."

"She's friendly," Steve said, holding out his hand to the dog, then rubbing its head. It stopped barking and snuffled Steve's legs. Lou touched its back with the very tips of her fingers.

"Hey," Shannon said to her with a smile.

"Hi." Lou offered a smile back and tried not to stare. Shannon was so pretty in a strong, tall, big way, with that very short hair that showed her eyes and ears and neck. She had on a long black T-shirt over flowy pants. Flip-flops.

Toenails painted dark red. Mom looked more gray and plain next to her.

"How are you guys settling in?" Shannon asked.

"We're getting there," Mom said. "It's an adjustment."

"I bet."

She invited them in. The kids were napping and Marcus was out, so they chatted in the kitchen. Mom admired the appliances and asked Shannon if she was happy with her refrigerator. She also said, "Love the cabinets." Lou had never heard Mom talk as much about house stuff as she had in the last twenty-four hours.

After a few more minutes of talking, Steve said, "Thanks for letting us pop in."

Lou wondered if she should say anything about guitar lessons but worried Shannon had already forgotten the whole thing. What if she had? And what if Marcus forgot, too? And what if Lou had to learn on her own and couldn't do it and then they'd finally get ahold of Dad and she'd have to say the guitar had just been sitting there in her room and he'd think she didn't care and he'd get sad and drink and—

"Belle, Shannon is speaking to you."

Lou had tuned out. Gone a little bit into her bubble without even realizing it.

"I was just saying I'll get in touch soon about meeting the kids and babysitting and everything."

"Oh, okay."

"And you can set up a guitar lesson with Marcus, if you're still interested in that. Maybe a little barter for babysitting?"

She nodded her head vigorously.

"I guess that's a yes," Shannon said with a laugh.

That afternoon, Lou propped herself up with pillows and read by the window over her bed. It was just as she'd imagined it could be: the sharp February air coming in, the protection of her blankets, the last afternoon light on the pages of her book.

Every few paragraphs, Lou glanced over at the guitar leaning in the corner of her room. She should take it out. She should get used to holding it. She should see if she could teach herself something before her first lesson.

It scared her, though, the kind of scared she sometimes felt before a quiz at school or in the waiting room at the doctor's office. The guitar was a test. Or a message. Dad was saying . . . he loved her but wasn't good at showing it, so here was something special to tell her that *she* was special. Or . . . he believed she could learn how to play it and be good at it and then he'd be really proud. Or . . .

She turned away from the guitar and looked out the window.

She didn't want to think about it yet. She didn't like that nervous feeling in the pit of her stomach. But now she couldn't concentrate on reading, so she got up and found her fleece vest in a pile on her desk chair. She lined up the lip gloss, the marker, the acorn, the red envelope, and her newest possession—not stolen, but given—her own key to Steve's house. A place she'd have to learn to call home.

13

EVERY DAY FOR THE NEXT week, Lou woke up disoriented. She was not in the bottom bunk. Casey was not above her. The window was at the side of the bed, not across the room. The closet was shallow and wide and with double doors, instead of deep with a single door.

Then, in the dim chill of morning, she would slowly remember.

She was in Steve's house, and Steve's house was home. Casey was down the hall. They couldn't walk to school.

And she had to get up *now*.

Since Mom had to drive them into the city on her way to work, the morning routine started an hour earlier than they'd been used to. Waking. Breakfast. Casey taking her daily shower, drying her hair, picking her clothes, putting on makeup. Every day, they were running late because of Casey, and every day, Mom was irritated by it.

Lou didn't mind the mornings once she was up. Steve had to leave long before them to beat traffic across the Bay Bridge, so those mornings were just the three of them and in some ways it felt like it used to. Except for Mom and Casey arguing.

"I don't like getting up earlier, either, Casey, but I do it so we can all be on time."

"It wasn't my idea to move here."

"I hate to break it to you, Case, but you usually ran late before we moved, too. It just didn't mean I'd be late for work every time."

Lou ate her peanut butter toast at the table—Steve's table, not their yellow one—while Mom and Casey rushed around, snapping at each other. Lou still took baths, usually at night before bed. Someday she'd probably get up and shower in the mornings like Casey and Mom and Steve.

"Oh, Belle," Mom said as she passed through the kitchen. "Marcus called about guitar lessons. He can start next week—Monday or Thursday evening for sure are options; probably other days if you plan ahead."

"Really?"

She'd figured a few things out on her own with videos she could look at on Mom's computer. She'd learned the names of the strings and parts of the guitar, and tried some easy chords, but they sounded wrong and she got scared again that she'd never learn. Last night she'd put the guitar in her closet after a particularly bad try when the whole thing just slid off her lap and onto the floor with an echoey thud.

Mom swished by again in a work skirt and sweater, and filled her car cup with coffee. "Yes, but remember, for every hour of lessons, you're trading an hour of helping Casey with babysitting."

"I know."

Casey came in and opened the fridge, closed it again, opened it again.

"We don't have *time* for you to be indecisive about breakfast," Mom said to her.

"I'm not indecisive! I thought we had boiled eggs!"

"Well, there were two in there last night. Maybe Steve took them."

"Seriously?" Casey spun around. "Does he *know*?"

"Does he know that's the only thing I can get you to eat before school? No, Casey, it hasn't come up. Maybe you should make your own and write your name on them."

She stomped back to her room.

"I hope you're getting your school stuff!" Mom called after her.

"I *am*!"

Lou's backpack and jacket were already by the door. She had her sneakers and fleece vest on. She got up to rinse her plate and put it in the dishwasher. They hadn't had a dishwasher at the apartment, and it still felt strange to her to rinse a dish and put it in the dishwasher when she could just wash it right then and it would be done.

But, she was getting used to it.

Beth waited for her out in front of school every day. Today, she waved frantically for Lou to hurry up when she saw Mom's car. Lou ran and Beth grabbed her hand and they scrambled up the stairs.

"You're always ten seconds from being late!" Beth said as they opened the door to Ms. Tom's room.

"I know. It's Casey's fault."

Ms. Tom smiled at them but also pointed at the clock. "Okay, girls, take your seats and settle down."

The day started with quiet reading. Lou shrugged off her fleece, hung it on the back of her chair, and got out her copy of *Where the Red Fern Grows*. Mom had read it when she was their age, and warned them it was super sad, which made Beth and Lou want to read it even more. They both loved sad books. It was one of those things that made them best friends. They were planning a joint report on the theme of "Sad Books."

"What page are you on?" Beth whispered.

"I just started chapter seven."

"Okay, but slow down a little."

Ms. Tom strolled toward them with her finger pressed to her lips. When she'd passed by, Lou took a break from reading so Beth could catch up, and looked around the room. This had been her room last year, too, also with Ms. Tom. It was a combined fourth and fifth grade class and now, more than halfway through the second year, it felt like home with its bookshelves, art table, the sink where they'd all rinsed papier-mâché paste off their hands last year. But the school only went up to fifth.

Lou always thought she and Beth would be at Roosevelt Middle School together for sixth, wearing the blue-and-gold gym outfits and jackets they'd seen older kids wearing on the bus around the neighborhood. Part of her still hoped that could happen. She'd been praying, and the desire of her heart was that God would fix it so the city school district would let her and Casey stay in their schools for as long as they wanted. Or, if God didn't do it, maybe they could use Dad's address to say they still lived there.

If Dad even had an address. They still hadn't heard from him and Lou kept remembering what Mom had said to him the day of the wedding: *Do you have a home to go to?* And she remembered his answer: *I don't know.*

Joey Levoy looked at her and bugged his eyes out. She'd been accidentally staring while her mind wandered. She grimaced at the thought that Joey might think she was looking at *him* and returned her eyes to her book.

When it was time to transition to science, Beth passed her a note written in purple gel pen: "We're going out of town this weekend to see my grandma but can you come over after school next Friday and spend the night?"

Lou wrote *YES* in bubble letters and slid the note back, sure it would be fine with Mom. Mom never said no to a sleepover at Beth's. She especially wouldn't say no *now*, when it used to be that Beth and Lou walked home together and they could go to Beth's house, where her mom was home, and there they would: do homework, run up and down the hall jumping over higher and higher stacks of pillows, sneak almond cookies from the pink tin in the cupboard, draw, barricade Beth's room with her dresser to keep Alan out, play jacks, try to get Rex to chase the jacks ball, play Nintendo, read their books with Rex moving from one of their laps to the other.

She hadn't even been over there since the day she took the lip balm. And the money.

Mom would definitely say yes.

And maybe, eventually, Beth would be able to come to Steve's. She'd never really been allowed at Lou's after school because Mom was always at work and the apartment was usually either empty or, before he'd moved out, Dad would be there. And Beth's parents knew that Lou's dad wasn't the kind of parent who could be responsible for his own kids, let alone someone else's.

Now, Lou couldn't even go over to Beth's house for a little bit on a regular day. She and Casey had to meet right after school—either Casey walking to her school or Lou walking to Casey's—and then together take a bus to the Stonestown shopping center. That was a safe place they could wait until Steve picked them up on his way home from work. It was still out of his way, but not as much as their schools, and it was the best solution he and Mom could come up with.

So they'd spend the half-hour ride home in his truck, sitting three across with Casey by the door and Lou in the middle, feeling how much Steve hoped Casey would like him, and how much she didn't.

Tonight, at dinner, Casey said, "We could just wait for you, Mom, then Lou can hang out with Beth and I can see Daniel."

"I already go out of my way in the mornings to drop you off. If we did it that way, with traffic we might not get home until six thirty or seven."

"So we can go downtown and meet you at your office, then."

"Casey." Mom said her name like a sigh.

Steve said, "We think this is the best plan for now, all things considered."

We.

Casey stared at her plate while she sawed into a piece of chicken like she was mad at it. It *was* pretty dry.

"It gets you home sooner, for one thing, and for another it gives you three time to get to know each other," Mom said.

Casey kept sawing. Lou felt a little bad for Steve in the silence, so she said, "Yeah," and then he kind of smiled at her in a sad way and no one said anything else until she asked for more noodles.

14

ON THE WEDNESDAY OF THE second week at Steve's, Beth walked with Lou to meet Casey near the high school. Not *too* near, because they didn't like being noticed by high school kids. They talked the whole way but Lou was only partly there. The entire day had been like that—Lou half in school and talking and playing and doing classwork, and half somewhere else, thinking about Dad, thinking about the apartment.

It had started with a dream she'd had last night where Dad was playing records for Lou. The apartment in the dream didn't look like the real apartment, but Lou knew that's where they were. Dad had on ironed jeans and cowboy boots like Steve, and he would play a song on a record and then Lou played it back perfectly on her guitar. Dad smiled, put his arm around her, held her tight. It felt so good and she knew he loved her. But the closer he got in the dream, the more she became aware of the sour smell of alcohol on him, and the good feeling went away. When she woke up, she felt sadness like an ache, homesickness for a home that only existed in the dream and even then, not for long.

"Can you imagine living in the country?" Beth was saying. "Hunting raccoons and running around barefoot? I guess it was olden times."

They were talking about *Where the Red Fern Grows*. The character lived way out in the middle of nowhere with his hound dogs and seemed to have all the freedom in the world, and he wasn't even that much older than them.

"Steve's house used to be sort of in the country," Lou said. She tried to pull herself out of her sadness and be there with Beth. "Compared to the city, anyway. He has a huge backyard and a front yard, too. The backyard goes all the way up a hill. It's the house he grew up in and he said he had a *horse* back there when he was our age."

Beth stopped walking and held Lou's arm. "He had a *horse*?"

"Yeah," Lou said. "Right in the backyard."

"Do you think *you* could get a horse?"

"No. It's not like that anymore. It's just a suburb."

They started to walk again. After a block of quiet, Beth asked, "Is it okay there, though? You have your own room and everything."

"Yeah. It's okay." Her room was all right and she *was* getting used to being in it alone. But she still missed Casey. Who was nowhere to be seen at their usual meetup corner.

"I'm starting guitar lessons tomorrow," Lou said, to try to tally up more okay things about being at Steve's. "Remember the guy who played guitar at the wedding? And sang? He's the one giving me lessons. He's Steve's neighbor."

"Ohhh," Beth said, "the one with the tattoos. By the way, I'm sorry we couldn't stay for the reception. I forgot to tell you. Alan had a soccer game."

"It's okay," Lou said quickly, even though it seemed strange for Beth to bring that up two weeks later, like maybe it wasn't really true. It was just as well that Beth and her family hadn't been there to see what happened with Dad. She looked down the street for Casey. "I bet she's with Daniel. I wish I had a phone."

"Do you want to call her from mine?" Beth had an emergency phone her parents made her take when she left the house. All it could do was make calls.

"I don't even know her number." Lou sighed and sat on the curb.

Beth checked her Hello Kitty watch, which Lou desperately wanted all of a sudden. "I have to be home soon. Don't forget to ask about sleeping over and tell me tomorrow."

Lou watched Beth walk down the street, imagining a ghost of herself from the past—just weeks ago—walking next to her.

During the time Lou and Beth had been talking, a bunch of kids from the high school had walked past, gotten on buses. Casey hadn't been *this* late before. Maybe she'd forgotten the plan and had walked over to Lou's school instead of waiting for Lou at hers? She walked the blocks back to her school to check. The only people there were some kids playing on the basketball court.

What if Casey had gone a different way and they'd passed each other without knowing it?

They'd been doing this routine for two weeks, though. Alternating days for who walked where, and taking the same route each time.

The ache she'd felt when she woke from her dream about Dad brushed against her now.

She had her bus pass and knew how to get to the shopping center on her own, but that wasn't the point. Casey was supposed to be there. More and more it seemed like she didn't care about rules, like going off with Daniel at the wedding without asking, and missing a couple of family dinners by simply saying "I'm not hungry," and staying in her room even though Steve and Mom had once said family dinner together at the table was "not optional." It wasn't fair.

Along with not caring about the rules, it seemed like more and more Casey didn't really care about Lou. She was a *we* with Daniel. She was sometimes even a *we* with only herself. Or maybe that was just a *me*.

Lou's face got hot; her eyes burned.

While she walked to the bus stop, she put her hand into the special inside pocket of her fleece vest. The mango lip balm was there, the red envelope, the acorn, Steve's black permanent marker. She took the marker out and the lid off.

Now that she and Casey had their own rooms, they didn't do the kind of talking they used to after lights-out. The sleepy kind of talking where you say whatever is in your head, including things you might not say if the lights were on. Casey's door was always closed.

Lou let the marker hang from her hand, and found herself walking closer and closer to the parked cars.

She wanted her sister. She wanted her dad. She wanted the apartment. She wanted her own *we* and to be good at playing guitar and then she wouldn't care if Casey forgot all about her.

The marker in her hand bumped against a blue car, leaving a small black streak. It bumped the next car, too, a green one. A woman pushing a stroller came down the street; Lou moved away from the cars. When the woman had passed, Lou saw a white car halfway down the block. She glanced across the street. No one was paying any attention.

She walked very, very close to the white car with the marker in her hand. She felt it touch the car and pressed it closer. She left it there for a count of three without looking, then moved away from the car, put the lid on the marker and the marker back in her pocket, and crossed the street to wait for the bus.

Lou got to their meeting spot at the shopping center ten minutes before Steve usually got there. No Casey. All the possible disasters spun through her mind. Casey was somewhere with Daniel doing something she wasn't supposed to be doing. Casey had gotten hit by a car. Casey had been kidnapped. Casey had run away.

Or, Casey was just late and it was going to be one more thing for Casey and Mom and Steve to fight about.

Praying to God to let Casey not be dead seemed like bad luck. If she didn't think it, it couldn't be true. Pastor Richards said they weren't supposed to believe in luck, they were supposed to believe in God's will. But he also said thoughts were important and you should have more thoughts about good things than bad.

A good thought: maybe Casey had already texted Steve or Mom to explain whatever had gone wrong and there wasn't a way to reach Lou.

Another good thought: Mom *had* to get Lou a phone after this. Their emergency plan right now was "wait in McDonald's if Steve is late," which wasn't much of a plan.

She looked in McDonald's now. Still no Casey. The smell of fries made her stomach growl.

After a couple more minutes of Lou trying to drown out bad thoughts, a small yellow car zoomed into the parking lot and stopped suddenly at the curb a few feet away from her. Casey tumbled out, laughing, then slammed the door behind her and ran to Lou.

"Oh my gosh, Lulu, I'm *so* sorry." She was still laughing, though, and didn't sound sorry. "For a second I didn't think I was going to beat Steve here. My heart is racing!" She gripped Lou's shoulders and searched her eyes. "You're mad. Don't be mad at me."

Lou swallowed. Her sister wasn't dead or running away. "Where were you?"

"Nowhere." Casey raked her hand through her hair and kind of fluffed the back of it, a thing she did about every five minutes in general. "Just hanging out."

"I waited for you where we were supposed to meet."

"I know. I know. I'm sorry. But I figured you would come here if I didn't show up, because you're smart like that. And look, you did, and it all worked out." She pulled an open KitKat out of her pocket and offered it to Lou. "I saved half for you."

Lou shivered. The fog was coming in extra thick.

Casey shook the candy at her. "Don't you want it?"

"No."

"Fine." Casey took a couple of steps away from Lou and bit into the KitKat. Then she turned to Lou again. "I said I'm sorry. I hardly get to see my friends outside of school anymore. It's one day, okay? You're old enough to take the bus on your own and I don't see why I have to be on your schedule. You're not a baby, Lulu."

"Tell that to Mom so I can get my own phone."

"You know she'll say no until you can pay for it yourself." Casey put her arm around her. Lou pushed it off and saw Steve's truck waiting to turn into the lot. "Don't say anything to Steve," Casey said. "About this whole thing."

Lou pressed her lips together.

"Come on," Casey begged. "Please."

"I won't tell Steve. I'm telling Mom, though."

Steve's truck turned. He waved at them. Casey grabbed Lou's arm. "If you tell Mom, she'll tell Steve, you know she will. And he's too strict and I'll get in big trouble!"

"He's not that strict. You just miss being able to do whatever you want without anyone knowing." They both knew that Casey would sometimes only get back to the apartment fifteen minutes before Mom got home from work, and then act like she'd been there all afternoon. Lou had never told on her, not once.

The truck pulled up and Lou opened the door to climb in. Casey got in after her. Steve made his usual small talk—asking about school and talking about his day and reporting on the traffic, which for some reason he thought was an interesting topic. "Not too bad today," he said. "A little tangle on eight eighty but I've seen worse."

Casey typed furiously on her phone and passed it to Lou. She'd written:

I'm so sorry. I shouldn't have done that. I guess I wasn't worried about you bc I know you can take care of yourself. But I know it was probably upsetting. I'M SORRY. It won't

111

happen again!!!!! PLEASE don't tell this time and I promise
x100 it will NEVER HAPPEN AGAIN.

Lou passed the phone back without answering.

Steve said, "I was thinking about grilling out tonight. I
know it's kind of cold, but burgers sound good to me. How
about you guys?"

"Whatever you want," Casey said. "I don't care."

"That sounds good," Lou said.

"Great. I'll need to stop at the store for burger buns."

"Can I pick out ice cream?" Lou asked.

It was the first time she'd ever asked Steve directly for
something. She was still more comfortable talking to him
through Mom if she needed a ride, permission, or help.
She hadn't even tried the record player again because she
couldn't remember how he'd said to do it and she didn't
want to ask.

"You sure can," Steve said, and gave her a friendly nudge
with his elbow.

Casey fumed beside her.

Mom and Lou had kept up a tuck-in routine similar to what
they had at the apartment. Even though Casey wasn't above
them and Lou's bed here was bigger, Mom still lay down
close and held Lou in the crook of her arm most nights.

"You and Steve seemed to be getting along well tonight,"
Mom said now.

"Mom . . ." Lou didn't want her to *notice* everything like

that so much. Or if she did, to not talk about it. It was hard enough to get used to a new life without feeling like every little thing was being watched and analyzed.

"Okay, I'm just saying. It was nice." Mom kissed her head. "Tell me two things."

Lou was so tired. Her dream last night had left an achy residue all day, and now that was combining with leftover feelings about waiting for Casey and not being sure if she should tell on her or not and the guilt of having marked up the cars. With permanent marker. Did permanent mean those marks would be on those cars *forever*? She felt suddenly hot, and moved away from Mom.

"You go first," she said to Mom.

"Well," Mom replied, "for one, a client said a nice thing about me to my boss, and that made me feel good."

"What did they say?"

"That I'm very reliable. They never worry I'm not going to do what I say."

Too bad Casey wasn't like that.

"What's the second thing?"

"That I took the wrong exit coming home," Mom said, "and started to go to the apartment."

Lou shifted so she could see Mom's face. "You did?"

"Yeah. I miss it, too, you know."

"I didn't know."

"I lived there almost my whole adult life." Mom pulled Lou back in. "And it's where you were a little baby. Just a teeny, tiny, squinty little baby."

"Mom," she said, squirming away.

"All right, what about your two things?"

Lou closed her eyes. "One is . . . can I sleep over at Beth's on Friday?"

Mom paused. "Saturday might be better, because then you can walk to church from Beth's house on Sunday morning and meet us there? Though I guess either way I don't get a day off driving to the city."

"I'll ask Beth." Then she was quiet a long time, thinking about her second thing of the day. She could talk about her dream, but she didn't want to. She could talk about *Where the Red Fern Grows* or how frustrating math was right now (multiplying fractions), but she didn't care. "Two is . . . I wish I had my own phone."

Mom sighed. "I am aware of this wish. And you know how I feel about that. What was it about today that made you especially wish it?"

"I was thinking, after school," she started, carefully, "what if something happened to Casey and she couldn't meet me? How would anyone know I was stuck and needed a ride or something? Like if I couldn't get a bus for some reason?"

"I think we have a pretty good plan in place for that. Your schools are less than ten blocks apart. You would go back to your school and use the office phone."

"I know, but what if Casey was late and I waited too long

and the school office was closed?"

Mom paused. "Was Casey late?"

"Kind of."

Mom rolled over and propped herself on her elbow. "How late? Is that why you're mad at her?"

"How did you know I'm mad at her?"

"Usually you two are exchanging all sorts of looks during dinner. Silent sister code. Tonight you were acting like she wasn't there."

"Oh."

"What happened, Belle?"

"Nothing."

"Are you sure?"

It all came out in a rush of words. "She was just late and not that sorry about it and what would I do if she didn't show up at all or something, or like if she broke her leg at school and couldn't meet me . . ."

"We'd find a way to collect you," Mom insisted. "We would not forget about you, honey."

"Most people in my class have phones."

"Maybe *half* do. I've asked other parents. That's not most. Sixth grade isn't that far off, and that's when you'll get one." Mom pushed Lou's hair out of her face. In a voice that said *New topic, starting now,* she asked, "Are you ready for your first guitar lesson tomorrow? It's all set up. You'll walk over to Marcus and Shannon's after dinner, so make sure you get your homework done before that."

"I will."

She paused again. "You know, Belle, you don't *have* to learn the guitar if you don't want to."

"I do want to!"

"Okay. But . . . you never said anything about guitar before. You shouldn't feel obligated just because—"

"Mom, I want to."

"Okay," Mom said repeated, sitting up. "I'm going to go say good night to your sister."

15

"WHAT DID YOU SAY TO Mom?"

Casey stood over Lou, shaking her awake.

"What did you say, you little fink?" she repeated as she sat on the edge of the bed.

"Nothing," Lou said groggily.

"Now you're a tattletale *and* a liar?" Casey snapped on the small lamp clipped to Lou's headboard. She had on her moons-and-stars leggings and an SF State T-shirt from Goodwill and the headband she wore at night to keep her hair off her face because she thought letting hair touch her skin gave her pimples. "Did you tell her about me riding around with seniors?"

"I didn't know you were riding around with seniors. I didn't say anything about that." Lou pulled her blankets up over her head. "I only told her you were kind of late. Because you were."

Casey stayed silent a moment, then lifted the blankets to look at Lou. "That's all you said? Then why am I grounded?"

"I don't know! I didn't tell her I had to take the bus to Stonestown myself or that you barely got there in time for Steve. All I said was you were *late*." Lou clicked the light back off. "Get out of my room."

Lou felt Casey's weight lift from the bed, heard her footsteps as she stomped out.

On Thursday after school, Casey showed up exactly on time, exactly where she was supposed to. But she made a point of texting with Daniel for the whole bus ride and then didn't talk to either Lou or Steve on the drive home.

It wasn't fair. Casey was the one who messed up, and Mom was the one who punished her, and now *Lou* was the one she was mad at. She'd barely even told Mom anything; it wasn't *her* fault that Mom always knew when something was up with Casey.

Before this year, they hadn't been the kind of sisters who fought very much about anything. They didn't call each other names, like Casey had done last night. They didn't give each other the silent treatment, for more than ten minutes. They didn't blame each other for stuff their parents did.

They stuck together when they were the only *we* they

had and now that was changing, too.

At dinner that night, Mom and Steve did lots of talking and tried to pull them both into the conversation, but Casey stayed as silent as she could without being outright rude, which would only get her in more trouble. Lou did the same.

Near the end of the meal, Mom said, "You two are off the hook for clearing the table so you can get over to Marcus and Shannon's for Lou's lesson."

Casey looked up from her plate. "Wait, I didn't know *I* was going."

"Yes, honey, we talked about this." Mom sounded impatient.

"No, we didn't."

"Yes. We did. You need to go over with Lou tonight so you can meet the kids and all of that, because you chose not to go last time."

"So I have to sit through the whole guitar lesson . . . why?"

Steve opened his mouth but Mom touched his arm and said, "Because I said so, Casey. The end. Take your homework with you."

"And leave your phone here," Steve added.

"Is he serious?" Casey asked Mom.

"Yes," Mom said. "You'll just be down the street and you can live without your phone for one hour."

Casey shoved herself away from the table and clomped

out of the kitchen in her boots. Lou went to her room to get the guitar and put on her fleece vest, because what if Mom took it to do laundry and found the stolen things in the pocket and held up the marker and asked, *What did you do with this, Belle?* And then the red envelope with the change from the cab. *Where did you get this much money?* And the acorn. *Steve has been looking all over for this!*

She checked herself in the mirror that hung on the back of her bedroom door. Would the Merritt-Mendozas be able to tell she was a thief and a vandal and sometimes a liar? If Mom couldn't see it, how could anyone? She could barely see it herself. Anyone could see that her hair was a nest of cowlicks and frizz, though. She mashed it down the best she could.

As she and Casey walked down the street, Lou defended herself again. "I didn't tell on you."

"I know." Casey said it so quiet that Lou wasn't sure she heard right. "I thought you did when Mom came to talk to me and so I ended up telling her everything. Then she grounded me."

They walked a few more steps. "How come you're mad at *me*, then?"

Casey shrugged. "I don't know. I just . . . yesterday when you were all 'Ooh, can I pick out ice cream' and being all buddy-buddy with Steve . . . it was like you were taking his side."

"I'm not."

Casey stopped walking and looked up at the sky. The night was clear and you could see more stars here than in the city. "I miss home," she said. "I miss the apartment. I miss Daniel. I miss my friends. I miss living in the city." Her voice broke a little on "living in the city."

"So do I."

They started walking again.

"I hate having to come home every day right after school and all that," Casey said. "I used to be free from after school to dinner."

"Me too!"

Casey laughed. "Sort of. You'll know what I mean when you're older. And you proved yesterday that you're totally fine taking the bus on your own to meet Steve. Why can't they let me live my life?"

Lou stopped in front of the Merritt-Mendozas'. "This is it."

"Here?"

They stood on the sidewalk. It seemed different at night than it had in the day. Smaller and cozier. A glow came from inside that made you want to be invited in.

"They have a dog," Lou warned, just as Bossy started barking.

The door opened and Shannon stood there, holding Bossy's collar. "Hey, girls! Bossy here is just excited to have visitors. I am, too. Come on in."

Casey seemed to relax immediately on hearing the

warmth of Shannon's voice. Lou did, too.

"What kind of dog is that?" Casey asked.

"Goldendoodle. A very embarrassing word to say."

"But it's black," Lou pointed out.

"The golden part is named for the golden retriever half of the breed. But they can get different coloring from the poodle side. Anyway, come in, come in!"

Shannon opened the door wider. Casey went first and Lou followed.

"I just took some oatmeal cookies out of the oven," Shannon said over her shoulder. "Lou, you can leave your guitar in the hall here."

They all went into the kitchen. "I love this countertop," Casey said, running her hand on the surface.

"I love it, too," Shannon said. "Green quartz. It's my favorite thing in the house. Marcus is upstairs dealing with bath time but he'll be down soon with Rosie and Tala. Noodle—sorry, Derek—is already in bed."

"Do these have raisins?" Casey asked, leaning over the plate of cookies.

"No, chocolate chips. I'm not a monster!"

Casey laughed. Her whole mood had changed since they walked in. She'd always been good at sliding into any situation and seeming to fit right in. Lou wanted to be more like that, but she would get stuck in her thoughts and lose track of what was happening around her. Like now, Casey was saying, "Go ahead, Lulu," pointing at the cookies, and both Casey and Shannon were staring at her.

She took one. "Thanks."

Then she watched as Casey wandered around the kitchen, poked her head in other rooms, asked Shannon a bunch of questions about the house and various bits of furniture and the pictures in the picture frames, while Lou stood there, forgetting that the next thing to do with a cookie was take a bite.

Casey asked where the bathroom was and disappeared. Lou turned back to Shannon, who asked, "How are you doing? I've been wanting to check in on you after everything that happened at the wedding, but when you were here with Steve and your mom, it didn't feel like the right time. So . . ." She smiled. "How are you?"

"Fine." Lou nibbled at her cookie.

"Have you heard from your dad?"

Shannon was the first one to directly ask about or talk about Dad since the wedding. It felt like a thing they weren't supposed to bring up, and Lou didn't know how to ask Mom about it or even what to ask. Even in the quiet moments when Mom tucked her in at night, something had stopped her because they were in *this* life now, not *that* life, and Mom loved Steve. Without anyone saying it, it seemed like they weren't supposed to look back.

"Not really." She quickly added: "It's okay, it's just been busy. We're not even totally unpacked yet and I think he's probably busy, too—"

Casey came back in the room then, and Lou stopped talking and took a big bite of cookie. And a few seconds later, Marcus came in carrying a toddler and holding the hand of a kid a little bit older.

Lou caught her breath as a pain radiated from her heart to her hands. This happened sometimes when she saw kids with a dad, a dad who was obviously safe and warm and strong. It hurt.

The older kid let go and ran straight for the cookies.

"Hi, guys," Marcus said. "Good to see you. Rosie . . . say hello to Lou and Casey first, okay?"

Rosie, golden skinned and with a halo of dark curls, looked straight at Lou. "Hello." Then took a cookie.

Lou took in a breath, trying to unhitch the pain.

"And this is Tala; she's a little shy," Marcus said, trying to slide Tala down to the floor, even as she didn't want to let go of him. He smiled at Lou. "How about we get started, and Shannon can attempt to explain the kids to Casey for now. Good?"

Lou could only nod.

16

THE GUITAR CASE BUMPED AGAINST Lou's knees as she followed Marcus into a room right off the kitchen, like a family TV room and playroom combined. There were several guitars in one corner and an electric piano against the wall. Marcus apologized for the mess as he gently kicked toys out of the way. There were inside double doors with little panes of glass—French doors, just like in the old apartment. When the doors were closed, they could see into the kitchen but the noise of Shannon and the kids was muted.

It felt cozy and friendly, and the pain was forgotten for now. Lou sat on the sofa and kind of sank in deeper than expected. "Whoa," she said, embarrassed.

"Yeah, that couch will eat you if you're not careful. You'll do better if you sit on the very edge."

She scooted up; he sat on the ottoman directly across from her.

"Let me take a look at your instrument." Marcus opened the case and took Lou's guitar out, put it on his lap. He had on a short-sleeve T-shirt, and Lou could see even more tattoos than she'd seen at the wedding. Geometric shapes, vines, a starfish. "What do you know about guitars?" he asked.

"I watched some videos." She pointed to the different parts of it that she could remember the names of: the body, the neck, the pegs, the bridge, the pick guard.

"Nice," he said. "And these are the frets."

"I forgot that one. I tried learning some chords but it didn't sound very good."

He picked each string and then strummed them all together, made some different chords, kept strumming. When he stopped, he looked at her and wrinkled up his nose. "Did it sound good when I did it?"

"Um . . . I think . . . no?"

"That is correct. You know why?"

A worm of shame wriggled around in Lou's stomach. "Is there something wrong with the guitar?" Maybe Dad had gotten her a bad gift, some sort of fake guitar, not even a real one.

"No, no. It's a little big for you, but it's fine. Where'd you get it?"

"My dad."

Marcus glanced at her, then back down at the guitar.

"Well, there's nothing at all wrong with this instrument. It's just out of tune. Listen." He plucked each string and turned the shiny silver pegs on the end of the guitar, with his head bent down. Every time he turned a peg, the sound of the strings changed a little. "Your dad . . . how he was at the wedding, is that kind of normal for him?" Marcus kept his head bent, kept plucking strings.

"Yes," she said quietly.

"There." He strummed again, and looked at her with raised eyebrows. "How's that?"

Lou smiled. "Better."

"Right. Guitars get out of tune when they're new, or when they sit unplayed for a long time, or when you put new strings on, or even after just playing it normally for a while. It takes some time to develop your ear so that you can tune it yourself, but we'll work on that." He passed her the guitar and got one of his own. "What kind of music do you like?" he asked while he tuned it.

She listed all the records she had in the tote bag in her closet.

"Really? Do you like anything from . . . this century?"

Were Dad's records not good? Her face warmed. "Yeah. I don't really know the names of songs and stuff."

"That's okay. I don't think I even started getting into music until high school. It can take a while to find your own taste, and until then, your parents' records and CDs and whatever else you have in the house are great." He started playing a song she recognized from one of Dad's Neil Young records. "This one isn't too hard. It's pretty much basic chords." He stopped. "What do you know about chords?"

"Nothing. I watched some videos. But . . . yeah," she said, laughing nervously, "nothing."

He talked about chords, playing them as he went, mostly looking at his guitar or at hers. Something about triads. Something about root notes. Major, minor, diminished, dominant. It was a jumble of words and Lou started to get the same feeling she got when she was doing math problems, how Ms. Tom would talk about them like they were easy and obvious and Lou could barely follow.

Finally he stopped, and looked at her. "Don't worry. You're not going to remember most of this. It's just an overview. Let's see if you can play a chord, an easy one. I want to see if your hands are big enough to make an E minor. That's the first chord in Neil's 'Heart of Gold.' Watch me and see if you can copy it."

The chord only required her to press down two strings, and they were right next to each other. She had to stretch her left hand around the neck as far as she could. With her right hand, she strummed. It sounded bad and muffled.

"Press harder. Hard as you can."

She did, and strummed again, and a musical sound came out of her guitar.

"Great! Now try this." He demonstrated another one, moving one finger slightly, and she copied it again. "Very good. One more? Do your fingers hurt?"

They did hurt a little, and she worried she was too small and weak. What she said, though, was "I can do one more."

"Let's try an A."

That one was harder; she had to hold three strings down at once, but she got something to come out of the guitar. Then she shook out her hand, trying to ease the burn.

"Yeah," Marcus said. "It actually hurts a lot when you start out because the skin on your fingers isn't used to it. But you develop calluses—your skin gets thicker and tougher—and after a while you don't even feel it."

He held his left hand out for her to touch. The skin on the tips of all the fingers had hardened. She looked at her own, pale but now turning red.

"So, you won't be able to practice for *that* long until you get good calluses. It will just hurt and you'll be frustrated, but if you stick with it—even ten minutes at a time, a couple of times a day—you'll get there. And the best way to stick with it like that is learning songs you know, ones that you like."

Lou, the person so good at not crying, felt her eyes sting. Even though she'd hardly played anything yet, her fingers ached. Learning whole songs seemed impossible. Couldn't anything ever be easy? Couldn't anything ever not hurt?

Marcus dipped his head. "You okay?"

She nodded. Pressed her lips together. All she wanted was to do a good job at this and have something to play for Dad someday, to give him a reason to think about her.

"You sure?"

"Yeah." A tear got out. She brushed it away.

"You've got a lot going on right now, huh?" His voice was kind. "Moving. New family member. A lot of changes."

Another tear, same eye. How could she go all week with everything at home and the fight with Casey and all of it without crying, until *now*, in front of Marcus?

He absently picked out a tune on his guitar. "There's always some pain with instruments. Trumpet players get blisters on their lips. Piano players get sore fingers. Clarinetists get thumb pain. Professional singers can have problems with their vocal cords . . ."

While Marcus talked, Lou tried mashing out the A chord again.

"Hey, not bad."

It was, though. It was bad.

"Then there's the *emotional* pain of learning something new," he continued. "Trust me, I've cried over learning a really difficult tab. Tabs—tablatures—are for when you're learning a song note by note instead of in groups of chords."

Lou sniffled; the danger of any more tears falling had passed. "Really? You cry?"

"All the time," he said with a laugh. "Ask Shannon."

He gave her a chord chart to study and showed her how

she could practice the hand positions without actually pressing down if her fingers hurt too much. Then he asked, "You want to sing a little? Just for fun? The kids love it." Before she could answer, Marcus opened the French doors and said, "Everyone get in here for a little pretend campfire."

Rosie and Tala ran into the room. Rosie said, "'On Top of Spaghetti'!"

Casey came in and looked at Lou. Could she tell Lou'd been crying?

The Merritt-Mendozas all sang a silly song about a mountain of spaghetti. Rosie sang *loud* and Tala tried to, but only got about every fifth word right. Lou was used to sitting around in a room with people singing; they did it at church and they did it when they went to home Bible studies sometimes. Casey seemed embarrassed and wasn't singing along, but even she had to laugh at the nonsense words Tala used when she didn't know the real one.

During "Baby Beluga," Lou sang louder and did the hand motions. On the first chorus, she stole a glance at Casey. *Everyone* knew this one, even Casey.

Casey just sat with her arms wrapped around her knees and her eyes on the floor.

Lou could see her lips moving, though.

When they got home, Casey went to her room and Lou went to the kitchen to find a snack. Steve was sitting at the table reading the manual for his truck. It was the only thing she'd seen him read besides the Bible.

"Hi," Steve said.

"Hi."

Lou still felt awkward whenever she ran into Steve in the house and it was just them. With family, you didn't say hi every time you walked into a room and found each other there. You didn't say "How are you?" six times in a day. But that's what kept happening with Steve. What else were they supposed to say?

She got out some crackers and the jar of peanut butter. Steve flipped through the corners of the pages of his manual while he watched her spread the peanut butter.

"How'd it go? With the guitar?"

"Fine." A cracker broke under the force of the knife. She put both halves in her mouth.

"Marcus is pretty good, huh?"

"Mm-hmm."

"Did he say anything about the guitar? Like, is it a good one? Is it okay?"

She nodded and started on a new cracker. The same thing happened.

"Because if it's not, we could always sell or trade yours and get one that's a better fit for you. If you need."

Why would he say that? She *had* a guitar and Marcus said it was good and Dad gave it to her. It was the same thing Steve wanted to do with everything from the apartment: sell it or give it away or stick it somewhere none of them had to look at it anymore. Instead of answering, she put the cracker pieces in her mouth.

One more try. She put the cracker down on the counter and very, very carefully spread it with peanut butter, without pressing down too hard. It broke.

"I hate it when that happens," Steve said. He started to get up. "Do you want me to . . ."

"No!" She clapped the lid back on the jar and crumpled the bag of crackers back into its box. "I like it when they're broken."

"Oh." He sat back down. "Okay."

"They're easier to eat."

He nodded, and flipped through his book again. "That's a good point."

17

SATURDAY, MOM DROVE LOU OVER to Beth's. On the way, they listened to the radio. Lou listened for songs that had guitar and tried to guess how hard or easy they'd be to learn. When they were almost to Beth's, Lou asked the question that had been on her mind for days.

"Have you talked to Dad since the wedding?"

"No, Belle. I haven't heard from him." Mom's hands tightened around the steering wheel. "Casey hasn't, either, from what I understand."

Lou realized she was holding her breath. She let it out. It wasn't the answer she wanted but she was relieved to have finally asked.

"Okay," Mom said, "so you'll walk over to church in the morning? Be on time."

"I will."

"Have fun." She leaned over and gave Lou a kiss, and it was like they'd never mentioned Dad.

They took their roller skates to a freshly paved schoolyard a couple of blocks away. It was sunny out and a little warmer than it had been during the week. On the walk over, Lou told Beth about her guitar lesson. She realized as she was talking that she left out the parts where she cried, where she put the guitar in her closet because it scared her, where she worried Dad would never hear her play. Sometimes she liked it better when she could make her life sound more like Beth's. None of the stuff about feeling awkward with Steve or not knowing where her dad was or hiding from her own guitar.

"Pretty soon I'll get my calluses and I'll be able to play whole songs. Maybe even play and sing at the same time."

"Then you could start a video channel and get famous and discovered," Beth said excitedly. "I could do your hair and makeup and pick your outfits and everything."

"Then we can buy a mansion by the ocean!"

"And have a hundred cats!"

At the schoolyard, they pretended to be Olympic figure skaters, balancing on one skate, making dramatic arm gestures, attempting to skate backward. After a while, they got hot in the sun. Beth took off her denim jacket and Lou took off her fleece vest and they tossed them on top of their shoes. Then they changed the game to racing around the perimeter, seeing who could get back to their pile of shoes and jackets first after going once around. Beth won first, then Lou won twice.

"My feet hurt," Lou said. "And my ankles." She'd gotten her skates from Goodwill and they were a little too big.

"Yeah. My mom is probably wondering why we aren't home yet."

Earlier, they'd promised to be back to help Mrs. Tsai make dumplings, but they'd lost track of time. Beth bent down to get her shoes from under the jackets. Her jacket had gotten tangled up with Lou's fleece, and Beth gave her jacket an exuberant shake to separate the two. The mango lip balm flew out, along with the wooden acorn and the marker, and Casey's partially used eyeliner and an amber marble that Joey Levoy had left on the ground at recess without noticing.

The corner of the red envelope peeked out.

Lou dropped to her knees and tried to put everything back in, but it was too late.

"Is that my lip balm?" Beth sounded confused. "I've been looking for that."

"No. I have one just like it. After I saw yours, I bought one." Even as she lied, Lou knew it would only make things worse.

"Is that . . ." Beth tore the vest out of Lou's hands and skated a few feet away before pulling the red envelope all the way out.

"It's the one your mom gave me," Lou said, pleading.

Cheeks flushed and eyes flashing, Beth pulled the bills—the change from the cab fare the night of her birthday—out of the envelope. "This is way more than my mom put in your envelope."

"How do you know?"

"Because I *know*. And I also know that Alan lost one that had fifty dollars from my grandma in it. He got in trouble!" She stared at the money in her hands and then back at Lou. "You took it. You took it last time you slept over."

Lou skated toward her. "I didn't! I like the envelope and I've been using it like a wallet for my own money. And I swear to God I bought that lip balm myself." *I swear to God*. Her lie was serious now.

Beth shoved the money back in the envelope and the envelope back in the vest, then threw the vest at Lou. It fell to the pavement between them. Beth skated back to her jacket and shoes and sat on the ground to take off her skates. Lou searched the blacktop and found the marker and the acorn and the eyeliner. The marble must have rolled away. She slipped the vest back on and sank down next to Beth to change into her shoes. Beth scooted away from her.

"Beth," Lou said, her voice small, "I swear. I didn't steal anything."

Why did she keep lying to Beth's face? Normally, she didn't lie any more than anyone else did. Little things here and there to keep from getting in trouble or hurting someone's feelings. This lie was for both those reasons, but it felt bigger.

She had to decide in the split second of *now* whether to back out of the lie or keep going. If she backed out, Beth would know for sure she'd betrayed her. If she stuck with it, maybe there was a tiny chance that some part of Beth might doubt the truth.

"I didn't do it," Lou said again.

Beth walked away with her jacket and skates bundled in her arms. Lou followed, the ground feeling extra hard on her wobbly legs after gliding so easily beneath her skates a moment ago.

They helped Mrs. Tsai make the dumplings, and Beth barely talked to her. At dinner, even though the dumplings turned out good, Lou couldn't enjoy them.

She helped Alan load the dishwasher after, which made Beth's dad give her a funny look and say, "You don't have to do that, Lou. That's Alan's job."

"I know. I don't mind."

Beth passed through the kitchen with her plate and said something in Mandarin under her breath. Alan replied, "Am not!" and Beth said, "I'm not talking to *you*."

When Beth was gone, Lou asked Alan what she'd said.

"It's like . . . cheater. Liar."

"Oh."

Alan ran off with the job half finished, and Lou did the rest and wiped out the sink and put away the condiments and swept the floor. Mrs. Tsai came in and watched with her arms folded. "Going the extra mile," she said. She handed Lou the dustpan. "How come Beth is mad at you?"

How was she supposed to answer that without the whole rest of the family getting mad at her, too? She'd be banned from Beth's house forever.

"We got in an argument while we were skating. It was my fault." She swept the crumbs and dirt into the dustpan, but a thin line of dirt got left behind. She moved slightly and swept that in. Another line, thinner now, remained. She tried to get it all, only to leave behind a still thinner line of dust.

"Here." Mrs. Tsai bent down with a damp rag and made the last bit disappear. "Maybe Beth is mad at you for moving. You know? It's not your fault, but it's still difficult for her to accept."

"Maybe." She hung the broom back on its hook by the fridge.

"She has a quick temper, too, you know that."

"I know. But . . . this *was* my fault."

Mrs. Tsai reached into the top cupboard and got down the almond cookies. She opened the tin and handed two of them to Lou. "Take her a cookie and apologize."

As if he had bionic hearing for the sound of the tin being opened, Alan raced into the kitchen to get his cookie, and

Lou walked down the hallway. Beth's door loomed in front of her.

She knocked. In a few seconds, Beth opened the door. "I guess I have to let you in because you're my guest. But I wish you still lived in the city so you could just walk home."

Lou held out the cookies. "You can have mine, too."

Beth took both, hesitated, and handed one back to Lou. She closed the door behind them and Lou sat cross-legged on the carpet, while Beth sat on her bed with her back pressed to the wall. Lou stared at her feet until they got blurry, then asked, "Are you going to tell on me?"

"Tell what? You didn't do anything, right? You swore. To *God*."

God would forgive her; she wasn't so sure about Beth. "You remember when you kept getting in trouble for hitting Alan? And you told your mom, 'I can't help it'? It's like—"

"I stopped! I haven't hit him in over a year!"

"I know. I was going to say . . . taking something feels like that. Like I can't help it."

"Taking something?" Beth said. "You mean stealing."

"Yeah." Stealing. One of the "Thou shalt nots" in the Ten Commandments.

"You *can* help it, though. Like I *can* not hit Alan. Or not yell at my dad when he's not listening to me. Or not do a lot of other stuff I want to." Beth flopped her hands against the blanket for emphasis. "We're not little kids anymore! It's called self-control!"

"I know. I'll stop. I'll . . . I can stop."

Beth sighed. "What about Alan? My dad got really mad at him for losing the envelope from my grandma. But he didn't lose it. It's not fair."

How many times had Alan been bad and not gotten caught? How many times had Mr. Tsai taken Alan's side instead of Beth's? Or made her responsible for Alan doing dumb kid stuff just because she was older and a girl?

"If I promise to never steal anything again," Lou said, "maybe we could just . . . let Alan be in trouble? For once?"

That wasn't how fairness and justice worked but she could not face anyone else knowing what she'd done. The fear of kids at school finding out—or even worse, *Mom*—made her get up on her knees and put her hands together to beg. The fingertips of her left hand still stung from her guitar lesson.

"Please, Beth. Pleasepleaseplease."

Beth wasn't finished. "I've never stolen anything. Why would you *do* that? Is it because of being poor?"

Now Lou felt *her* cheeks get hot. They never talked about this. They didn't talk about it when, at the beginning of fourth grade, Mrs. Tsai took Lou shopping for some back-to-school clothes so she didn't have to only wear Casey's old clothes. They didn't talk about it that one summer, when they did horse camp together and the only reason Lou could do it was because the Tsais paid her way.

They both knew Lou's family didn't have money, but Beth had never spoken one word about it.

"No," Lou said fiercely, even though she didn't know what the real answer was.

Rex meowed at the door. Lou got up and let him in and scratched behind his ears with her back to Beth. Now she, too, wished she still lived close enough to walk home. Though she wouldn't have been allowed to anyway, now that it was dark out.

Lou turned around, her guilt only letting her look into Beth's face for a few quick seconds.

"I'm sorry," Lou said. She focused on Rex's ears and the tufts of fur that grew around them. "I'm sorry. For stealing and then also for lying about it. I didn't . . . I don't *want* to be like that." Was that true? She didn't try very hard to stop herself.

"I know."

"Please don't tell." The Tsais would know and Mom would know and Steve would know, and none of them would ever forget.

Finally, Beth furrowed her eyebrows and said, "I won't tell. But that makes me feel like *I'm* lying now, too."

"I'm sorry," Lou repeated.

When it became clear Beth wasn't going to say "It's okay" or "I forgive you," they brushed their teeth and changed into their pj's, and separately and quietly read their copies of *Where the Red Fern Grows*. When Beth started sniffling, Lou didn't know if it was because of a sad part in the book or the sad part in their friendship.

18

Mrs. Tsai got them up in the morning with a knock on the door and the promise of cocktail buns fresh from the bakery. Lou had already been awake, and Beth must have been, too, because she flung her blankets back right away and jumped over Lou in the trundle. When they got to the dining room, Mr. Tsai was just opening the bakery box. Alan and Beth stood close to their dad to look in the box, excited and grabbing.

And Lou suddenly hurt, right in the center of her chest.

Like she did when she saw Marcus with Rosie and Tala.

Like a bruise inside herself was being pressed.

Mr. Tsai was a dad who would go out early to the bakery and bring back something to make his kids happy. And Alan and Beth weren't scared to stand close, whine, grab, be sad, be mad, be frustrated.

The bruise was: she'd never had that.

With a dad like Lou's, you held your breath. You watched and waited to see what was okay to feel and to say. You kept yourself small in case his feelings and actions needed to be big. You stayed still in case he decided to move.

Never easy, never warm. Never totally safe.

"Okay, okay, okay," Mr. Tsai said, breaking her from the spell. "Offer to our guest first."

Beth and Alan both looked over at Lou.

"It's all right," Lou said, still covered in a film of guilt from being caught by Beth. "Go ahead."

But Beth picked up the box and carried it to her. "You pick."

The whole family watched, and Lou wondered how they'd feel if they knew the truth, but it seemed like Beth was saying—with her eyes, with the bakery box—it was over. She really wasn't going to tell, and maybe Lou was even forgiven. Her mouth watered at the sight of the row of golden buns, which she knew were made of sweet, soft dough and had a buttery, coconutty center.

She took one and said thank you, and sat in her usual seat at the table while Mrs. Tsai passed around napkins.

But the bruise stayed tender.

She walked to church with her roller skates heavy in her backpack. Her arms and legs felt heavy, too, and her walk got slower and slower.

Beth would never think of her the same way again. Even if she did, Lou would know the truth about herself and know that Beth knew it, too. She'd hardly slept last night and she didn't take a bath and she felt grimy inside and out.

Steve was in their usual pew. Lou scooted in, leaving a big gap between them. Mom would want to sit next to him after she finished talking to people in the back, and there'd also be Casey. Pastor Richards smiled at her from the pulpit, where he was doing a sound test on his lapel mic while Barbara played pre-service music at the piano.

Steve slid down toward her and patted her shoulder once, tentatively. "How was the sleepover?"

"Fine."

"You should have brought Beth to church!"

"They have their own beliefs."

"Sure, but everyone has their own beliefs before they meet Jesus."

She didn't want to talk to him. She stared at her church bulletin with the songs and Bible verses listed on it. Steve believed that their religion was the right one, even when they were doing it wrong. And he believed it was the right one for *everybody*, they just didn't know it yet. That was not exactly how Lou believed, but Steve had a way of talking like he thought you agreed with him.

She replied with a sound like "Mmph," to end the conversation.

Soon, Mom sat between Lou and Steve, and Casey on

the other side of Lou. No Daniel because of Casey being grounded, which included no Daniel on the weekends. They went through the order of service: songs, readings, prayers, a sermon, offering, more songs. Some weeks there was a special "prayer of confession" that everyone would read aloud together. In the middle there'd be a pause, and that's when each person was supposed to quietly confess their sins.

Pastor Richards always let the pause go long enough that you really had time to scour inside yourself for the ways you'd been mean, dishonest, greedy, or uncaring. You listed them in your head and then Pastor Richards said a prayer to remind you that if you were really sorry, you'd been forgiven.

There was no prayer of confession this week, right when Lou really needed it.

After the service was over, they went downstairs for cookies and grapes and cheese cubes. Casey leaned against a wall in the corner and her arms were folded in a way that made Lou think of Dad. Like she was on her own island and you weren't invited. Lou took a cookie over anyway, not sure whether she was still mad at her.

"Thanks." Casey's eyes settled on Lou. "You look like crap."

Lou pressed her lips together. Casey sighed and slumped even lower against the wall, letting her feet slowly slide in front of her. Her gaze was over Lou's head now, and Lou turned to see what Casey saw. Steve and Mom, talking to

Barbara over by the coffee urn. Steve's arm was around Mom, rubbing her shoulder.

"I can't believe Mom made me leave my phone at home," Casey said. "Well, I can believe it. I just wish . . ."

"What?" Lou asked.

"I was going to say I wish I could live with Dad. But I don't." Steve's big laugh echoed through the fellowship hall. Casey grimaced, then continued. "More what I wish is we had the *kind* of dad we could live with sometimes. You know? Or at least the kind of dad we weren't always trying to track down on the phone. For once I'd like to feel like he wanted to talk to *us*." Her voice broke and she stopped, then said, steady, "But we don't have that kind of dad."

Lou knew then that Casey wasn't mad at her anymore. Casey was sad. And she was right. They didn't have that kind of dad.

She wanted to make her sister feel better but knew she couldn't. That wasn't how this kind of sadness worked, because you couldn't change the thing causing it.

So it hung on and hung on. It became a part of you.

That afternoon, Mom and Steve took a Sunday nap and Casey closed herself in her room. Lou got out the bag of Dad's records. She was looking for a particular one that had a song Dad once played over and over and over and over again when he was drunk, until late into the night when Lou was sure the neighbors would call the police.

Eventually he passed out or fell asleep and it stopped.

Cross-legged on the floor of her room now, she found it. It was on an R.E.M. record with a stark black-and-white picture on the front, and another picture on the back along with the song listings.

She'd never forget the words. Not just from hearing them so many times that night on the record, but also because Casey, in the bunk above her, had finally shouted to the ceiling, "Yeah, Dad, we get it! *Everybody hurts!*"

And somehow that made them laugh so much and for so long that it made it not feel so terrible to be so sad.

Now, she got Steve's marker from her pocket and drew a circle around "Everybody Hurts" on the back of the album cover. She walked down the hall and slid it under Casey's door. Then she knocked once and ran back to her room, unable to keep herself from giggling.

In a minute, Casey burst into her room, and she was laughing, too. It had worked.

"You crack me up, Lulu." She waved the record. "Where did you get this?"

"I wanted to save them from the garage. So I packed them with my stuff." She showed Casey the small collection.

"You probably just ruined a collector's item by drawing on it," Casey said, then tossed the R.E.M. album onto the floor with the rest. "But if you learn that one on your guitar, I promise I'll sing along."

19

LOU'S STOMACH HURT ON THE whole Monday ride to school. Not from carsickness but from how she couldn't stop her thoughts from going over and over and over the moment when Beth saw all the stolen things fall out of the pocket of the fleece vest. Each time she saw it in her mind, another ripple of shame went through her gut.

Casey hummed the melody of "Everybody Hurts" for part of the drive, and that did make Lou laugh for a second.

"What's funny?" Mom asked.

"Nothing," they said.

Beth stood in front of school waiting for Lou like always, but she didn't wave when Mom pulled up.

And then, after Ms. Tom did the announcements and passed back some book reports and told everyone to look over her comments, she came to Lou's desk. "Mr. Sturgess wants to see you in the office."

"Oh." Automatically, she starting putting her notebook and pencil case back into her bag. She didn't dare look at Beth. What if Beth had told on her after all, and now she was in some kind of bigger trouble than she ever imagined? What if they searched her and found the permanent marker in her pocket and asked, "Why do you need this?"

"You can leave your things," Ms. Tom said. "I think it's just a little administrative question."

"Okay." Lou walked out with the wooden hall pass in hand and felt everyone's eyes on her, but especially Beth's.

Mr. Sturgess was older than Mom and Steve, with white hair and a beard that was darker than the hair on his head. He wasn't the kind of principal you liked or hated; he was just *there*.

"Louisa!" he exclaimed, as if happy to see her. "Step in here for a sec, I have a quick question."

She perched on the edge of one of the three chairs across from him. Last year, she had to come into his office after Alex Rubin pushed her onto the ground at recess and some skin scraped off her cheek. Other than that, she'd hardly ever talked to him.

She waited.

He smiled and put his hands on the desk. "Okay. So where are you living right now?"

Where was she living? At Steve's. That's what she said. "Steve's."

"Steve's? And who is Steve?" Before she could answer, he said in his concerned voice, "Listen, Louisa, if your family has been evicted, or anything like that, we have—"

"No," she said, her face hot.

Mr. Sturgess knew which kids got lunch assistance. Which kids had "extra challenges" at home. Lou had always been on all the lists. She had sat for meetings with teachers about missed work, and for Mom explaining that Dad wasn't allowed to come to the school after the divorce, and one time when she got called in because Dad fell when getting off the bus and hit his head on the curb and was in the emergency room and Mom was going to have Mrs. Tsai pick her up.

But for once, this wasn't anything bad—she thought—and she didn't hesitate to say, "My mom got married. We moved to my stepdad's house in Pacifica."

"Oh, okay." He pushed his lower lip out and nodded. "Pacifica. Okay. Nice." He spun in his chair and typed something in his computer. "Sorry. I'm just . . . hmm." He clicked and moused. "All right. Okay. That's what I thought." After he turned his chair toward her again, he handed her a piece of mail. "We sent this health department update out to all students' families, and yours came back. Maybe it was supposed to be forwarded and the post office missed it. So I just wanted to check. Will you make sure your mom gets this?"

Lou took the piece of mail. Someone had written *No such person* next to their name and the apartment address. Her stomach kept hurting.

151

On the drive home, Steve was quiet. Casey was allowed to use her phone again and stayed hunched against the car door, scrolling and typing. Steve didn't ask his usual questions about their days, and didn't talk about his. When they hit bad traffic going into Pacifica and another car cut him off, he swore under his breath and then said, "Sorry."

Lou could tell something wasn't right. The mood felt off, like when Dad would lose another job but not tell Mom for days, or when he'd break a stretch of sobriety and disappear.

The off mood continued through dinner. They had lasagna, which was one of the things Steve liked to cook. He'd done two big pans of it over the weekend so they could have easy dinners and lunches for a few days. It was good—cheesy and tangy—except it had black olives in it, which Lou had to pick out.

It seemed like Mom wouldn't really look at Lou. Like Beth today at school.

Finally, when they were almost done eating, Mom said, "Um . . . all right, well, we have to tell you girls something."

Lou looked at Casey, whose face had gone blank.

Mom took a deep breath and continued. "The school district realized we've moved. We, well, *I* was supposed to submit a change of address form within fourteen days of moving, and apply for an interdistrict permit from the school district *here*, and—"

"And you didn't," Casey said in a flat voice.

"With the packing and the wedding and everything, I . . . no, I didn't." She stared down at her plate. "I assumed you could stay through the school year and it wouldn't be a big deal, and the paperwork fell through the cracks."

"Wait," Casey said. "What do you mean?"

Mom looked up. "I'm sorry, Casey."

"Are you saying we *can't* stay at our schools?"

"I messed up."

"Well," Steve said quickly, "we don't know if they would have approved it even if you did do the forms."

Lou tried to catch up, read the faces, interpret the words. "Are we in trouble?" she asked.

"No," Steve and Mom said simultaneously. "But . . ."

"But we have to *change schools*." Casey stood up, shoved her chair back. "As if all this didn't suck *enough*."

Had Lou caused this by answering Mr. Sturgess's question? The lasagna churned. She clutched her stomach and said, "May I be excused?"

"Belle." Mom reached her hand out and touched Lou's arm. "I'm sorry. You were changing anyway next year. It's just happening sooner now."

"*How* soon?" Casey asked.

The icy rage in her eyes made Lou afraid. She checked Mom's face, then Steve's, for any sign of warning or of comfort.

"This week will be your last week at the city schools," Mom said.

"What?"

"That will give us time to deal with the enrollment process here."

"One *week*?" Casey said.

She smashed her hand down on the table, which made Lou jump up, fear bouncing through her body like a loose pinball. Casey said the f-word and kicked her chair over. Steve stood and moved toward Casey but Mom pulled him back down by the arm. In a calm voice, Mom said to Lou, "You may be excused to your room. Everything is okay."

Lou retreated, wondering how everything could be okay when Casey was kicking things and saying those words, and screaming, "It's not *fair*! It's not fair! It's not fair!"

20

Lou paced her room. Maybe she should sit still. Maybe she should practice her guitar chords. Maybe she should read her book for school. Her body shook as if she was cold, but she wasn't. She pressed one ear to her door.

Casey stomping down the hall. Mom's voice close behind. Casey's door clicking closed. Their voices: Casey's loud and angry; Mom's quieter and calmer most of the time, with a few loud moments.

Her whole life, when something got scary, Casey had been in the room with her. When Dad drank and yelled. When Dad was sober and yelled. When they heard crashing or crying, Casey was there.

Now, Casey *was* the scary thing, and Lou felt so alone. This time she couldn't solve it with an inside joke about a song.

She opened her door just a crack and crept toward the kitchen. Steve stood at the sink, rinsing dinner dishes and loading the dishwasher. She stood there until he seemed to sense her presence and turned.

"Hey," he said softly. "You okay?"

Lou came in closer. "Yeah," she said, and wrapped her arms around herself.

She watched him. He was a careful rinser. The dishes he put in the washer were nearly clean.

"So you don't like olives, huh?" he asked, pointing to the little pile of shiny black slices on her plate.

"They taste like salty soap."

He laughed. "Fair enough."

"Green olives are okay, though."

"Noted."

The ache in Lou's stomach was starting to feel permanent, even though the sounds from Casey's room had gotten quieter.

"Is Casey in trouble?" she asked. "Are you mad at her?"

After thinking for a few seconds, he said, "No. I think I'd probably feel like she does if I were her. Your mom knew this was going to be hard news. That's why she didn't want me to say anything on the drive home, even though I already knew."

"I think it's my fault. Principal Sturgess asked me today where we live."

Steve set a glass carefully on the top rack. "It's not your fault." He sounded certain. "All you did was answer his

156

question honestly. Either way, he was going to call us to find out why the letter came back."

"But I could have said . . . or, like, *not* said . . . and then maybe warned Mom and then . . ." Then, what? They could have made up a lie together?

"No. We were supposed to fill in a form and let both districts know, and we didn't. Even if we had, you might still have had to change schools. It might have delayed things a couple more weeks but there's a good chance this was going to happen anyway."

Her stomach hurt a tiny bit less.

"But I was thinking," Steve continued, his voice lifting, "maybe the silver lining is you'll get to know some kids in your new school before sixth grade. Make some friends around here for the summer? Then when you start sixth, it'll be easy."

"I don't think it will be easy," she said.

"Maybe 'easy' isn't the right word." He leaned against the sink. Now that he was done with the dishes, he seemed less comfortable. He glanced at his watch. "Should we have some ice cream?"

Lou's stomach was still upset enough that she said no. "I think I'll practice my guitar."

She brought the fingertips of her left hand together, feeling the raw and red parts, the sore parts.

When would she get the calluses Marcus promised? When would it stop hurting?

* * *

157

Casey's face was puffy and splotchy in the morning, and she didn't eat any breakfast. Lou peeked at her from behind the cereal box and wondered if she knew about the conversation with Mr. Sturgess. She didn't want Casey to be mad at her for another thing that wasn't really her fault.

But Casey only sat there with her jacket on and her backpack in her lap, staring at nothing, not even her phone.

When Mom came into the kitchen to fill her car mug with coffee, she didn't try to cheer Casey up. She didn't try to tell either of them that things weren't so bad. All she said was, "Do you want some of my oatmeal, Case?"

Casey shook her head and Mom scooped out one serving of oatmeal from the batch she cooked every weekend, and heated it up in the microwave before adding a little maple syrup and some chopped nuts. She ate it standing while Lou rinsed her bowl and put away the cereal.

No rushing or fighting. Casey didn't stomp or slam. Mom didn't scold. They all left on time in a sad, single-file line from the door to the car. There were questions Lou wanted to ask on the drive to the city—like should she tell Ms. Tom what was happening? Would she have to do her homework this week if she was about to change schools anyway? When would she see Beth again?

It didn't feel like there was room in the car for her questions; Casey's silence took up all the space.

When they got to Lou's school, Casey suddenly spoke: "Lulu. When's your next guitar lesson?"

Lou looked to Mom, who said, "Do you want me to try to set one up for tonight, Belle?"

She said yes, mostly because she felt that's what Casey wanted her to say.

21

TODAY, BETH WASN'T WAITING FOR her.

Lou walked to class alone, and found Beth in her usual seat next to Lou's, opening her pencil box to line up her cute erasers. They looked and smelled like pieces of fruit: a watermelon slice, a grape, an orange wedge. Lou's fingers itched to reach out and take the small orange wedge and smell it. The pencil case was full of adorable things—tiny gel pens in their own little plastic case, a miniature pink stapler, a notebook no bigger than one-inch square.

"Stop staring at my stuff," Beth said, and slid her case farther away.

Lou turned to face Ms. Tom at the front of the room. She had on her blue polka-dot blouse with orange pants and tan flats, an outfit that Lou and Beth had once agreed was one of her best. She was writing the quote of the day on the whiteboard.

"Never bend your head. Always hold it high.
Look the world straight in the eye."—Helen Keller

"That rhymes," Joey Levoy said.

"Hold it high. Straight in the eye," Charles chanted. "Ms. Tom, how are we going to do silent reading without bending our heads?" Everyone watched him as he held his book right in front of his face, keeping his neck rigid. Joey and a few other people laughed and started to do the same thing with their books, pointing out that you couldn't look the world straight in the eye while holding a book in front of your face.

"How do you even bend your head?" Joey asked. "You bend your *neck*."

Beth sighed. "So stupid," she muttered.

"Missing the point," Lou whispered.

"Okay," Ms. Tom said, "that's enough. We are looking at this quote metaphorically."

She had them do their silent reading. When Lou opened her book, Beth leaned over to see what page she was on, and then showed Lou what page *she* was on, with a smile.

They were in the exact same spot.

By lunch, it felt normal between them again. Beth gave Lou two of her Oreos from the lunch Mrs. Tsai packed her, and Lou shared her cafeteria chicken strips because she knew how much Beth liked them. Also, maybe one of Beth's favorite foods would make the bad news go down easier.

Lou dipped her last chicken strip into the little cup of barbecue sauce that came with it, and handed it to Beth.

"Are you sure?" Beth asked.

Lou nodded. She tried to take the top off her Oreo in one piece, but it broke. "Remember yesterday? When I got called into the office?"

"Were you in trouble?"

"Mr. Sturgess found out we moved. My mom was supposed to tell the school, and she didn't, and now . . ."

Beth's eyes widened. She swallowed. "Now . . . what?"

"I have to change schools. To my new district."

"Next year."

"Next week."

Beth suspended the second half of the chicken finger over the sauce. Tears were gathering in the corners of her eyes.

Lou piled the crumbled bits of cookie onto the filling and put the whole thing in her mouth, then let the sweet mass sweep the salty slime of almost-crying down her throat.

Beth lowered the chicken finger into the sauce and dunked and dunked and dunked and dunked without ever eating it.

"It's not fair," she said. She shook her head. "It's not fair."

Joey Levoy ran by their table, picked up Lou's second Oreo, and crammed it into his mouth before they even knew what was happening. Infuriated, Beth threw the half chicken finger and sauce as hard as she could, and it hit Joey in the neck.

Then Beth buried her head in her hands and sobbed. Lou wished she could undo stealing from Beth and Alan, getting caught, being jealous of Beth's erasers and father. Wished she could undo every time she had ever been anything less than a perfect friend to someone who was going to miss her this much.

22

WHEN THEY GOT TO THE Merritt-Mendoza house, they were greeted by Rosie and Tala with Shannon standing behind them in the doorway. She didn't have on lipstick this time, and wore a long, fluffy red sweater and black yoga pants and clogs with flowers etched into the leather.

"Rosie's been asking about you two all day," Shannon said. "After your mom called, I told them the big girls were coming over and I haven't heard the end of it since."

Rosie slipped her hand into Lou's the second she put her guitar down and pulled her toward the stairs. "See my bunnies."

"Go ahead," Shannon said. "Marcus is on a run with the dog, but they'll be back any minute." She turned to Casey. "You want to hang with me in the kitchen?" Casey followed her and didn't look back.

Lou climbed the stairs with Rosie and stopped with her at an open door. "See my room," Rosie said, tugging her hand.

But Lou froze in the doorway.

Against the wall was the bunk bed. Lou and Casey's bunk bed, from the apartment. It had a blanket hanging from the top, to make a private fort out of the bottom bunk.

Lou pulled her hand out of Rosie's. "Is that a new bed? Did you just get it?"

"Yeah. My bunk bed. I don't even have to share." She ran over to it and crawled behind the blanket.

"It's *my* bunk bed," Lou said to the blanket.

"My bunk bed," came Rosie's voice.

Lou looked around the room in an effort to distract herself and stop feeling what she was feeling. Her eyes fell on a troll doll on a jumbled toy shelf and, barely thinking, she closed her hand around it and put it in her pocket.

Rosie crawled back out and looked at Lou as if she knew what had just happened.

"You don't share with Tala?" Lou asked.

"No."

"Okay." She wanted to get out. First, she looked around once more in case Steve had discarded any other of her belongings, but she didn't see anything else familiar. "Show me Tala's room."

Rosie skipped out and down the hall two doors. Tala's room was much smaller and simpler. There were no piles of toys and games and clothes, just a smooth wooden box that had been stenciled or painted with red and blue balloons and held a few stuffed animals.

"Where are the bunnies?" Lou asked.

"See my closet." Rosie ran back to her room and Lou followed. Inside her closet was a cage with two rabbits, who looked sleepy. "Bill and Phil."

Lou crouched down and pretended to be interested in the rabbits. She tried to tell herself Rosie was a little kid and why wouldn't she think the bunk bed was hers now, if that's what her parents told her? But her head still buzzed with anger.

Then she heard her name. It was Marcus, his voice getting closer until he was there in the doorway. "Hey, Lou. Just going to take a two-minute shower and I'll meet you downstairs. Cool?"

Did you know this bunk bed belonged to me and I didn't say you could have it?

"Cool."

"How are the calluses?"

Marcus and Lou were in the same room where they'd had their last lesson, and, like before, Casey and Shannon were on the other side of the French doors, talking and eating cookies fresh from the oven. The smell in the room was a mix of sugar and vanilla and whatever soap Marcus had used in the shower.

They sat facing each other, and both had their guitars in their laps.

Lou held out her hand. "I don't think I have calluses yet. It mostly just hurts."

Marcus pressed a couple of her fingers between his. "You're getting there. You gotta be patient." He let go. "Been practicing with the chord chart?"

"Yeah," she said. "I mean, not that much."

"A little?" He raised his eyebrows with a smile, teasing.

"Yeah."

"A little is better than nothing." He strummed the strings of his guitar, then picked at the lowest string, his cheek practically touching the guitar body. "Do you want to learn how to tune?"

"Can I?"

"We can try. Let's see if you've got an ear."

She could tell he didn't mean literal ears. She tried a joke. "I've got two."

He laughed and glanced up. "You're in a better mood than last week."

"No, I'm not," she blurted. "Worse." She'd only wanted to make him laugh.

"Worse! I'm sorry."

"It's okay."

He bent over his guitar case, then held up a little black box. "We'll start with this. It's an electronic tuner. It'll give us a perfect version of the note, and we'll adjust until we match it."

He demonstrated with his guitar, playing the note on the

tuner and then turning the pegs as he plucked the string, depending on whether the note was coming out sharp or flat. "Sharp is when it's really close but a tiny bit too high, so we need to loosen the string. Flat is the opposite—a little too low and the string needs tightening. But first you just want to listen to your gut and see if the note sounds right to you, compared to the tuner, or off in some way."

She tried it with her guitar—playing an E on the tuner and plucking the bottom E on her guitar. She listened.

"How does that sound to you?" Marcus asked.

It sounded bad. She played the tuner again, plucked the string again. "It sounds . . . off," she said.

"Good. *Real* off. That happens with new strings and new guitars. They go out of tune easily. So does it sound too low to you or too high, compared to the tuner?"

"I don't know."

"Listen again. Close your eyes."

She did.

"Now try turning the peg and see which way gets you closer to the note and which way gets further."

She turned the peg one way and then the other and closed her eyes and played the note on the tuner again. Marcus waited, quiet. The more Lou tried to find the note, the more lost it seemed. Her frustration grew and she felt Marcus watching her and she thought about the bunk bed up in Rosie's room and finally she hit the top of the guitar and said, "I can't do it!"

Immediately, she was embarrassed for losing her temper.

"Well, you're not supposed to get it right the first time," Marcus said. "It doesn't work that way, usually."

Lou worried he was only saying that to make her feel better.

"You're frustrated," he added.

"I'm doing it wrong."

"No, you're *learning*. There's a difference." He pressed a button on the tuner. "Try the A."

She went through the whole process again for each string, concentrating with all her might on listening to the true tone and trying to match it. Marcus and the room and the distant sound of Casey talking in the kitchen faded out, and then she was done—having tried and failed at tuning all six strings.

"Great," Marcus said.

"It's still out of tune."

"Great that you know that. And you didn't give up. *And you were really into it!*"

She blew a big breath out through her mouth.

He laughed and said, "Not in the mood for my positivity?"

"Not really."

The right notes were lost, she was lost, the bunk bed, school, Beth . . . her life as she knew it was as lost as these stupid notes. He tuned her guitar for her, and showed her one more chord to add to the ones she'd already learned—a G— and then Casey tapped on the door and said it was time to go.

Lou wondered if they were going to do family singing time like before. But Shannon was already carrying Tala up the stairs. Marcus grabbed a cookie off the plate on the counter. "How's everything over at Steve's?" he asked both Lou and Casey.

Casey shrugged. "It's whatever."

"I've known that guy a pretty long time. Ever since we moved in. He was the first one on the block offering us his truck if we needed it during the move. Took care of his mom for a long time, too. He throws this great block party the first weekend in May. He probably told you."

Casey didn't say anything. Lou took a cookie. They'd never heard of any block party.

"Sorry," Marcus said, glancing from Casey to Lou and back again. "I'm not trying to sell you on him. Just mentioning it. I know it must be complicated."

"We have to go," Casey said.

"Sure." Marcus slipped his hands into his jeans pockets and nodded. He looked like he wanted to say more about Steve or the neighborhood, but maybe he'd had enough of wasting his optimism on them for today.

But then, he did smile at Lou and say, "Keep up the good work."

23

"SO ARE YOU REALLY LEARNING how to play that thing?"

The walk back from the Merritt-Mendozas was the first time Casey had talked to her all day.

"I've only had two lessons. It takes time." The guitar in its case got heavy quickly. She switched it to her other hand.

Casey's steps slowed. "I always wanted to learn the saxophone but there was never money for it."

"I didn't know that."

"Yeah. I think sax is kind of cool. Or drums." She stopped walking a few houses away from Steve's. "I have to tell you something, Lulu."

"Okay." Her fingers hurt from the guitar case handle and the tuning lesson. She set the guitar down on the sidewalk. Casey's face was pretty in the streetlight, with her dark hair curling against her pale skin.

"Dad's phone number is working again. I talked to him today." She paused a moment before continuing. "I wanted to ask him if . . . well, I wanted to see if I could live with him the rest of the school year. Or if I could use his address to at least say I lived in the city. For the school district."

Lou held still, listening hard, like she had listened to the tones coming from the electronic tuner.

What she heard was *I*, not *we*.

"Would you really live with him?" Lou whispered. Him drunk. Him disappearing. Him and the strange people that came and went out of his life. Would she really do that?

"If I could, yeah," she said, an edge of anger in her voice. "I don't want to change schools."

Neither did Lou, but she would never think about living with *Dad*. "Mom wouldn't let you," is what she said.

"Lou, just—" Casey turned away from her and looked up at the sky. When she turned back, she said, "It doesn't matter, because what I wanted to tell you is he lost his apartment."

So he *had* had somewhere to live. But now he'd lost it.

It had happened before. He'd gone from an okay one-bedroom right before and after the divorce, when he had one of his better jobs, to an okay studio when he lost that job, to a smaller one-bedroom where Lou once saw a rat, to a week-to-week studio with a hot plate and tiny sink for a kitchen, then to a big house with roommates. All of that in just one year. Then somehow he got a pretty good job and was staying in a nice furnished studio, but he lost that job and had to move. It was always something.

"Where did he move to?"

"Nowhere." Casey pushed her bangs back and kept her hand there on top of her head. "One of his friends loaned him a van to live in." She let her hair fall down again. "He says he likes it. He said if he doesn't like his neighbors he can just drive to another street."

Lou listened. It sounded off. *Real off*, she heard Marcus's voice in her mind. It sounded out of tune with what life was supposed to be.

Casey dug at some weeds growing in a crack in the sidewalk with the toe of her boot. "I still want to figure something out so I can stay at school, but . . . I don't know what. I just thought you should know I talked to Dad."

"Does he have a job?" Lou asked.

"Some delivery gigs and stuff. As long as he has a phone, he can do that kind of work. Enough to get food and gas."

And alcohol.

Lou picked up her guitar case. "I'm cold."

A few dozen steps and she'd be at Steve's and it would be warm inside. There'd be food if she wanted a snack before bed. There'd be her room and her books and blankets. She heard Casey's boots on the sidewalk behind her and thought about Dad in a van.

* * *

When Mom came to tuck her in, she started to lie down next to Lou like usual but Lou stopped her. "You can just sit on the bed."

"Oh. Okay."

"I told Beth today that I might be changing schools."

Mom stayed quiet for a few seconds. "How did that feel?"

"She cried."

"How did it feel for *you*? Did you cry?"

Lou shook her head.

"You know it's okay to cry, if you feel like you want to."

"Dad always says not to."

Mom got stiff and still, then she breathed in and said, "Dad isn't very good with feelings. That's one reason he drinks. Do you understand?"

She didn't, really. Did drinking make you not feel? Because it seemed like drinking gave Dad big feelings, and let loose his sadness and his anger and his everything else. She pressed her index finger into one of the pearly blue buttons of Mom's cardigan.

"Did you give our bunk bed to Marcus and Shannon?"

That made Mom go quiet again.

"Did you?" Lou repeated.

"Steve—we—we offered it to them," Mom said carefully. "There really wasn't room in the garage for some of the bigger things."

Things? Lou pulled at the button. "What else wasn't there room for?"

"Well . . . the dresser from my bedroom. One of the shelves that was starting to break anyway. Nothing you would miss."

How would Mom know if she'd miss it or not? She missed everything.

"Is the kitchen table in the garage?"

"The one from the apartment?" Mom asked. She pulled Lou's hand away from the button. "You're going to rip it off, honey."

"Our old table. The yellow table."

"The yellow table went to the Goodwill."

Lou froze, then rolled away. It felt as though something had been torn right from her hands.

"It was just a table, Belle."

Just a table. Their table. The table they sat at for nearly every meal when Dad was there, sober, when he was drunk and eating with his eyes closed, and when he wasn't there at all. Where Lou and Casey cooled their Shrinky Dinks and dyed Easter eggs. Where Mom told them about the divorce. Before Steve. Always.

How could Mom call it "just a table"?

She pulled herself into a ball as far away from Mom as possible. When Mom touched her back, she scrunched down smaller.

"Do you want me to leave you alone now?" Mom asked softly.

"Yes," Lou said, in her quietest voice.

Mom had said it was okay to cry but she also said "just a table," and Lou didn't know how to sort it all out. The feelings about the table and the bunk bed and the apartment, the feelings about Dad living in a van, the feelings of hope and new beginnings that were creeping in when she thought of what Steve said about changing schools and making friends for the summer . . . all of these things were loud inside her, like a hundred songs playing at once.

And she didn't know how to pick one apart from the other and really hear it.

24

By Thursday morning, Ms. Tom had made a sign-up sheet for kids to say what they'd bring to Lou's going-away party.

On Friday, the class had the party at the end of the school day. Joey Levoy brought potato chips and Lawrence Lee brought a tray of cheese and crackers from the store. Beth and her mom made cupcakes. The last time Beth brought cupcakes was Lou's birthday. The sleepover coupons Beth had given her then were in Lou's junk drawer, where she'd buried them after Beth discovered the stolen things.

Ms. Tom asked if anyone in the class wanted to say something nice about Lou. "Starting a new school is hard," she said, "and this is a good chance for you to give Lou some encouragement."

Hands went up so quickly that Lou thought Ms. Tom

had probably talked to the other kids about it ahead of time.

Joey went first and Lou elbowed Beth, dreading whatever joke he was going to make. Even Ms. Tom looked skeptical. But then he said, "When we do reading aloud, Lou is the best. She never messes up. She knows how to say all the words and everything."

A few other kids said, "Yeah," or nodded. Lou stared down at her plate of chips and cheese, embarrassed in a good way. She did like reading aloud.

Charles Poza talked about the time last year when a bird flew into the classroom and got trapped there and Lou was the one who was able to get it to fly out again. Really that had been luck, and the bird pooped on her bare hand, but it was nice that he remembered.

Lawrence went, then Daisy Dobrov, then a couple of other kids. Lou listened hard. Then, Beth's hand went up. Ms. Tom said, "Yes, Beth?"

Lou held her breath.

"I like Lou because she's real," Beth said. "She's not perfect. She's just herself." Then Beth started crying again, like she had at lunch on Tuesday, her head down on her desk. Lou put her arm across Beth's shoulder and a few more kids came over to pat Beth on the back and tell her it would be okay. They would still be there to be her friends when Lou was gone.

That's when it hit her that they were all going to go on without her. This classroom would still exist and everyone else would still be in it and Joey would still be making jokes and all the usual games and conversations at recess and lunch would happen. It didn't seem real or possible, but that's how it would be.

She walked with Beth to where she was supposed to meet Casey, like they'd been doing since the move. Lou carried a shopping bag that contained leftover cupcakes, a card from Ms. Tom, and a jumble of pens and pencils and erasers and markers and paper and drawings from inside her desk.

"Can you come over this weekend?" Beth asked.

"I have to babysit . . ." Saturday would be her and Casey's first real babysitting job for the Merritt-Mendozas now that the kids and the dog knew who they were. "Maybe the next weekend?"

"Make sure to ask ahead and I will, too."

"Or you could come to Steve's house," Lou suggested for the second time in as many weeks.

"You know how my parents are. It's easier if you come to mine."

They walked a little more. It was a gray day, but not too cold. Casey and Daniel were ahead of them at the corner, leaning into one another against a mailbox. Beth watched them and asked, "Are they in love?"

"I think so. I don't know. They say 'I love you' to each other all the time."

They were really kissing now and Beth and Lou could

see Casey running her hands all through Daniel's hair, and Daniel's hands under Casey's jacket. Beth giggled a little. Lou was about to tell her they should stop watching when Casey saw them over Daniel's shoulder and gently pushed him away.

"Oops," Beth said, and laughed again. She looked at Lou. "I should get home."

"Okay."

"But we're not saying goodbye!"

"I know."

Beth put her hand in the pocket of her jacket and pulled out a round lip balm, like the one Lou had taken and then given back when she was caught. "Here. This one is green apple."

A wave of shame washed over Lou when she knew she was supposed to be thankful and she wasn't. She hadn't taken the lip balm because she really wanted or needed lip balm. Now this one would always remind her of what she did, and how Beth knew. But she couldn't ruin this last day of school with Beth after the cupcakes and the nice thing Beth had said about her in class.

She thanked her and took it.

Casey had started down the street toward them while Daniel went the other way.

"I guess I'll . . . see you," Lou said. "Or talk to you."

"Or write me."

"Yeah." Lou nodded. "Bye."

"Bye-not-bye," Beth answered. She waved at Casey, too, then headed in the direction of her house.

Lou cupped her hands around her mouth and shouted, "Bye-not-bye!" and Beth turned and jumped up and down, waving her hands over her head wildly, turning their goodbye into a chance to laugh.

When Steve picked them up, he asked if they wanted to go into the shopping center and get ice cream. He offered to buy a coffee drink for Casey from Peet's. He offered to get anything from the food court: noodles, pizza, curry, anything.

Casey asked, "Why can't we just go home?"

"We can," Steve answered. "But we don't have to. It's Friday. It's the last day at your schools. Kind of a big day."

"Traffic is only going to get worse if we stop."

"We can handle it."

Lou sat in the middle of the truck seat as usual, stuck between Steve's trying and Casey's refusing. She would have liked a green tea ice cream or some fries, but if she accepted the offer from Steve it would only make Casey think she was taking Steve's side. She didn't want to take anyone's side.

"Let's go home," Lou said. "I'm tired. My class had a party and I have leftover cupcakes." She passed the bag to Casey. "You can have one if you want."

Casey shook her head.

"Well, all right," Steve said, and pulled away to leave the parking lot. After they got through the jam-up before the freeway entrance, Steve said, "So, Lou, your classroom had a party?"

"Mm-hmm." She stopped herself from adding any details.

"I bet that was nice." He sounded like he wanted to say something more and Lou had the feeling he shouldn't say it.

Casey shrank away from Lou until her face was practically pressed against the window on the passenger side.

"How about you, Casey?" Steve asked, leaning forward for a second to see past Lou.

That was exactly the kind of thing Lou had worried he would say. She was frustrated at Casey for being so stubborn, and at Steve for not knowing when to leave her alone.

"Nope. No party. I haven't even told anyone I'm leaving."

Sounding surprised, Steve said, "So . . . you're just gonna not show up on Monday and your friends won't have any warning?"

"Pretty much."

He didn't have an answer to that. There probably wasn't one.

In bed that night, after tuck-in and after the house got very quiet, Lou did one of her long prayers. She hadn't done that since before the wedding when she prayed for it to not happen, and God had let it happen anyway, and Dad was worse, and Casey was still mad at her more often than not, and they had to leave their schools . . . It was hard to know if God was even listening.

But one thing she really liked about her religion was the idea that every day, you got a chance to start over. You could be forgiven and everything could be new just by asking.

She told God she was sorry about stealing and also sorry that she wasn't more sorry. She was thankful Beth had given her another chance. She was glad Dad's phone was working again, even though she hadn't gotten to talk to him and even though he was living in a van. She asked God to watch over him and—like always—to make him stop drinking. Make him better.

She asked God to help her get calluses and a better ear and learn the guitar and find a song that she'd be able to play from start to finish without messing up. She was still mad about the bunk bed, she told God, and she knew it wasn't Rosie's fault and would try not to take it out on her tomorrow.

When she ran through her list of things and people she was thankful for, she found herself saying them aloud, a whisper into the dark:

"Mom and Casey."

"Beth and Rex."

"Cupcakes."

"Fog."

"Having my own room."

She did like it, she'd decided. The privacy and the good light from the window for reading in bed.

"Steve."

That one surprised her. Steve?

She said it again to make sure.

"Steve."

She rolled over in bed and finished her list quietly, in her head. *The ocean, eucalyptus trees, Ms. Tom, her guitar, Marcus, cookies, horses and all cats, some dogs, ice cream . . .*

Soon, she was asleep.

PART IV

The New Girls

25

ON SATURDAY MORNING, STEVE TAPPED on Lou's door. "Breakfast quesadillas in ten minutes!" Then he did the same at Casey's door.

Lou was hungry for those quesadillas. Steve had made them before: scrambled eggs and black beans and cheese and salsa between crispy tortillas. He cut them into wedges and served them with sour cream and guacamole on the side, two things Casey loved even though she acted like she didn't care when Steve was the one offering.

She got up and went to Casey's door. "Casey? Case?"

A grumpy-sounding "What" came from the other side.

"Can I come in?"

After a long pause, Casey said, "Yeah."

Her room looked as if they'd just moved yesterday and

not a month ago. Clothes still spilled out of cardboard boxes, and she hadn't hung any of her posters or draped her scarves on the bedposts or put books on the shelf.

She was a lump under two comforters. Lou pushed the lump. "His breakfasts are good."

"I don't care."

He's actually nice, Lou wanted to say. *He's trying.*

What she said was "Did you really not tell your friends about changing schools?"

She emerged from the blankets and sat up. "They'll figure it out. I don't have that many friends, you know. The ones I care about besides Daniel have cars, and they'll drive down here all the time and get me and we can text and it won't even be that different."

Lou listened and decided that sounded about half true. Casey hadn't said anything else all week about Dad and his van or what she was "figuring out" about not having to actually change schools, so maybe there hadn't been any figuring out or more calls to Dad.

The smell of frying tortillas floated down the hall and right up Lou's nose.

"Just come eat breakfast with me. Please?"

Casey sighed. "Fine. Only because I'm hungry, not because I want to talk to Mom or Steve."

"Mom isn't even up." They had gotten into a Saturday routine where Steve made breakfast for him and Lou and Casey, and Mom slept late. "You have to talk to Steve a *little*, though, since he cooked for us and everything."

"Okay!" Casey said with a huge fake smile. She flung her covers back and danced around the room saying "Thank you, dear stepfather, for this *wonderful meal*; I shall never forget your generosity!"

It was supposed to be funny. And it *was*, a little bit. Lou allowed a short giggle but hoped Casey would stop.

"What a *good, good* man," Casey continued, pressing her hands in front of her as if praying, "to take in the needy." She put a corner of her blanket over her head and held it together under her chin. "A miserable, downcast woman such as our poor mother and her wretched children."

"Stop," Lou blurted.

Casey let the blanket fall. "Sorry, I didn't know Steve was your new best friend."

"He's not."

"You like him."

"So?" After a pause, she added, "I don't like him *that* much."

"Just wait till the honeymoon is over and the *real* Steve comes out and we're all stuck here."

Steve's voice boomed down the hall. "Order's up!" That was his way of saying the food was on the table and ready to eat.

Casey picked a bra up off the floor and wiggled into it under her shirt. She watched Lou watching her and said, "You're going to need one of these pretty soon." She shook her head. "Sixth grade in the suburbs. Nightmare."

Lou hated when Casey got this way. What did she even mean, *the real Steve*?

"Let's go eat," Casey said. She brushed past Lou, who followed her down the hall. But Lou had lost her appetite.

26

Lou stared into her closet.

There were some hand-me-downs from Casey, some things from Goodwill. Most of the rest of her wardrobe came from the sales racks at stores where everything was already discounted. Clothes weren't that big a deal to her or to most other kids at her school. Her *old* school, that is. Those kids had known her since kindergarten and didn't judge her based on what she wore.

But in a new school . . .

What Casey had said about sixth grade being a "nightmare" was eating at her. Even in fifth grade, where she was now, kids could be mean. And *now* was when she'd be making her first impression on the ones she'd probably be in school with for the rest of fifth until high school, at least.

She took everything out of her closet and put it on her bed, then did the same thing with all the clothes in her dresser drawers.

Back at the apartment, Casey and Lou would do this sort of thing together: go through their clothes and toys and games, take bags of stuff to Goodwill and pick up different things from the shelves and racks there. Then they'd come home and rearrange their bedroom furniture and wash their new used clothes at the laundromat. Those were some of their favorite days together.

Casey was still in her mood from this morning, closed back up in her own room the minute breakfast was over. This left Lou on her own in trying to figure out what to keep and what to give away, what to make new outfits from, what looked good and what looked babyish or wrong.

The pile of clothes on her bed overwhelmed her. Casey was the one who always knew how to start a big project like this.

She picked up a T-shirt she'd gotten at the Santa Cruz Beach Boardwalk last summer, with a unicorn on the front and Lou's name ironed onto the back. Beth's mom had paid for them to get matching shirts and it was also her idea to pay extra to have their names put on. It was too small now and maybe too fourth grade. She dropped it on the floor and it landed with the back facing up.

L-O-U.

Joey Levoy used to tease her by saying that Lou was his

grandpa's name. For a while he called her Grandpa. It didn't catch on with anyone else at school, so he dropped it. She was named after Mom's grandma—Lou's great-grandma—who had also been Louisa, and also went by Lou her whole life. But maybe kids at her new school would think it was an old man's name, too.

Louisa was kind of different in its own way, but didn't feel like *her*.

She put her toe over the O on the T-shirt.

L-U.

Lu.

Sounded the same. Was still her. Yet it felt different when she looked at the letters.

She sat at her desk and got out a piece of notebook paper and wrote *Lu Emerson* in her best cursive, then did it again. Twice, three times, four times, until it filled the paper. On a new piece of paper, she wrote it big in block printing with a purple marker.

As she was taping the paper to her bedroom door, Mom walked by with a few rolls of toilet paper. She stopped to read the sign. "*Lu Emerson*. Hmm. I guess the O *is* a bit superfluous."

"What's that?"

"Unnecessary, basically. Lu. I like it." Mom nodded in approval. "It's jaunty. Look that one up if you need to."

Lou—Lu—glanced down the hall at Casey's closed door. "Mom, can you cut my hair today?"

"I can do it right now." She handed Lu the rolls of toilet paper. "Put these under the sink in your bathroom and I'll go get my shears."

Casey came out of her room while Lu put the TP in the cabinet. She stood in the bathroom doorway.

"How come you didn't ask *me* to cut your hair?"

"You were listening?"

"I heard."

Casey had cut Lu's hair the last few times and she liked doing it. Usually it only meant cutting an inch or so off the bottom.

"I want bangs."

"I can do bangs."

"I want Mom to do it."

"Fine." When Casey turned to go back into her room, she noticed the sign on Lu's door and walked over to it. "'Lu.' That's cute, I guess. Do I still get to call you Lulu?"

"If you want."

"I guess I should go through my clothes and stuff, too," Casey said, leaning into Lu's room. "Or at least put them away. Since we're stuck here." She crossed her arms and rested her hip on the wall. "Do you want to try on anything I don't want anymore?"

"Okay."

"You can fashion-show for me. I'll help you make outfits if you want."

"Just leave it all in a bag by my door." Casey seemed out

of her bad mood but Lu didn't trust it to stick.

Casey paused a few seconds, then pushed herself off the wall and said, "Sure. Will do."

Lu sat on a chair in the kitchen while Mom circled her with the scissors. She had a gotten a good set of cutting shears—one for cutting and one for thinning—way back when she was in college, and had them sharpened every year. She'd been cutting her own hair as well as Lu and Casey's forever.

"What are we thinking?" Mom asked.

"Something different."

"How different?"

"Bangs."

Mom nodded. "I can see that. How about shorter, too? Like Ramona? About here?" Mom placed her fingers on Lu's neck, right above her shoulder.

"Not that much."

Mom moved her fingers down a couple of inches. "Here?"

"Yeah."

She started snipping the back and Lu watched chunks of her light brown hair fall onto the beige linoleum of Steve's kitchen. "There's a nice layer of reddish hair underneath, close to your neck," Mom said. "Maybe that will be your color as you get older."

"My hair color is going to change?" She looked up at Mom.

"Hold still, Belle." She did another snip. "Maybe. A lot

of times our hair is lighter when we're kids, then it gets darker. Sometimes the reverse."

Her hair was going to change. She'd need a bra. She'd grown out of most of her fourth-grade clothes. She *could* get her period soon, too. Their life in the apartment was fading so fast, into what felt almost like a dream. She sniffed.

"You okay?"

"Yeah. I got a hair in my nose."

Mom moved around in front of her and bent low to do the bangs. She combed some of Lu's hair over her face. Lu closed her eyes, felt Mom's breath on her cheek. "Ready?" Mom asked.

"Yes."

27

"IT LOOKS SO GOOD," CASEY said again.

They were walking to Marcus and Shannon's to babysit. Casey's mood was even better—she liked going to the Merritt-Mendoza house now.

She kept staring at Lu. "You just look . . . different. In a good way."

"Thanks."

"Not that you looked bad before."

Lu knew what Casey meant. There was something about the haircut that had changed her face. And she had on an old black-and-pink striped T-shirt of Casey's. It was a little big and hung slightly off one shoulder so you could see she also had on her own pink undershirt—a lighter pink than the pink in the T-shirt.

Altogether, the removal of one O and several inches of hair left her feeling light. Half her wardrobe was stuffed into garbage bags by the door of her room, ready to be donated.

Marcus came to the door first. He dropped his jaw in an exaggerated way when he saw Lu. "Who's this little punk-rocker?"

Casey laughed. "You need to get her into a band, right?"

He stepped back. "Come on in. Shannon's walking the dog but should be back in a minute." They followed him into the kitchen. "The kids have had dinner and baths. Noodle is in bed but will probably need a diaper change at some point. Tala and Rosie are upstairs. They're allowed to run wild for another hour, then they need to get in bed, too."

"Are they already in pj's?" Casey asked.

"Yep. And they know the rules. They can take books with them to bed and read quietly for fifteen minutes, then it's lights-out." Marcus tapped a piece of paper on the kitchen island. "Both our cells, pediatrician, vet, and of course there's 911."

Lu felt nervous all of a sudden thinking about all the things that could go wrong, but Casey seemed confident as she asked if any of the kids had any allergies.

"Tala had to go to the ER after a bee sting once, but I don't think you need to worry about that tonight." Marcus opened the fridge. "They can have *one* cookie or pudding each if they ask and say please. You guys can have as many as you want. Or anything in here. There's some leftover Filipino barbecue if you're into that. My mom made enough to feed the block." He closed the fridge and turned around, then grinned at Lu again. "Love the hair."

"My mom did it."

"And she changed her name," Casey said. "It's Lu, *L-U*, now, not *L-O-U*."

"I dig it."

The dog came bounding in to greet them, and Shannon followed. She made a big deal over Lu's new hair, too. "Your eyes are so pretty! Ooh, I can't *wait* to put makeup on you."

"I'm not allowed," Lu said. "Till seventh grade."

"Just for fun." Shannon reached over and tucked a strand of Lu's hair behind her ear. "We won't let anyone see."

Shannon looked beautiful, as always. She had on a flowy dress, cherry red with little black roses all over it. It hung perfectly on her full body. She had her short hair slicked back and wore dark lipstick.

"I can do yours, too, Case," Shannon added. "Though you do a pretty good job on your own." She glanced at Marcus. "I'm obsessed with these girls right now. Do we have to go out? We could stay in and play makeover."

Casey seemed to blush, or maybe it was the glow she always got around Shannon and Marcus.

Marcus laughed and put his strong arm around Shannon's shoulder. "Uh, *no*. I haven't been out alone with you in, like, two weeks."

"Well, okay," Shannon teased. To Casey and Lu she said, "I'll go up to Rosie and Tala and break the news that we're leaving."

Tala cried a little bit after Marcus and Shannon were gone and stopped when Casey told her they could have a snack. Then Lu and Casey played zoo with them. Lu chose to be an elephant because it was easy and fun to make her arm into a trunk. Rosie was a tiger, Casey a seal, and Tala was a dog even though they tried to explain to her dogs weren't zoo animals.

Tala threw a small tantrum when it was time for them to get in bed. Casey lured them upstairs by still acting like a seal, flopping up the stairs on her belly and making seal noises. She was really good at it.

Lu followed them up. When they got to Rosie's room, Casey froze and went back to her human form.

Lu realized: she'd just seen the bunk bed.

"Um . . ." Casey said, still staring into the room. "What?"

Rosie skipped over to the bottom bunk and jumped in.

"Mom said they needed it and there wasn't room in the garage." Lu was careful to leave Steve's name out of it. Casey didn't need more reasons to dislike him.

"You knew?"

"I saw it last time. I wanted to tell you but you were already mad about something."

"Read me!" Rosie shouted.

"Read to yourself," Casey muttered. She scooped up Tala and took her to her own bed.

Rosie was waving a small book at Lu now, chanting, "Read, read, read!"

Lu looked down at Rosie. She had everything she wanted. Her own room. A bunk bed. Cookies and pudding and a dog. A fun, loving dad and a cool mom. Lu had to fight through the feeling of being mad at her.

"It's almost lights-out," she said to Rosie. "Your dad said you can be quiet in your bed."

"Daddy reads me." Rosie was crumbling now instead of being demanding, her voice weaker and eyes uncertain.

Lu swallowed her anger and sat on the edge of Rosie's bed with the book, and read to her.

When the kids were all asleep, Casey and Lu sat at the kitchen island and sampled leftovers and snacks and treats. Casey's good mood had disappeared again. It seemed it could never stay. Her face was cloudy as she tried bites of barbecue and half slices of pizza and two different flavors of Goldfish crackers and washed them down with a diet root beer.

Lu found herself trying to talk Casey out of her feelings even though she was just as mad about the bunk bed, if not madder.

"It's not like we were ever going to use the bed again," she said.

"That's not the point."

"I know, but . . ."

"But what? But Steve and Mom should be able to do whatever they want with our stuff without asking first?" She got up and opened cupboards until she found a bag of potato chips. "That's not right and you know it."

"Maybe they just—"

"No. Stop."

Lu had been going to say that maybe Mom and Steve just didn't think about asking since they had new beds at Steve's, and the week they moved had been so busy with the rain and the wedding on top of it. Also, what was it about the bed that belonged to Lu and Casey? They hadn't bought it. They hadn't assembled it. They hadn't painted it. No one had said, *This is yours now for all time.*

Still, Mom should have told them. It *wasn't* right and Lu *did* know it, but all she wanted was for Casey to go back to being happier. Lu definitely wouldn't tell her about what had happened to the yellow table.

Casey crunched chips, three or four at a time, her cheeks puffing out from her mouth being full of food. Lu reached for the bag and Casey tilted it toward her. She got a handful and crammed them into her mouth. Shattered bits of chip stuck to her lips and chin, fell to the counter. Casey laughed a little.

After they'd eaten most of the stuff they'd taken out, Casey held her stomach and groaned. "I feel gross."

Lu cleaned up and hoped Marcus meant it when he said

they could have as much of anything they wanted. Casey watched without helping, while she twisted back and forth on the kitchen stool.

"Remember Covered Wagon?" she asked.

"Yeah."

Before Casey had grown out of make-believe games, they'd drape blankets over the bunk bed and put two kitchen chairs at one end and pretend they were pioneer girls. The bed was their covered wagon. They had to imagine the team of horses.

Lu added her own memory: "Remember when we put the top mattress on the floor, and turned the upper bunk into a reading loft?"

Casey's face brightened. "Oh yeah! We had snacks up there and all our stuffed animals and kept our library books organized by due date."

"I used to think the robes and sweaters we hung on the post looked like monsters in the night."

"I liked hearing Mom tuck you in right underneath me, after I was too old for it myself."

Lu finished washing the empty leftover containers and set them on a towel. "Everything's different now."

"Obviously."

Warm water from the tap coursed over Lu's hands as she got the last of the potato chip grease off them. "I'm nervous about school on Monday." It was easier to say with her back to Casey.

"You've got your new name, your new hair . . ." Casey's phone chimed before she finished. "It's Shannon," she said when Lu turned around.

Shannon had texted to ask how things were going and that they'd be home in about an hour or so. After Casey texted back, she spun her phone around on the countertop.

"I'm nervous, too, Lu. I don't think anyone's going to like me. They'll like you. But me . . ." She shrugged.

"Why not? Why would they like me more than you?"

"Reasons." She rested her chin in her hands. "Fifth graders are generally nice people. Compared to tenth. And you're sweet. I'm not sweet."

"*I'm* not sweet," Lu argued. She'd stolen from her best friend! She'd vandalized cars with a permanent marker! She'd hated tiny Rosie for just existing. But she didn't know how to say any of those things out loud, even to Casey, who would probably understand better than anyone.

"Well, you do a better job faking it, then."

Maybe. She *did* try to be what people wanted, not make waves. Casey liked making waves. Or maybe she didn't like it, but it seemed she couldn't help it.

"Sorry I didn't let you cut my hair," Lu said. She still just wanted to make Casey feel better.

"Mom did a good job. I bet you'll be super popular by Wednesday."

"You too."

Casey made a scoffing sound, then stood up and

stretched her arms overhead. "Let's go watch TV."

They half watched the TV in the music room while Casey texted Daniel, and Lu looked through Marcus's guitar music for a song he could teach her—something she could have ready to maybe play for Dad over the phone, or at least to be able to tell him she'd learned.

Already? he'd ask. *Wow. It seems like I just gave it to you, and here you are, already knowing a whole song.*

She put Marcus's music back on the shelf and nestled into the deep couch, imagining how she'd tell Dad about her favorite songs from his records, the ones in the tote bag in the closet.

You have those records? That's great—I thought I'd lost them.

He'd thank her for saving them. And he'd say his favorites were the same as hers.

I should find a guitar for me, too. Then we could get together and play. I bet I still remember stuff from when I was pretty good.

Here, she was adding fiction to her fantasy. She didn't actually know if he'd ever played guitar himself; Mom probably would have mentioned it by now if he had. But she liked to imagine it. How her playing would make *him* want to play again, and it would be a healthy hobby away from drinking, and also it would be something for them to have in common. He would want to see her regularly to work on their music.

These are my favorite times together, Loula, he'd say, looking at her over the top of his guitar the way Marcus did.

Mine, too.

Marcus would be impressed with Dad. *Now I know where you get your talent!* he'd say to Lu.

She melted deeper into the couch and her fantasy dissolved into a dream where she had red hair and was in a band with Dad and Marcus and, for some reason, Daisy Dobrov from school. They were on a stage but they were also in a house and a small audience was gathered. The song they played was nothing Lu recognized from real life, but it reminded her of home, and somehow she knew all the words.

28

A FEW PEOPLE AT CHURCH on Sunday made a fuss over Lu's haircut, which left her feeling self-conscious. She wished you could just make a change and *be* the After version of yourself without everyone pointing it out. At least at the new school, no one would know about her Before. She would simply show up and be Lu.

Pastor Richards squinted at her and asked, "Did you get taller since last Sunday?"

"No. It's my hair."

"Ohhhhhh, the *hair*." He winked and Lu realized his question hadn't been serious. She hated that kind of teasing question, because how were you supposed to know? If you didn't answer seriously, you might end up being rude, and if you did, you might end up feeling stupid.

The sermon was about trusting God in times of uncertainty, and it seemed specifically written for people who were starting a new school the next day. Lu glanced at Casey to see if she noticed it, too, but she had her phone hidden under her jacket in her lap and kept looking at that.

". . . you can tell what's inside a wet sponge by giving it a good hard squeeze," Pastor Richards was saying. "Sometimes that's what God lets life do to us. Life presses and squeezes and we learn a lot about what's inside us. Faith or fear, love or hate, obedience or rebellion. Are we full of clean, fresh water, or old dirty dishpan water?"

Her mind wandered before she heard Pastor Richards's solution to the whole thing and now everyone was standing up to sing the closing hymn. Casey seemed surprised, too, that time had passed so quickly, and she fumbled with her phone and jacket as Mom looked at her sideways.

As soon as the benediction got to "Amen," Casey walked fast down the aisle between the rows of pews. Lu followed while Mom and Steve stood around to chat. Soon, Casey was out the front doors of the church and headed toward the park.

Mom and Steve liked to stay to the very end of coffee hour. They somehow had a lot to talk about with people every week. There were no other kids Lu's age in their small church and if Casey could go off to the park to meet Daniel, Lu should be able to run over to Beth's for a little while. She started back in to ask. Then decided that would waste too much time. They probably wouldn't even notice she was gone.

Mr. Tsai came to the door after Lu rang the bell. He had on his maroon tracksuit.

His eyebrows went up in surprise. "Hi there."

"Is Beth home?"

"Yes," he said, opening the door wider. "Come in."

Alan was in his pj's in the front room, playing video games. He glanced at Lu, then back to the screen. "She's with Daisy in her room."

Daisy? Daisy Dobrov?

"I'll tell them you're here," Mr. Tsai said.

"Okay." She perched on the edge of the sofa like a stranger, hands folded in her lap while she watched Alan's game.

"You can use the other controller if you want to play," he said.

"No, thanks."

After what felt like too long, Beth came down the hall with Daisy close behind. Lu could tell they'd been doing each other's hair and playing with makeup. Mrs. Tsai sometimes gave Beth her almost-used-up eye shadows and lipsticks.

"What are you doing here?" Beth asked. She said it in a nice way, but the question was still uncomfortable. What *was* she doing there?

Daisy stood behind Beth, silent and serious.

"It's coffee hour at church. I just thought . . . just saying hi."

"Hi."

Daisy laughed and also said, "Hi!"

"You were in my dream last night," Lu told Daisy. "We were in a band."

She wrinkled her nose. "Weird."

Maybe Beth always had someone else sleep over when Lu couldn't come. It seemed like she would have mentioned it, though, one of those times.

Mr. Tsai cleared his throat and said something in Mandarin.

"Oh," Beth said. "Do you want to stay over for lunch?"

"Um, I probably can't." Beth looked relieved. "I didn't tell my mom I was coming over."

Mr. Tsai frowned. "You should go back if you didn't get permission."

"I know. Sorry. It's okay. I'm allowed to." Maybe. Probably. "Well, bye," she said to Beth.

Daisy said "Bye!" and giggled.

Beth stepped forward. "Did you ask about sleeping over next weekend?"

"Not yet."

"Don't forget." Beth smiled. "I like your hair."

Lu had forgotten. She touched her neck and thanked Beth, then said goodbye to Mr. Tsai and Alan, and walked down the stairs to the sidewalk. She felt hollowed out and a little angry. She pictured envy and possessiveness squishing out of her like dirty water from a kitchen sponge.

On the way back to the church she passed the corner store she and Beth often went to for candy. All the kids from the neighborhood came here because the owners had every kind of candy including stuff that was hard to find, like Jolly Rancher sticks for just a quarter. Joey Levoy and some of the other boys would lick them into sharp points and then try to stab each other. Lu and Beth like to suck on them until they took the shape of the roof of their mouths and pretend they were retainers.

She went inside and wandered some of the aisles. At the candy display she scanned all the options until she found a watermelon Jolly Rancher stick and held it in her hand. She had change in the pocket of her birthday jacket. More than enough.

After checking to see if the cashier was watching, she put the hand with the Jolly Rancher stick into the pocket with the change. She could pull a quarter out with the stick and put it on the counter.

She didn't, though. She kept it in her pocket with her hand and the quarter and walked out the door.

29

MOM TOOK MONDAY OFF AND drove Lu to school half an
hour early; they had an appointment with Lu's new teacher.
They checked in at the office and met the principal. The
school felt small and bright compared to the big, old beige-
ness of her city school—each classroom door painted a
bright color, the linoleum clean and shiny.

"I think you'll like Mr. Wealer," Mom said. "When I
spoke with him on the phone, it sounded like he gives a lot
of thought to how to help new students adjust." She looked
at her phone, where she kept notes to herself. "Your room
should be at the end of the hall. . . ."

Lu's fingertips buzzed from the inside, even though
the surface of her skin was getting tough from guitar.
Sometimes when she got nervous, she felt it in her hands

and arms and fingers. They got hot and tingly and achy all at once.

A yellow door, the color of their old kitchen table, opened at the end of the hallway.

"There he is," Mom said, relieved.

A man with dark brown skin, a bald head, and a short, graying beard waved at them. He had a green sweater-vest over a white shirt, jeans, and sneakers. Lu waved back.

When they got to the classroom, Mr. Wealer extended his hand. "Hi, Louisa," he said.

She shook his hand. "Hi. It's Lu. *L-U*. No O."

"Sorry," Mom said. "I know her forms say Louisa."

"No problem. I'll make a note of it. Also, we have a class photo wall where you can put your preferred name, your pronouns, some of your favorite things. Should we take your picture right now?"

"Okay." She smoothed her hair down while Mr. Wealer got an instant camera out of his desk. She'd always wanted one of those, and wondered if he ever let the students use it.

"Smile," he said. "If you want."

She did, and he handed her the photo that had popped out of the camera. While Mr. Wealer talked to Mom, Lu watched her picture emerge, pale and ghostly at first, then turning darker and more solid. Her eyes got squinty when she smiled. It made her look so happy! Was this what she looked like to other people?

He gave them a tour of the room: long tables with

cubbies and chairs just like at Lu's old school, a reading corner with a classroom library, and a shelf with some musical instruments.

"I play guitar."

"Oh yeah? That's great."

"I mean, I'm learning. I'm not very good."

"Let's sit down." He indicated one of the tables. "We had a class meeting on Friday and everyone's expecting you. We talked about how it's hard to start a new school in the middle of the year. Past the middle, really. And I've got two classroom ambassadors coming in a few minutes for you to meet. You'll sit at the same table, and they'll take you to lunch and basically make sure you start to get comfortable here."

"That's great," Mom said. "She's not too shy. A little reserved, maybe, and she's been at the same school since kindergarten so I guess it's hard to know how this will go."

Lu stared at Mom and frowned.

"What, Belle?"

Mr. Wealer stood up. "Our ambassadors should be turning up in a sec. I think we've got this," he said to Mom. Then he looked at Lu. "What do you think, Lu?"

"Yeah. Mom, you'd better get home to take Casey."

"Right, I haven't forgotten."

"I'm okay."

Mom nodded, then put her hand on Lu's head and kissed her cheek. "Have a great day, sweetheart."

As Mom went out, two kids were coming in. One had long blond hair in two braids. She was taller and bigger than Lu and when she smiled you could see she had braces on her teeth. The other had shaggy brown hair and a long tie-dye T-shirt over jeans, and slip-on white Converse.

"Lu with just a *U*, this is Kyra and Jase. Why don't you three get to know each other a little while I set up for the day."

"I like your hair," Kyra said quickly.

"Me too," Jase said.

"I like yours," Lu said to them both.

"Follow me!" Kyra said, and started to walk the perimeter of the classroom.

Jase and Lu followed while Kyra pointed out everything in the room, some of which Mr. Wealer had already told her about and some he hadn't. "Reading corner. You can check out books from the class library here," she said, tapping a clipboard that sat on one of the shelves. "Over here is the penalty box." She pointed to a table against the wall with just one chair at it. "If you break a classroom rule and you've already had a warning, you have to come sit over here and work quietly. I've been in it twice."

"I've never been in it," Jase added. "This year."

"You're not supposed to touch the instruments unless we're doing music," Kyra said, indicating the shelf of tambourines, small drums, and a couple of ukuleles.

"Mr. Wealer said that you moved here from the city?"

Jase said. "Why? I would never move out of the city."

"I—we didn't—" Lu stumbled over her words. It wasn't like she'd had a choice. "My mom got married. Remarried. My stepdad lives here."

Jase made a face. "I do *not* like my stepdad."

"Mine is okay."

"Water fountain," Kyra said, pointing. "You don't have to ask for permission but don't get up and use if it someone is in the middle of talking. Out of respect." Kyra glanced at Lu and said quietly, "My parents are divorced, too, but there's no steps. I live with my mom."

"Here's the photo wall," Jase said, and gently slapped the big piece of butcher paper that acted as a background for all the pictures. Jase pointed to the photo in Lu's hand. "Just peel off the back and stick it on."

Mr. Wealer chimed in from behind his desk. "There's space for you right near the middle."

Lu peeled the backing off her photo and pressed it against the paper. Seeing her own face among the others already helped her feel a part of the class.

"What color marker do you want?" Kyra asked. "To write your name and stuff?"

"Um . . . purple?"

While Kyra got the marker, Lu scanned the wall to see what other kids had written. She quickly found Kyra's photo—she was the only one in two braids—and read: *Kyra. (KEE-ra.) She/her. Favorites: Siberian tiger, Muppets, cheese.*

Jase's said: *Jase. They/them. Favorites: all pachyderms, some Star Wars, french fries.*

Kyra put the purple marker in Lu's hand. She wrote: *Lu. She/her.* She would have rather had time to think about her favorites instead of writing them with Kyra and Jase watching over her shoulder, but she heard the sounds of other students coming down the hall and wanted to have a version of herself all done and on the board when they got there. *Favorites: cats, sad books, peanut butter.*

"Do you have a cat?" Jase asked.

"No. My sister is allergic."

Kyra showed her their table, and that's when other students started coming in. Lu slipped inside her bubble. Sounds faded. She saw herself at the table and felt small next to Kyra, and even smaller as more people came in.

Kyra broke into Lu's bubble by leaning over to say, "Remind me to tell you later about the school talent show."

Mom picked her up after school, only because it was the first day. Starting tomorrow, she would walk.

Lu buckled herself into the passenger seat.

"Well?" Mom asked, smiling.

"It was good."

"That's all?"

Good was good. Nothing bad had happened, and Kyra and Jase were nice, and some other kids ate with them at lunch, too. Kyra had asked Lu if she wanted to do something for the talent show with her, and Lu had said maybe while thinking *probably not.* At recess she learned a new jump-rope game. There was a girl in the class she could already tell was the mean one. Her name was Wren and she told Kyra her braids were "really crooked, you should look in a mirror." They *were* kind of crooked, but Kyra explained to Lu that she'd done it herself and braiding your own hair was hard.

"They're not *that* crooked," Lu had assured her.

All that was inside of the word "good" when she said it to Mom. She didn't need to tell all the details.

Mom touched Lu's hair now. "Did you make friends?"

Lu pulled her head back. "Mom . . ."

"All right, all right." The car inched forward in the pickup line. "Should we go get Casey? We'll be a little early, but if I drop you at home first, we might be late."

"Don't be late." Casey wouldn't like that, not today.

They moved forward another few inches. "Well *I* had a good day. I finally got to spend some good time in the yard with some weeding. Then I fell asleep in one of the lawn chairs. It was delicious, being alone. I realized it's been a long time since I had that much time totally to myself."

Finally, they made it out to the main street. The high school wasn't too far away, and soon they were in another pickup line.

"Oh boy," Mom sighed. "This is worse than city traffic." She turned on the radio and found a news station. Then she said "Oh boy" again at some news and changed it to the Christian station. A man was giving a sermon about "fruit of the spirit." Like love, joy, peace, and patience. Then the radio preacher said, *"Gentleness. Now gentleness is important, especially for all you gals out there,"* and Mom said "Oh boy" one more time and changed to the classical music station.

The sermon on the radio made Lu think of what Pastor Richards said yesterday. "Mom, do you think I'm a dirty sponge?"

"What?"

"Like when life squeezes me, does dirty water come out? Like Pastor Richards was talking about?"

She felt Mom glance at her. "No, Belle, I don't think that."

They crept forward. "Even if I do bad things?"

Lu spotted Casey sitting on the curb a few cars up, legs out, arms folded, phone in one hand and her earbuds in, scrolling. Lu felt unusually happy to see her. She rolled down the window and waved her hand, shouting, "Casey!" to try to get her attention.

A couple of kids turned and looked, and then Casey noticed them and jogged over to the car.

"Honey, Pastor Richards was using a metaphor, and not a great one."

"Hi!" Lu said as Casey climbed into the back.

After Casey had closed the door, she pulled an earbud

out and asked, "Why did you *yell* like that?"

"Sorry. I wanted to make sure you saw us."

"And heard you, apparently."

"How was it?" Mom asked.

"Fine."

Mom didn't say *That's all?* this time, and Casey put her earbud back in.

"Belle, I don't want you thinking you're dirty inside if you do bad things. You're—"

"What are you guys talking about?"

"Nothing," Lu said.

They inched and inched, and Mom said in a low voice, "You're good, Belle."

When they got out of the pickup line Mom asked if they wanted to get drive-through fries and shakes.

"Really?" Lu said. "Yeah!"

Mom smiled. "Great!"

"I just want to go home," Casey said. Whenever she had her earbuds in, she could decide what to hear and pretend not to hear.

"We're going to the drive-through. It will be fast and we'll go home and I want to hear about your days."

"They gave me *so* much homework."

"It won't take long," Mom said. "Ten minutes isn't going to make or break you."

"I don't—"

"Case."

"Fine."

Lu snuck a peek at Casey in the side mirror. Her head was bent low over her phone. Lu wanted to know about her day, too.

When they pulled into the drive-through, Mom asked what kind of shakes they wanted.

"Vanilla," Lu said.

"Casey?"

No response.

"Great," Mom said, "I'll get you strawberry."

Casey hated strawberry and Mom knew it. She said, "Mom!"

"Oh, so you *can* hear."

Mom ordered two chocolate shakes and one vanilla, and two large fries to share. She passed Casey's chocolate shake back to her. When Casey took it, she said, almost too quiet to hear, "Thanks."

By the time they got back to Steve's house, Casey was crying.

30

"NOTHING HAPPENED," CASEY SAID THROUGH her tears. "Nothing, like, *specific*."

The three of them were on Casey's bed. Mom in the middle, and Lu and Casey on either side, with the greasy bag of fries ripped open in their laps and packets of salt all around.

"No one *talked* to me," she continued. "It was like I was invisible."

"Oh, honey. Did you introduce yourself to anyone?"

"Mom!"

"Okay! I'm just asking!"

Lu sipped her shake. Mr. Wealer had been so prepared for her, had talked to the class ahead of time and everything. Did they not do that in high school?

She felt bad that Casey was upset but at the same time she couldn't remember when they'd last all sat together like this. Sharing some junk food and talking. The three of them. The original *we*.

"I want to go back to my school," Casey said, angry.

"I know you do. I wish change wasn't so hard."

That made Casey cry more. She shrunk down on the bed and buried her face in Mom's side. "Why couldn't Dad, like . . . I don't know." Her voice crumbled. "Be better."

Mom didn't say anything, just held Casey tighter.

"Why'd you even marry him?" Casey wailed.

"Casey, honey, we've been over this so many times. . . ."

"No, not *Steve*." Casey's voice had gotten smaller. *"Dad."*

"Oh." Mom sighed. She took a sip of her shake and said, "Well, I loved him. Brilliant. Handsome. Charming. We were wild about each other. Maybe some part of me ignored the things I should have worried about because I did love him so much. I thought my love could fix him. We *were* happy sometimes, you know. And both you girls were brought into this world out of love." Mom turned her head to kiss Lu's temple. "Whatever happened after, as hard as things were, I want you to know that. Dad and I loved each other and wanted both of you. We planned for you. We were so happy to see you."

Casey's shoulders shook and she kept sniffling. Even Mom was crying a little now. Lu felt a weight on her chest like if she really let the words Mom said come in, she could cry, too.

She stopped herself from thinking about it too much, like she always did. She sipped her shake. Ate two more fries in tiny nibbles.

Steve's truck pulled into the driveway; they all recognized the sound. Mom shifted away from Casey, and Lou got off the bed so that Mom could, too. She brushed salt from the fries off her shirt and wiped tears off her face. "It will get better, Case, I promise."

Mom left the room, and then Casey told Lu she wanted to be alone, so Lu went to hers.

She thought about Mom and Dad in love. The versions of them from Mom's special photo album, her in all her dark makeup and him on a mountaintop.

After dinner, Lu read from *Where the Red Fern Grows*. She didn't know if reading it would count for anything now in Mr. Wealer's class, but she was into the story now and wanted to finish.

She wondered if Kyra liked sad books.

She read the worst and saddest part about Old Dan the hound, and the tears came so fast and so many, she had to put the book down. For the first time in her life, she wondered if a book could be *too* sad. Maybe she would like more stories where good things happened. As long as they weren't fake. As long they were the kinds of good things you could believe in and imagine happening to *you*, not just to a perfect person in a book.

She put the unfinished book on the floor next to her bed and said a short, silent prayer for Dad. For something real for him, for something not so sad. It wasn't the kind of long talk with God she did sometimes. This prayer was more like picturing Dad and imagining God tucking him into bed. In the van, in a park, wherever he was.

31

LU WALKED TO SCHOOL BY herself on Tuesday.

If they were city blocks, it would feel closer, but these streets curved and meandered. The sidewalks were empty and narrow compared to city sidewalks. Some streets didn't even *have* sidewalks. Instead, front yards spilled juniper bushes and ice plant and flowers right up to the edge of the street.

The closer she got to school, the more kids she saw. Lu recognized one from her class. But her mind was mostly on Casey. She wanted Casey to find a friend. For someone to *see* her so she didn't feel invisible again today. She wanted Casey to come home this afternoon and not be sad or mad.

Kyra was standing outside Mr. Wealer's classroom,

waiting. Her hair was in braids again. Maybe the same braids as yesterday—they looked even more crooked and frizzy.

"Hi!" she said to Lu. She bounced slightly on the tips of her toes. When Lu got to her, Kyra said, "You forgot to ask me more about the talent show. And I forgot to remind you to ask me." She glanced over Lu's shoulder, then pulled Lu into the room. "Do you have a talent?" she asked in a low voice.

"I . . . I don't know." No one had ever asked Lu that before, and she'd never really thought about it. "I'm taking guitar lessons, but I've only had two so far. I only really know tuning, and how to play a few chords."

"That's a talent! How soon can you learn another chord, or maybe two more?"

"Probably pretty soon?" Her calluses were building up. She could practice for longer periods of time before her hands started to hurt.

"Okay." Kyra led her by the elbow to their table. "We can sign up together. I want to sing but not by myself."

Lu hung her backpack on her chair and sat down. "In front of people?"

"Yeah. It's a show for the whole school. And parents and stuff."

The classroom started to fill. Mr. Wealer came over and asked Lu if she had questions about anything so far.

"Do we have free reading time?"

"Yes! Not every day but we'll do it today after lunch. You can pick something from the class library if you didn't bring a book, or you can go to the school library at lunch and look around."

"I brought one."

"Which one?" Kyra asked.

"*Where the Red Fern Grows*."

Mr. Wealer sucked breath through his teeth. "Ooh, you're tougher than me, Lu."

"Why? What is it?" Kyra asked them both.

"It's just really sad," Lu said. "I . . ." She had planned to say *I like sad stories*, because that's what she always said. Maybe she'd changed. "I might not finish it."

"You don't have to," Mr. Wealer said. "We have lots of other options." He tapped his knuckles on Lu's desk. "Okay. Let me know if you have any questions."

Jase walked in, red-faced and breathing heavy. They shrugged their backpack off and let it fall onto the floor with a heavy *thunk*, then went to the water fountain while saying "Sorry I'm late" to Mr. Wealer.

"They're always almost late," Kyra told Lu. "Except yesterday when we had to be here for you."

While they waited for Jase to come back, Kyra put the tip of one of her braids in her mouth and someone whispered, "Mmm, braid," and there were giggles.

"I can hear you," Kyra said loudly, the braid dropping. Quieter, she added, "So shut up."

Lu unpacked her notebook and pens, while trying to slyly see who was teasing Kyra. She wanted to know who was mean. At the same time, just because Kyra and Jase were the ones Mr. Wealer assigned to be her friends didn't mean they were the best people for her. She'd prefer to observe and decide on her own.

Jase returned and Kyra bent backward and let her braids fall practically in Lu's lap and said, "So what about the talent show?"

"Maybe I'll do it next year. When I know more people."

Jase said, "You can't. Next year is sixth grade. We'll be in middle school. The talent show is only for fourth and fifth grades."

"Oh. Well, that's okay." Lu asked Jase, "Are you going to be in it?"

"Definitely *not*," they said. "My talent is writing and I don't want to share."

"Pleeeeeeease, Lu?" Kyra sat up and faced her properly. "Don't decide yet. Come to my house after school and we can talk about it and I'll sing you some of my songs. My mom is picking me up."

Lu started to say no. She was curious, though, to see Kyra's house and do something different.

"Okay," she said. Technically she was supposed to ask permission, but she could call Mom later from Kyra's.

Kyra's eyes got bright and she said, "Yaaaaaaaaay," in a way that made Lu smile.

They stood in the pickup circle and watched car after car pull up, collect their classmates, and drive away. A few kids left like they were walking home and there were two at the bus stop, but most were waiting to get picked up.

"My mom isn't the most *punctual*." Kyra played with the end of one of her braids as she watched the cars. "She always shows up, though. Eventually."

It was hot out for spring. Bright and sunny and warmer than Lu had dressed for. She could take off the green-and-white striped sweater Casey had given her and just wear the tank top she had on underneath. Except ever since Casey said she'd need a bra soon, she'd been self-conscious about it.

More cars came and went.

"Only seven more weeks till I get my braces off," Kyra announced.

"Seven is a lot!" Lu said.

"Not really. Not after fifteen months." Kyra squatted down and sat on the curb. "When we get to my house, just remember we clean it on Wednesdays and today is Tuesday. So it's going to be messy."

"That's okay." Lu was starting to drip sweat. Maybe that's why they called it a *sweat*er.

There were only two more cars left in the pickup line. They watched a brother and sister from one of the younger grades get into the very last car. Lu started to get the same feeling she got that day she'd waited for Casey so long after school.

"Don't worry," Kyra said.

"I'm not."

Suddenly Kyra sprung up. "There she is."

A small car headed up the street and as it got closer, Lu could see it was a two-door, dirty white VW with rust along the edges of the passenger door. The woman behind the wheel was tall, like Kyra. Her head almost touched the roof of the car. Her hair was so blond it was nearly white, and pulled into a ponytail.

"Sorry!" she said, after Kyra opened the door.

"It's okay, but can Lu come over?"

"Oh! Um, sure, let me just . . ." She reached into the backseat and swept some clothes and papers off one side, and Kyra climbed in.

"Ow." One of her braids had caught in the seat belt. "Okay, I'm in."

Lu got in the front.

"Hi," Kyra's mom said. "I'm Meg." Her smile showed that one tooth was missing on the side, and Lu noticed a scar on her bottom lip. It was a memorable and likable face.

"Hi."

"Aren't you hot in that sweater, hon?"

"I'm okay."

32

KYRA'S HOUSE WAS ON A block where most of the houses were smaller than the ones on Steve's block. Hers had gray siding and a cracked cement patio in front. Instead of a garden, there were a few plants in terra-cotta pots on the steps to the door. Kyra's mom—Meg—unlocked it, then stopped and turned to Lu. "Pardon our dust, the maid comes tomorrow."

"I told her," Kyra said quickly.

Inside, the front room was dim, with mail in a pile on the floor and laundry on the sofa, half of it folded and half of it not. There were a few paper bags of recycling waiting to go out. It reminded Lu a little bit of how the old apartment could get when Mom was too tired to clean and too frustrated to keep reminding Lu and Casey to pitch in.

"You girls want a snack? What do you like, Lu?"

"Ooh, can we make grilled cheese?" Kyra asked.

"Let's find out if your guest even likes it, babe-lini."

Kyra looked at Lu. "You do, right? Everyone does."

"I like it."

"Okey-doke," Meg said. "Have at it. I've got to make some calls."

Kyra and Lu put their book bags down, and Lu finally peeled off the striped sweater. It felt good to have her skin out. She followed Kyra to the kitchen, where dishes were piled in the sink.

"I like to do it with a combination of cheddar and jack. Do you like mayo? Mustard? Some people don't but I usually put both." Kyra opened the fridge.

"I like mayo and mustard. But not too much mustard."

"Okay." Kyra got the sandwich stuff out. "Have you ever seen *The Muppet Movie*? The very, very first one?"

"I don't think so. . . ." Lu was looking at the fridge. Every inch was covered in magnets. Some were pictures of Kyra and her mom, some were there holding up coupons, some had little quotes and sayings on them like "One Day at a Time" and "First Things First" and "Let Go and Let God." Lu snuck a glance at Kyra. Did she believe in God, too?

Kyra was making the sandwiches, with careful dots of mustard and just the right amount of mayo. "There's a song in it I think would be good. I'll just have to sing it to you or we can get my mom to look it up on her phone." She turned the stove on under a pan and put a chunk of butter in it. "Can you go like this: 'Dooga-doon dooga-doon'?"

She set the sandwiches into the pan and waited for Lu to echo her.

"Dooga-doon dooga-doon," Lu tried.

"No, like: 'dooga-doon dooga-doon.'"

Lu made her voice low like Kyra's and did it again.

"I guess you'll have to hear it first," Kyra said as she pressed the sandwiches with the back of a spatula.

Lu still didn't know if she even wanted to be in the talent show but it seemed set in Kyra's mind. "I *barely* just started learning guitar. FYI."

"That's okay." Kyra turned the sandwiches over carefully.

"I got it for my birthday. Last month." Lu watched the back of Kyra's head, the crooked, frizzy part between the braids. "From my dad."

"Oh. Well, my dad is in Idaho now. He doesn't really keep in touch."

That made Lu feel safe enough to say, "Mine either."

Kyra turned to look at Lu, her eyes curious and sharp. "He gave you a guitar, though. Do you have any brothers or sisters or anything?"

"A sister. Casey. She's four years older."

"Is she like you? Do you get along?"

Lu shrugged. "We're different. But mostly we get along."

Kyra turned back to the stove and slid the spatula under one of the sandwiches to check. "The secret is you have to be patient. Low, low heat. Otherwise the bread burns before the cheese melts."

"I can make boiled eggs, cake from a mix, English muffin pizza, ramen, macaroni and cheese from a box . . ." Lu ticked these things off on her fingers, trying to think if she'd forgotten anything. "Hot dogs."

"Everyone can make hot dogs and cake from a mix."

"I know."

"And instant ramen. Like, just add boiling water!" Kyra checked the sandwiches again, then slid them both onto one plate she'd gotten out of the dishwasher. "I can make spaghetti with garlic and olive oil, chili, French toast, a bunch of different casseroles. Veggie soup, veggie burgers, veggie pasta, veggie enchiladas." She glanced at Lu. "We don't eat a lot of meat. Do you want these cut in triangles or rectangles? I do triangles."

"Either way."

Kyra cut one sandwich into rectangles and one into triangles. Cheese oozed out and the bread was buttery and perfectly toasted. "Do you like to dip into ketchup?"

Lu had never eaten grilled cheese that way. "Do you?"

"Yeah." She was already squeezing a perfect circle of ketchup onto its own small plate. Lu reached for the plate of triangles and Kyra stopped her. "You said either way."

"Oh . . ."

"I do triangles."

"Okay." Lu took the plate with rectangles, and Kyra

pushed a stack of books over to clear a space for them to sit at the table. Meg came through the kitchen, talking on her phone. "I can move you to Thursday afternoons but I can't do Wednesdays." She winked at Kyra. "That's my afternoon to do my own house and also go to a meeting. . . . Hang on." She pulled her phone away from her ear and looked something up. "Yep, that works. . . . Great. . . . See you then. Oh—payment due up-front. Cash or use this phone number to find me on payments apps. . . . Mm-hmm. Bye."

As soon as she'd hung up, Kyra said, "Mom, can I show Lu something on your phone?"

"Trade you for a bite of your sandwich."

"*One* bite. Not a point, though. You can eat from the crust."

Meg passed Kyra the phone and took a big bite of one of the triangles, from the crust side. After a minute, Kyra found what she was looking for. She got up and leaned right over Lu to put the phone in front of her face. The smell of toast and cheese and something sweatier was on Kyra's skin.

"That's Kermit and Fozzie," Kyra explained. "They're on a road trip."

Lu watched the clip and listened to the song. She liked it, but she also wasn't sure about doing it in front of everyone even if she could learn how to play it.

"Is it a little . . . babyish?" Lu asked.

Kyra frowned. "Just because it's Muppets? Even my mom still likes Muppets."

"I don't think I can learn to play that one, anyway."

236

"You don't even want to try?"

She looked at the video again while thinking how to answer, and noticed the time on the phone with a start. "I have to call my . . . Steve. And tell him where I am."

"Didn't you get permission to come over, honey?" Meg asked.

"Not yet."

Meg tensed, and Lu immediately regretted not asking first. "Go ahead and call who you need to, then I want to talk to them, too."

With Kyra and Meg staring, Lu couldn't remember Steve's cell phone number or the number at the house. Mom's work number was the only one she could think of. She glanced up at Meg, who was now biting the nail of one of her index fingers.

Mom didn't answer until the fifth ring.

"It's Lu."

"Is everything okay? Where are you calling from? I don't recognize this number."

"I'm over at a friend's house but I forgot to call first. And I forgot Steve's number."

"What friend?"

"Kyra. Here's her mom." Lu passed the phone to Meg.

"Hi, I'm Meg Hale, Lu's fine, I didn't know she hadn't gotten permission."

Meg walked out of the kitchen and her voice faded. Lu looked at Kyra. "I don't think I can do that song."

"Well, maybe there's another one we can do."

237

It was hard to say *I don't want to,* and hard to decide if she really wanted to be friends with Kyra this way. Going over to each other's houses and everything. She was so different from Beth, and the feeling of being in her house was so different from being at the Tsais.

Lu liked going to the Tsais because it was neat and clean, and Mr. and Mrs. Tsai were calm and predictable, and Beth liked to read as much as Lu did. Kyra's house was in chaos that reminded her of chaos at the apartment, and Kyra was asking her to get up in front of everyone at a brand-new school and play a song she didn't know.

"I'll try to think of one," she said, so that Kyra wouldn't keep asking.

Meg came back in. "Okay, Lu, Steve's going to come get you in about ten minutes, so you two wrap it up and clear your dishes."

"I'll do it later," Kyra said.

"Now, Kyra. And don't sulk."

Lu jumped up and took the sandwich plate over to the sink to rinse, feeling guilty about her failure to get permission and upsetting Meg.

"Honey, let Kyra do that. You're her guest." She took the plate from Lu and set it on the counter. "It turns out I know your stepdad. We went to high school together, and I used to clean his house back when his mom was still alive."

"Oh."

Meg said to Kyra, "Steve Cook. Steve is Lu's stepdad. Small world, huh?"

Kyra, at the sink, looked over her shoulder at Lu. "Steve? That's your stepdad?"

"Really, his mom was my client," Meg said.

"Oh," Lu replied, confused.

"I clean houses, honey," Meg said. "I'm a house cleaner. A maid."

"It's her own company," Kyra said. "Didn't you see the big magnet on the car door?"

"It's true, I'm an *entrepreneur*, so fancy. Anyway, I didn't know Steve had gotten married, that's great!" She tucked her fingertips into her jeans pockets. "I'm happy for him, and your mom sounded very nice on the phone."

"She is."

Meg laughed. "Okay, kid, get your stuff together."

Lu found her sweater, put it on, got her backpack.

Kyra stood in the front room with her, looking out the window while they waited for Steve. She suddenly blurted, "Do you want to be my best friend? I haven't had one in a long time. It's okay if you don't, but hopefully we can still do the talent show anyway."

"I have a best friend. Beth. In the city."

"Well, I can be your best Pacifica friend." She tried to smooth out the end of one braid. "Ever since I got taller than everyone . . . I don't know. Jase is sort of my best friend but mostly by accident. We don't have that much in common. Mr. Wealer sticks us together because neither of us have very many friends this year. Last year I had more, but . . ." She shrugged. "People change, my mom said."

239

Steve's truck pulled up to the curb.

"We can be friends," Lu said, reluctant to commit to "best," even just for Pacifica.

"Bye until tomorrow!"

Lu said goodbye and ran out to Steve's truck.

33

ON THE RIDE HOME, STEVE was quiet in a way that made it seem like he was mad.

When they got to the house, he turned to Lu with the engine still idling and said, "Your mom isn't going to be in the best mood when she gets home. Casey picked the same day as you to go somewhere after school and not tell us, and she's not answering her phone. Just wanted to give you a heads-up. I'm about to do a little drive in the neighborhood in case she's walking around."

Was he upset with her? "Should I come with you?"

"No, go on in and answer the house phone if it rings, okay?"

"Okay." She paused for a second. "Sorry."

"It's okay, El." He glanced at her. "Louisa, I mean."

El. Like the letter *L* for Lu and also kind of like Belle. She liked it. "You can call me El."

She slid out of the truck and ran into the house, where she paced and thought about Casey. Maybe she was just walking around, like Steve thought. Or maybe, like the day she'd been so late to meet Lu, she was in a car somewhere with her city friends. Or trying to see Dad?

Pacing around didn't help Lu feel better.

She went to her room and got the guitar out of its case. She sat on the floor with her back against her bed. It was easier to support the guitar that way.

E and A and D. Easier chords for her small hands. While she practiced them over and over in different order, a cloud of guilt hung over her. For not asking permission, for not wanting to be in the talent show with Kyra, for making Kyra want to be her best friend, for stealing from Beth, stealing from the store, marking the cars. For Steve being upset and Mom being in a bad mood and now for Casey not coming home, and for having a better first week of school than her. For them having to change schools in the first place. Even for Dad living in a van.

It was a catalog of bad things floating around her and bumping into her, and if she could figure out how they were her fault, she could organize them and put them away. Stealing and marking cars, that was easy. She'd done those things.

The rest, she wasn't sure. Each thing hovered and collided.

She tried to push them away from her and out of her room by playing harder, better. She strummed chords until the fingers on both hands stung and her wrists ached.

The house phone rang; she pushed the guitar off her lap and ran to answer.

"Lu? Hon, it's Shannon. Is Steve around? Or your mom? I tried Steve's cell but there was no answer."

"He's out looking for Casey."

"Yeah, about that. Casey's here."

Lu paused. Right down the street? "They've been trying to call her."

"She says she doesn't have her phone. She's *really* upset. She—listen, I'm going to try Steve again, but can you also give me your mom's number? Casey can't communicate very well right now."

"Is she okay?"

"She will be."

She gave Mom's work and cell numbers to Shannon and hung up, then stood still in the kitchen. The refrigerator hummed, and somewhere outside, a weed trimmer whined. She wasn't allowed to leave, probably. Even though she could be at Marcus and Shannon's in five minutes and see Casey for herself.

She paced again, back and forth between the living room and kitchen and her own room.

It reminded her of when Mom and Dad were married and they all lived together. There were days when Dad didn't come home at the usual time, or several hours after, or sometimes for the whole the night. Lu remembered: the sound of the phone ringing at two a.m., the way it echoed in a particular way in the dark, quiet apartment. Mom's low voice, hoping Lu and Casey wouldn't hear. The awareness that Casey was awake in the bunk above her, too, but pretending not to be. How they both lay silent and scared.

That feeling of waiting and waiting for the next bad thing to happen and trying to be good so that it didn't.

It was a feeling Lu had almost her whole life, so much that when it started to fade after Dad left, after the divorce, it seemed like something was missing. Not that she wanted it back—the waiting and waiting and the guilt and wondering if she'd caused the bad things. She remembered exactly how it felt because she felt it right now. She wanted some parts of her old life back, but not that.

34

STEVE CAME RIGHT BACK AFTER finding out Casey was all right, and told Lu he was taking her to the Taco Bell by the beach. He ordered them a lot of food and they sat in a booth, where he kept checking his phone. He asked her little questions about her day, but she could tell he wasn't really listening to her answers.

Finally, when all that was left were the crumpled wrappers on their trays, Steve said, "I guess I can just tell you. Daniel broke up with Casey. And she kind of lost it. It was a real shock to her."

Lu covered her mouth with her hand. It was a shock to her, too.

"You liked him, huh?" Steve said.

"He's nice" was all Lu could think to say. Daniel was

quiet and didn't talk to her more than he had to, but there was something about him that felt safe and comfortable.

"I thought they were a little too serious for high school. Your mom said I should stay out of it, so I did." He stabbed his straw into his cup to break up the ice. "Casey hates me enough as it is. I'm not going to tell her 'I told you so.' But . . ."

"Can we go home?" It seemed like forever ago that she'd been at Kyra's house, let alone school. The day had been eternal and Lu slammed into a wall of tiredness. And she wanted to see for herself that Casey would be all right.

Steve checked his phone again. "I'm supposed to wait for the all-clear but I think maybe your mom forgot. She wanted a chance to spend some time alone with Casey without us in their hair."

Us. Now Lu was an *us* with Steve.

They made the short drive home without talking. Casey's bedroom windows were dark. When they got inside, Mom met them in the living room and held her finger to her lips before whispering, "She cried herself to sleep, finally."

Lu's chest hurt, knowing that.

Mom gave her a hug and kissed the top of her head. "You okay?"

She nodded, even with the pain in her chest. Her stomach hurt, too, from tacos on top of grilled cheese on top of the cafeteria spaghetti from lunch.

"Sit in the kitchen with me and tell me about your new friend. Whose house you shouldn't have gone to without permission."

"Sorry."

To Steve, Mom said, "You can go watch one of your shows? In our room?"

"Oh," he said. "Sure." And he was gone.

Mom ate some leftover soup while explaining how Daniel had broken up with Casey through a text while Casey was in her geometry class. And she started crying and ran out of the room, and threw her phone down the hall.

"She doesn't know anyone there yet, so there was really no one for her to talk to after she broke her phone. *All* her friends are in the phone."

Lu could picture it and feel it and she couldn't stand it. It felt *too* sad, *too* terrible. How could Casey handle all of those feelings, alone, with no one to understand or talk to?

"Then she left school," Mom continued. "Just walked out. Apparently the school office didn't notice it until the end of the day when she'd turned up absent for all her afternoon classes. She'd walked to Marcus and Shannon's."

"Why didn't she just come here?"

"She didn't want to be alone. She felt more comfortable with Shannon. A lot of reasons."

If Lu hadn't gone to Kyra's without permission, she could have been home and Casey could have talked to Lu, maybe.

Or if Lu hadn't told Mr. Sturgess that they'd moved, they wouldn't have changed schools and Daniel wouldn't have broken up with Casey. Or even if he did, she'd still have been with her friends.

If Mom hadn't married Steve, they wouldn't have had to move and Lu wouldn't have had to tell and Beth wouldn't be inviting Daisy Dobrov over instead of her.

Mom put her spoon down and reached for Lu's hand. "Belle? You in there? You want to tell me about your new friend? Steve says her mom used to clean over here sometimes. They knew each other in high school."

She pulled her hand away. "We shouldn't have moved."

"Honey . . ."

"Casey could still be with her friends and Daniel wouldn't break up with her. And she wouldn't have to be sad."

Something like a smile showed in Mom's eyes. "Change is hard. Even good change. It just is."

The table in Steve's kitchen was tile and wood. Little tomatoey drops of soup speckled the surface around Mom's bowl. Lu missed their yellow table. "This isn't a good change."

Mom sighed and picked her spoon up again, scraped the rest of the soup out of her bowl. "Why don't you give it more time before you decide that?"

"I don't *want* to." Lu jumped up, gripped the back of her chair. What if she kicked it over like Casey had done? She couldn't.

"Come here," Mom said. She opened her arms like she wanted Lu to sit on her lap. "Belle, let me tell you something you don't know."

Lu sat back in her chair, not Mom's lap.

"What you don't know is that at this time last year, I was making plans to move us—you, me, and Casey—to Ohio. Back to my family."

Any trace of a smile had left her eyes. Lu listened.

"It was all *so* hard for me. I was *so* scared. Making rent every month on my own in one of the most expensive cities in the world . . . even with rent control and having been in the apartment so long, it was a struggle all the time. You know that."

Her mouth lost its normal shape and Lu knew Mom was going to cry. Lu didn't want to see that but she couldn't look away.

"I was so afraid of telling you and Casey because I knew it would be very upsetting. The idea of leaving everything. Your friends, your home. I felt like such a failure."

Mom wiped her eyes with the paper napkin crumpled next to her soup bowl.

Lu tried to imagine it. Them living in Ohio, where Lu had never been and Casey had only been when she was practically still a baby. "How many miles away is Ohio?" Lu asked.

"More than two thousand."

Way farther than Pacifica. Farther than she could even

imagine. "Dad would have still been here in California?"

"Unless he decided to find his own way to Ohio, yes." Mom moved toward Lu's hand again and this time Lu let her hold it. "So things were going to change anyway. No matter what. They always do. Even if we'd stayed in the apartment, even if there was no Steve. *Even* if Dad still lived with us. If not Ohio, somewhere else. If not Steve, something else. Things are always changing. It's one of those facts of life that you can fight and deny but you can't stop it."

Lu wished she had gotten into Mom's lap after all. She was tired, too full, anxious about Casey's sadness. Now all this. And what Mom was saying felt true.

"Does Casey know? About Ohio?"

Mom shook her head. "No. I never told anyone how close we were to leaving. Well, Steve, later. But not my parents, not Casey, not Pastor Richards, not anybody. That was another thing that made it hard. I was carrying it around all by myself. All that fear and not knowing what to do or how to know what was best for all of us."

Steve's big Bible was on the windowsill behind the chair where he always sat. Lu looked toward it now. So much of what was inside seemed to say that if you believed and you prayed and tried to follow God's rules, then you would automatically know what was best.

Now Mom was saying *she* didn't even know.

"Can I go to bed now?" Lu asked.

"Of course. I'll come tuck you in."

"I think . . . I just want to go by myself."

Mom tilted her head, as if to see if Lu wanted to say more, then nodded. "Okay, Belle. Good night."

35

IT WAS STRANGE GOING TO her next guitar lesson knowing Casey had a whole big thing happen at the Merritt-Mendozas' without her. Casey didn't talk on the walk there, and then when they arrived, Shannon hugged Casey and led her off to the living room with only a quick "hi" to Lu.

Lu stood alone in the kitchen. There weren't any cookies, but there was some kind of a fruit pie. She didn't like pie. She set her guitar down in its case and perched on an island stool.

It had been a hard day. That morning, Mom had said, "I might have underestimated how difficult this first week or so at new schools would be." So she was going to take them to school for a while, and go in a little late to work. Steve would go in even earlier than usual to his job so he could pick them up.

It seemed unnecessary when they could both easily walk from their schools to Steve's, but Lu was always happy for a ride. Casey acted like it was a punishment. "Please, Mom, I can get home on my own," she'd protested when Mom dropped her off that morning.

"Can you, though?"

Then Casey got out and slammed the car door closed.

When they'd pulled up to Lu's school, Kyra was waiting for her in front, the end of one of braid in her mouth. Lu worried this would be another day of her same braids without redoing them or washing her hair.

Kyra waved with both arms, making huge circles in the air.

"Is that your friend?" Mom asked.

"That's . . . Kyra."

"She's so excited to see you!"

Clusters of kids moved toward the entrance; a couple of them looked toward her to see what Kyra was waving at. Lu felt guilty for being embarrassed.

"Okay, Belle, have good day. Be right here when school is out and wait for Steve."

"I know."

The walk to Kyra had felt like a mile. Lu, suddenly extra conscious of being the new kid, imagined everyone staring and tried to see in her mind what they saw. Casey once told her she bounced on her toes when she walked. Kyra did that, too. Lu tried to walk flat. Her backpack thumped against her anyway and felt way too big. Now that her haircut was a few days old, the bangs weren't keeping straight like they'd done at first.

When Lu got close, Kyra ran to meet her the rest of the way. The braids looked more crooked and frizzy than before. Instead of saying hello, Lu blurted, "Do you want me to redo your hair? I have a brush in my bag."

"That's okay." Kyra tossed the braid she'd been sucking on over one shoulder.

"We have time." She added, "Me and my best friend in the city always do each other's hair."

Kyra checked her watch. "If you really want to."

They went to a tree along the side of the building, and Lu had Kyra sit cross-legged in front of her. Kyra worked the rubber bands off the ends of her braids and used her fingers to undo the right one while Lu worked on the left.

When Lu started brushing, Kyra said, "Just don't pull too hard. Sometimes it hurts when my mom does it."

"I won't. I start from the ends. When I was little I had really long hair and my mom would do it like this."

"Did you get knots?"

"Sometimes." Lu methodically worked through Kyra's blond tangles, then smoothed the brush over each section. "It's actually not that bad." When the sun hit her hair, strands of reddish-gold showed up, and the braids had left soft waves. She kept brushing and brushing, her mind wandering to Beth, Casey, Dad. Especially Casey.

When the bell rang, Lu was only halfway through redoing one braid.

Kyra had hopped up in a panic, feeling her head. "It's down, I can't leave it down!"

"It looks good down, though." Lu stood, too, and saw that Kyra was about to start crying.

"I never have it down." She shook her hands out, stepped from foot to foot. "I hate how it feels on my neck. I hate how it gets in my face."

"It's okay. It's okay." Lu glanced around. Two girls were watching as they walked toward the main door. "It's okay," she said again. "I'll fix it."

Kyra took in a big breath, let it out. Lu undid the half braid and brushed all the hair together, then used one elastic to make a thick ponytail. She put the second elastic around the middle of it to help it stay off her neck.

"There."

Kyra ran her hand down it and seemed to calm down. "I can still feel it a little."

"I can do the braids at lunch if you want."

She nodded. "Okay. Or morning recess."

They grabbed their bags and ran to class.

At lunch, when Kyra asked about the song for the talent show, Lu said, "I probably can't do it." She didn't want to hurt Kyra's feelings, but she had been thinking: What if she *could* learn a song in time for the talent show? And what if she invited Dad? And what if he said yes, and he'd know he had to be sober to get down to Pacifica so that would make him stop drinking at least for a couple of days, and then she'd be so good on the guitar that he'd realize he was really missing out and he'd maybe change some things and try really hard to keep a good job again and his own place, where she and Casey could visit, and she didn't want to be messing up in the background of someone else's song, she wanted her *own* song and—

"Lu? LU!"

How long had Kyra been talking to her? "Sorry. What?"

"I said, if it's too hard we can pick a different song."

"I don't know."

Later, as soon as the final bell had rung, she took off before Kyra could invite her to her house again, saying over her shoulder, "Steve is picking me up. I can't keep him waiting."

The whole day felt off, because she knew she should just tell Kyra what she was thinking and instead she was avoiding her. And she was still so tired from yesterday, and Casey was still miserable and taking it out on Mom and Steve by being sour and moody.

And now, Shannon had disappeared with Casey and there were no cookies. Only pie, with some kind of oozing orange filling.

She got off the stool and looked at the fridge magnets and what they were holding up. Family pictures of the Merritt-Mendozas on beaches and by lakes, one with the Golden Gate Bridge in the background, one around a Christmas tree. Drawings by Rosie and Tala. Baby pictures of them both; one of Rosie on Marcus's shoulders with her hands wrapped under his chin, both of them grinning.

"Hey, sorry to keep you waiting!"

Lu jumped and turned around at the sound of Marcus's voice, then they both laughed at her surprise.

"Sorry," he said again. "You good? Need anything before we start? Want some peach pie?"

"That's okay. Can I have a glass of water?"

"Sure." Marcus had on a Giants T-shirt and track pants and flip-flops. His hair was gelled back. Steve usually wore his ironed jeans or beige pants and a polo shirt, and his hair was thin and poofy. "How's your week going?" he asked as he handed her the water.

She answered with a shrug.

"Yesterday was kind of rough, huh?"

"Kind of."

Had *he* talked to Casey, too, about Daniel and everything? Had both Marcus and Shannon sat with Casey at their kitchen table, listening and giving her hugs and cookies and advice? Lu pictured it. Like Casey was part of *their* family. Like she belonged on the fridge, too.

She changed the subject.

"How long do you think it would take for me to learn a whole song?"

"Depends. There's actually a lot you can do with only two or three chords, but we really haven't done much with strumming and keeping time." He gestured with his head toward the room off the kitchen. "Let's get set up and tuned up and we can try it."

After they got their guitars all ready, Marcus said, "It helps a lot to start with a song you already know. The simpler, the better. Let's see . . ." He played a few chords while looking up toward the ceiling. "How about 'Row, Row, Row Your Boat'? You know that, right?"

"Yeah. But . . . what if I wanted a song I could do in front of people?" She was *not* going to play "Row, Row, Row Your Boat" in front of the whole school and Dad. "There's a girl at school who asked if I'd be in the talent show with her."

"Yeah? Well, we'll get to that. For now, try 'Row, Row, Row.' It's a G and a C and a D. I know C is still hard for you, but try."

They went through the chord sequence, Lu's C sounding more like a dull thud than a chord since she had a hard time pressing strings on three different frets hard enough.

"Oh, hang on . . ." Marcus leaned over his guitar case and then handed her a flat, plastic triangle with rounded edges. "Guitar pick. You can keep it, I have a ton. You might not like it but it can give you extra volume and help save your fingers."

She tried strumming the chords with the pick. It flew out of her fingers and landed on the floor. The second time she tried, she lost the grip again and it fell inside the guitar through the hole.

"Yeah, that happens," Marcus said. He took her guitar and shook it over his head until the pick fell out. "You can practice more with the pick at home if you want. For now, let's go back to fingers."

He taught her some different strumming techniques, and how to count the beats. That different songs had different rhythms, and sometimes you played things in twos or fours, and sometimes you played in threes. Sometimes you strummed on the beat, sometimes you strummed off the beat.

Lu could hear how just changing how you strummed could make even a simple song sound better.

"Great," Marcus said. "Most important things to remember: Try to keep your wrist loose. Don't tense up. You might think you're doing better by keeping rigid control of it, but one, you're gonna get a sore wrist, and two, it sounds better when you keep it loose."

She shook out her hand and strummed again.

"Better. Here." He reached over and circled her wrist with his thumb and index finger and made it strum the open strings, with no chord. "Feel that?"

She nodded and he took his hand away. She could still feel where he'd touched her wrist. It was nice. She thought of the picture of Rosie with her hands cupping his face like it belonged to her. She thought of Beth and Alan, jostling each other into Mr. Tsai, how he would rest his hand on Alan's neck or ruffle his hair. And she remembered one time when Dad carried her on his back to the doctor when she'd hurt her ankle roller-skating. The doctor was only two blocks away and Lu had been little. If she tried hard, she could still feel the warmth of his back radiating through his jacket, the safe grip he had on her legs so she couldn't fall.

". . . simplified down to three chords like that," Marcus was saying. "You'd be surprised."

She'd gone into her bubble and missed something. "Oh."

"So like I said, maybe listen to whatever music you have that you like. Maybe get online and find some stuff. Write down some song titles. Then you can come over and I'll figure out the chords and see if I can make it simple for you. We should be around tomorrow evening or whenever. Just have Case drop us a text."

"Okay. Thanks."

"Remember," he said. "Keep it loose. Things are going to be okay."

36

SEVERAL TIMES FRIDAY MORNING, LU felt herself getting comfortable in her new classroom and then would suddenly realize it was only her first week. It was kind of amazing how quickly you could get used to things that were brand-new only five days before.

For example: Mr. Wealer's face and voice now seemed almost as familiar as Ms. Tom's face and voice. Lu's seat at the table on the side of the room near the windows felt like hers almost as much as her and Beth's desk had.

Were Beth and all her other friends from school as used to her being gone as she was used to *being* gone? The idea of people missing her made her feel almost as bad as the idea of them not missing her. Like them missing her would be her fault.

At recess, she and Kyra practiced their flexed-arm hang on the play structure while Jase joined a kickball game. Kyra had her hair in a version of the double ponytail Lu had done the other day.

"I haven't tried anything but braids in, like, three years," Kyra said. "That's when I grew my hair out and then I didn't know what else to do with it."

Lu bent her elbows, trying to pull herself up a little. "With long hair like yours, you can do anything. Braids, one braid, high ponytail, low ponytail, side ponytail, ballet bun, low bun, wrap braids around your head, wear it down, barrettes . . . anything."

"I think my arms are going to pull out of their sockets."

"They won't."

"I just hate it when my hair touches my face. Or my neck. Or my shoulders."

"I know." *You told me that like five times already.* It was easy for Lu to lose patience with Kyra, she was learning. She was also learning that she liked being around Kyra anyway.

Kyra let herself drop to the ground. "You win." She looked up at Lu, and squinted against the sun. "Do you want to come over this weekend and practice?"

"I told you I can't do that song. Too many chords."

"Then come over and we can pick something else!"

The bell rang. Lu let go of the bar. When her sneakers hit the ground, a painful jolt went through her knees. "Ow." Lu's hands stung. She hated the metallic smell the bar left on her hands, but she couldn't stop herself from sniffing them.

They walked toward the school building. "Or you could come to my house," Lu suddenly thought to suggest. After so many years of not being able to have Beth over, she'd have to get used to doing the inviting. But with her own room and a house with a yard and not worrying about Dad showing up, it would be fun. And she might even work up the courage to tell Kyra she was thinking about doing a separate song.

"Yeah!" Kyra said excitedly. "I can ask my mom to drop me on the way to her meeting tomorrow morning. About nine forty-five? Then she can pick me up after."

"Okay!" There was a hop in Lu's step as they went back into their class.

That night at dinner, even Casey was in a good mood. Or, a better mood than she had been. Steve had surprised her with a new phone, and he helped her set it all up with her old number so she got all her missed texts from her friends in the city.

And they had takeout pizza. It wasn't as good as Giorgio's but it was still good. It was pizza, after all.

Lu was glad for Casey but wondered aloud if Steve would get *her* a phone, too.

"Sixth grade," Mom said for the hundredth time.

"But it's not fair. Also you told me before that you only

let Casey have one because she paid for it herself. She didn't pay for this one herself."

Steve jumped in. "This was a special circumstance."

The circumstance was that Casey broke her own phone. Lu frowned and took another piece of the cheese pizza, her favorite. The other one was sausage and mushroom—Casey and Steve's favorite.

When Mom tucked her in later, Lu was still thinking about the phone. "Casey broke her own phone and broke rules and cut school. Then you guys give her a new phone."

"Don't sulk, Belle. Casey's had a hard week and we wanted to do something extra nice, just because. Not a reward and not punishment. Just something nice."

"I had a hard week, too."

Mom pulled her in. "I know. But not too bad, right?"

No, it wasn't too bad. She liked her teacher and she already had a friend. "When Kyra comes tomorrow, can we make French toast?"

"Sure, Belle. As long as you clean it up."

"Kyra's a good cook. She can make casseroles."

"Wow."

"Her mom has her own business."

"Mmm." Mom sounded sleepy.

"I learned how to do different strumming on the guitar. Marcus gave me a pick. He's really nice. So's Shannon. Rosie can be a brat, though."

Mom's only response was to pat Lu's leg.

"I still miss the city. There aren't any corner stores here, and the sidewalks are so small. You can't roller-skate because of the tree roots and cracks and stuff."

Silently, Lu listed other things she missed: the squeaky wooden floors of the apartment, the pinging of the radiator at night, their bay windows. The bunk bed. The table.

As she drifted toward sleep, she imagined Dad in the talent show audience, Lu onstage, keeping her wrist loose and making perfect C chords.

Dad would think, *Lu sure has grown up since the wedding. That's my daughter!* Afterward, he'd tell her, *I always knew you were talented. I knew when I got you that guitar you'd learn it so fast.*

He might not say I love you. That was hard for him.

He'd hug her, though. She'd feel the warmth of him as he held her tight.

31

KYRA ARRIVED IN THE MORNING with fresh braids in damp hair.

Lu, who'd been sitting on the steps waiting, said, "You smell like oranges."

"We were just eating one in the car."

Meg waved at Lu; Lu waved back. Meg shouted through the open passenger window, "I'll stop and chat when I come back!" Then she drove off, fast.

"Running late again," Kyra said with a sigh.

"Do you want to make French toast?" Lu asked.

"I want to *eat* French toast. Do you know how to make it? Or are you asking me to?"

"Umm . . . can you teach me how?"

They scrambled up the stairs and into the house. Even

though Steve usually made breakfast on Saturdays, Lu had asked him to have cereal or something so she and Kyra could have the kitchen. He was in there now, holding two mugs of coffee: one for him, one for Mom.

"Hi, Steve," Kyra said.

"Hey, Keek, how's things?"

"Fine." Kyra turned to Lu. "Actually, Steve's the one who taught me French toast. He hasn't showed you yet?"

Lu shook her head, watching how easy they were together.

"Do you want to learn that stuff, El?" Steve asked. "I can show you how I do the breakfasts, and also my lasagna. No olives. Whatever you want."

"I want to learn the breakfast quesadilla."

"Anytime." Steve lifted one of the mugs of coffee. "I better get this up to your mom before she falls back to sleep."

Kyra already had her head in the fridge, pulling out bread, eggs, milk, butter, like it was her own house. She carried an armload of ingredients to the counter. "Can you get out one of those green plates? The really deep ones?"

Lu felt lost, back to being the new girl, but obeyed. When she turned toward the cupboard, she saw Casey in the kitchen doorway, with bedhead and smeared eyeliner.

"How do you know where everything is?" Casey asked Kyra.

"This is Casey," Lu said. "Casey, this is Kyra."

Kyra said, "My mom used to clean this house before Steve's mom died. Steve didn't care if I was here, too, because he's known me my whole life."

Casey narrowed her eyes. "Was your mom Steve's girlfriend?"

Kyra rolled her eyes. "Ew. No. Not since they were, like, fifteen."

"She's a maid," Lu said.

"A house cleaner," Kyra corrected. "She has her own business."

"Oh. Nice to meet you, and stay out of my room even if you've been in it a million times before." Casey brushed past Kyra and opened the fridge to get out one of her boiled eggs, then left.

Kyra didn't seem bothered by Casey's rudeness. She explained the French toast recipe, babbling and doing all the steps herself while Lu watched, not listening or remembering. She tried to picture Meg and Steve at fifteen. Steve knowing Kyra since she was a baby. Calling her "Keek" and all that. Why didn't Steve marry Meg, instead? Then he could be Kyra's stepdad and Lu and Casey could be back in their own apartment and schools.

Was that what she even wanted anymore? Sometimes she thought so. Other times, she wasn't so sure.

"Hello? You're not watching," Kyra said. "This part is important. The pan has to be the perfect temperature, otherwise the bread will either be soggy or burned."

"When did your parents get divorced?" Lu asked.

Kyra picked up a piece of bread dripping with the batter she'd mixed up in the green plate. She dropped it into the hot pan, then put another one in. "A long time ago. I was little. How about yours?"

"Only like two years ago."

"Why?"

"I just wondered."

"No," Kyra said, "I mean why did they get divorced?"

"Well . . ." Lu stood by Kyra and watched the edges of the bread sizzle. "Mostly because my dad is an alcoholic." She'd heard Mom say the words so many times but couldn't remember if she'd ever said them herself in that exact way.

Kyra seemed to freeze for a second, then turned to Lu and asked, "A real one?"

Lu wasn't sure what she meant. "He drank . . . drinks . . . a *lot*. He came to Mom and Steve's wedding drunk. He mostly always drinks and when he tries to stop—which has been a lot of times—it never lasts very long."

A wisp of smoke curled up from the pan. Lu pointed and Kyra flipped the bread, which now had some black spots.

"Does he go to AA?" Kyra asked. "Alcoholics Anonymous? Like meetings and stuff?"

"Oh. I think he tried it a few times. It didn't work, I guess."

Kyra kept her eyes on the pan now, her forehead pulled into a thinking-hard expression. "It works for my mom.

That's what her meeting is. This morning. She goes every Saturday. And sometimes other days of the week, too."

"Your mom is . . . an alcoholic?" But, Meg had a job. And she took care of Kyra.

"She's been sober three whole years. Almost four."

Lu held this information very still in her mind so she could get a good look at it. Meg, who had her own business; Meg, who drove her home from school that one day; Meg, who was friends with Steve, had the same problem as Dad.

Except not. Because she wasn't drinking anymore.

Of course the idea of Dad stopping drinking forever wasn't new or anything, but it felt like a wish or a dream or make-believe. She realized now that even after years of praying for it and imagining it, she didn't know for sure it could be real.

"I think if we put on enough syrup we won't taste the burnt parts," Kyra said, scooping the pieces of bread onto their plates. "Or we can cut them off."

"What about your father?" Lu asked as they sat down.

"What about him?"

"How come . . ." If Meg was an alcoholic, why did Kyra stay with her when their parents got divorced? "Was he, like, *worse*? Is that why your mom got custody?"

"He didn't want me." She shrugged. "His loss."

Maybe her body shrugged and her voice shrugged, but Lu could tell in Kyra's face that it hurt. It was in the way Kyra wouldn't look at her and how her forehead was still bunched up around her eyes and also how hard she squeezed the syrup bottle. Her plate flooded with amber liquid.

"Oops," she said. "Sorry."

"It's okay. I'll use some of yours." Lu spooned syrup from Kyra's plate onto hers.

She had so many questions. Before Meg stopped drinking, would Kyra come home and find her passed out on the sofa, like Dad? Did Meg walk through the house in no underwear when she forgot someone might see her? Had Meg ever gotten her driver's license taken away? How did she stop drinking? Just by going to those meetings? Did Kyra worry she'd start again?

The question that came out was, "Does Steve know about your mom?"

"About her drinking and stuff? Sure. It's not a secret. And I think my mom started drinking in high school, and he knew her then."

So Meg had started drinking when she was Casey's age.

"Taste it," Kyra said, pointing with her fork at Lu's French toast.

She cut off a piece. It was chewy, cinnamony, drenched in syrup. "Delicious. I don't taste any burned parts."

Kyra smiled. "Next time, you can do it." They ate some more, then Kyra said, "When I'm thirteen I'm going to go to Alateen."

"What's that?"

"It's for, like, if your mom or dad is an alcoholic. Or your grandma or uncle or whoever. It's a group. A group meeting like AA but for, you know . . . kids like us."

Kids like us. Lu was an *us* with Kyra now, in a way.

"About the talent show," Lu said. She needed a new topic to think about.

"Do you want to do it or not?"

"I do . . ."

Kyra's smiled and her eyebrows shot up.

"But," Lu continued, "I want to do a song by myself."

The smile fell. "Instead of with me?"

Lu swirled her last bite of French toast around in the syrup. "I think so."

"You *think* so or you *know* so?"

"I think I know."

Kyra sighed and stared into her plate a few seconds, then she asked, "Can you tell me for sure by Monday? Like by the end of school on Monday?"

"Yes."

"Even if you don't do the talent show, I think we're meant to at least be best—well, friends. Considering how many times I've already been in this house and considering how my mom and your dad are both alcoholics and considering we both like to cook and considering Mr. Wealer assigned me to you. Don't you think?"

It did seem like some kind of destiny, or even God's

plan. Lu nodded and Kyra smiled. They could be their own unique kind of *we*, at least for now.

In the afternoon, Lu took the bag of records out to the front room and tried to remember how to work the turntable. She thought she remembered: power, put the record on, flip the switch. The record spun and the needle landed, but no sound came out.

Her first instinct was to take the records back to her room before anyone noticed her trying. But she had to find a song soon or there was no way she could learn anything before the talent show.

Steve was in the family room watching TV. Lu stood at the top of the two stairs, heart thumping with nervousness, until he noticed her and said, "What's up, El?"

She wasn't used to asking for help. She didn't like to bother people and she didn't like to ask them for anything, especially.

"El?" Steve asked in an encouraging voice.

"I'm trying to play records but it's not working."

"Did you turn the power on?"

"Yeah."

He paused the TV. "Let's check it out."

She stood aside so he could come up the stairs, then she followed him to the front room. In less than a minute, he said, "Ah, here's your problem." He pointed to the little shelf speakers. "You have to turn on the speakers separately. See?" He showed her how they had their own power button.

"Oh," she said. "Sorry."

"Nothing to be sorry for." He smiled, and gave her shoulder a single pat.

38

THAT NIGHT, LU WAS BORED and restless. The Merritt-Mendozas didn't need babysitting, and Mom and Steve were watching a show about politics, and Casey was in her room.

Lu had already read her library books, and had spent what felt like forever listening to records. She did make a short list of songs she liked to take to Marcus, but there wasn't any particular song that called to her that felt like the *one* she would play for the talent show. She could use this time to practice. But practice what? And why? She put the guitar in her closet so she could stop thinking about the whole talent-show problem.

She went down the hall and tapped on Casey's door, holding her breath as she waited for the answer. When

Casey said, "Come in," she exhaled and opened the door. Casey sat cross-legged on her bed, looking at her new phone.

"Hi."

"Hi," Casey replied without looking up.

"What are you doing?"

"Nothing."

"Do you want to play Bananagrams?"

"No."

Lu looked around the room. Still a mess. "When are you going to finish unpacking?"

"Never."

"Have you talked to Dad since you got your new phone?"

She still didn't look up, but she stopped scrolling and paused before answering. "No. He doesn't answer my texts, and his number goes straight to a message saying his voicemail is full."

Lu sat in Casey's desk chair and swiveled back and forth. "Kyra said—"

"Who?"

"Kyra. My friend who was over."

"Oh, yeah." Casey was scrolling again. "She said what?"

"She said her mom is an alcoholic, too. Only she's been sober for almost four years."

Casey's finger hovered over her phone. "So?"

"She started drinking in high school. Her mom did." Lu swiveled a few more times. "Have you ever drank?"

That got Casey to look up. "Lulu, have you ever thought

of minding your own business?"

Lu picked on a splinter at the edge of Casey's desk. "Have you ever heard of Alateen?"

Another pause. "Yeah. I actually went to a meeting once."

"You did? When? What was it like?"

Casey finally put her phone down. "It was awkward. I didn't see the point. You might like it, though. Does Kyra go?"

"You have to be thirteen."

"Hm. I think I was twelve." She picked up her phone again and typed into it, then handed the phone to Lu. "Here. If you want to read about it. I'm going to get some ice cream. I'll bring you a spoon."

Lu stayed in the desk chair and read the screen. The top said:

Frequently Asked Questions

She read through some of the questions and the answers. She learned that all kinds of people are alcoholics, and they might drink even if they don't really want to. And sometimes they couldn't express love very well and had trouble loving themselves, too.

One question on the site was: *What can I do if my friends don't want to visit me?*

She thought about Beth. When they first became friends, in first grade, Beth would come over sometimes. Then in second grade, at Lu's birthday party, Dad had come home after he'd been gone for days. He walked right through the party, straight for the cake. He smelled really bad and he picked up a piece of cake with his bare hands and then stood in the room eating it without a fork or plate or anything while all the kids stared until Mom got him to go into their room and stay there. After that, Beth didn't come over.

Casey returned with the carton of Moose Tracks and two spoons, and sat on the floor. Lu put the phone down and got off the chair and sat across from her.

They passed the ice cream back and forth for a while. They hadn't done this since they moved, and even before that they didn't do it that often because Mom didn't keep ice cream around all the time. But Steve did.

"Do you think Dad could stop drinking for three whole years?" Lu asked. "Like Kyra's mom?"

Casey scoffed. "Doubtful." She looked at Lu. "I know I shouldn't say that. I wish he could. My whole life, Mom and Pastor Richards and people at church made it sound like him quitting was always probably *about* to happen. That with God's help, anything is possible—even miracles—and there was going to be a miracle for Dad any second."

Lu knew what she meant. It did feel like that. Or it had, even right up until the wedding.

"But then it never happened," Casey continued. "And I stopped thinking it would. I can't even imagine it, now. He's never stopped for more than a couple of weeks."

"You think it's . . . impossible?"

Casey thought for a second. "I would never say that. But

I'm not sitting around waiting for it. You know?"

Lu nodded. It just seemed like there *could* be a miracle any second. There was one for Kyra's mom. And Dad had gotten himself together at least enough to get Lu the guitar. And didn't him showing up for the wedding prove that he still cared, in some way? That he still thought about them, and wanted to see them?

"He has it really bad, I guess," Lu said quietly.

"Yeah. He does." Casey looked into the carton and dragged her spoon through to scoop up one more cashew. "We better save some for Steve." She got up off the floor. On her way out of the room, she stopped at a half-unpacked box and pulled out the yellow Bananagrams bag. She tossed it onto the floor in front of Lu. "Set this up. I'll be right back."

39

Lu took her list of songs to Marcus on Sunday after church. They stood in the kitchen with Tala in her high chair eating macaroni with her fingers. He looked through them, nodding to himself, or saying "I don't know this one," or "Yeah, good song, pretty advanced, though," or "Possible," before he asked her, "Which one do *you* love?"

She shrugged. "I don't know."

"You don't know?" He picked a piece of macaroni off the floor and tossed it into the sink. "What's up? You're not into these?" he asked, pointing at the list.

"Do you think I could do any of those really good? In time for the talent show?"

"You could probably learn one good enough. Show off what you've learned so far; you can be proud of yourself for that."

She didn't want to be good enough. *Good enough* wasn't what impressed people and made your dad think, *Wow!* Ever since her talk with Casey last night, she was even more unsure about her whole talent show idea. Unsure about the point of even learning the guitar at all.

"Maybe I'm never going to be good at it," she said.

Marcus laughed, then stopped when he saw she wasn't. "You literally just started. You're gonna be bad before you're good. You could take the talent show off the table if it's stressing you out, and just focus on learning and practicing."

Lu glanced at Tala, who was looking at her with big eyes, chewing macaroni. Marcus probably loved her just for existing.

"I want to invite my dad," she said, staring down at her hands while she felt the calluses. "I want to play something and be good at it for him."

He waited to see if she'd say more, but that was it.

"Mm," he said. "I can understand that." He got a towel and wiped off Tala's face and hands, then got her out of the chair and put her on the floor. She stayed sitting there next to his legs. "But . . ."

Lu looked up at him.

He continued, "It's a lot to put on yourself."

The list of songs sat there on the counter. Any one of them would impress Dad—they were from his records— but she knew Marcus was right. She couldn't learn these in the short time before the talent show.

"Didn't you tell me you were doing something with a friend?" Marcus asked.

"I was thinking about it. She really wants me to."

"How about this: I'll tell you what I think, and then you can decide and let me know how I can help."

Tala reached for him; he reflexively bent down and lifted her to his chest. Lu wondered if Dad had ever been that kind of dad. If there was a time when he would automatically feed her, pick her up, hold her.

". . . and then you kind of share the whole thing." Marcus had been talking; she tuned back in. "The planning, the stage fright, the good parts, and the mistakes. Playing with other people is cool and a lot less pressure than playing solo."

She nodded, unsure of what to say. It was true, playing something with Kyra would probably be easier and more fun. But it would mean the whole talent show the way she'd pictured it wasn't real, that Dad really was just a person who lived in a van and didn't care to answer his phone when his daughters called, that she had no way of knowing when any sort of miracle would come, if ever.

"And hey," Marcus said, "if your dad does show up, he'll just be happy to see you." He kissed Tala on the cheek. "Trust me."

She got her list of songs and went home, holding on to those words.

* * *

Monday was when she promised Kyra she'd give her final answer about the talent show. Kyra asked at the beginning of the day, and at recess, and again at lunch.

"You said *end* of the school day," Lu reminded her.

"I know! Sorry!"

She already knew what she was going to say. She was 95 percent sure, anyway. The other 5 percent was her thinking that the safest thing to do was nothing, and never play the guitar again, never want Dad to care, never hope he'd stop drinking or be different.

But she couldn't help wanting it.

When the last bell of the day rung, Kyra spun in her chair and grinned at Lu so hard that it made Lu laugh.

"O-*kay*," Lu said, "I'll do it."

"Finally!"

PART V

Spring

40

By April, Lu knew four chords really well, and a few more not so well. She could strum with a pick. She could almost sing and play at the same time. At least "Row, Row, Row Your Boat." She and Kyra had been practicing the Muppet song, "Movin' Right Along," and Casey assured her it wasn't just for little kids; everyone liked the Muppets. She said, "Muppets are eternal beings."

She'd had one sleepover at Beth's, but it was for Beth's birthday and there were three other girls there, too, including Daisy Dobrov. Beth ate too many hot Takis and threw up and Daisy laughed at her for it, and by bedtime she and Beth weren't speaking. In the morning, Daisy apologized and Beth forgave her. A little too easily, if you asked Lu.

Lu had gone to a birthday party, too, for a boy at her new

school, a Saturday party where the parents had rented a big cotton-candy machine and everyone got a turn spinning sugar in the yard. Kyra hadn't been invited to that one and Lu felt bad on Monday when so many of the kids were talking about the cotton candy and also the make-your-own pizzas. Kyra's feelings were hurt about not being invited. Jase said, "Everyone gets left out sometimes." And Kyra said, "Yeah. My mom says it's part of the 'human experience.'" She made big air quotes with her fingers and then they got the giggles and everything was okay.

Lu and Casey still hadn't heard from Dad.

And Casey was still unhappy. Getting along a little better with Steve, but unhappy.

When Lu thought of the apartment, her arms and legs still ached, but she also liked the house. Steve had been right—she liked having her own room once she got used to it. And she liked her new school and Mr. Wealer, and Kyra and Meg and going to the Merritt-Mendozas'.

She even liked Steve. But liking Steve didn't mean she didn't wish Dad would call.

Most days now, Lu and Casey were supposed to find their own ways home, which meant walking or waiting for the bus. From Lu's school, the bus took longer than walking, and sometimes Casey walked all the way home, too. Some days, though, Steve worked a shorter shift and would pick them both up.

Like today. Steve got Lu first, and Kyra hung her arms in the passenger window of the truck to talk to him a little while she was waiting for Meg.

"Have you taught Lu how to make tamale pie yet?" she asked him now. "Because that's one of my favorites."

"Not yet, Keek." He looked at Lu. "How about we make it soon and Kyra and her mom can come over for dinner to help us eat it?"

"Okay!" Lu didn't like cooking as much as Kyra wanted her to, but she liked hanging out in the kitchen with Steve. It was kind of relaxing, and "relaxing" was one word she could never, ever use to describe any time she'd spent with Dad.

"We better get moving," Steve said to Kyra, who stepped away from the truck as she said goodbye.

When they pulled up to where Casey was supposed to be, she wasn't there. Steve made a sound somewhere between a sigh and a growl. "Do you see her coming out of the building?" he asked.

"Not yet. . . ."

Steve stayed silent while they both craned their necks in search of Casey. Then he said, "What am I doing wrong, Lu?"

The car crept forward.

"I don't need Casey to *like* me," he said. "I only wish she'd trust me a little. Wouldn't see me as the bad guy."

Lu tried to remember what Casey had said not long after they'd moved. "She said . . . she's waiting for the 'real Steve' to come out." She used the same air quotes Kyra had the other day. "After the honeymoon is over."

Steve kind of laughed. "What?"

Lu sat up straighter, leaned forward. "There she is."

Casey, in her black jeans and boots and denim jacket, was jogging across the lawn in front of the high school. And someone else ran beside her—a girl dressed a lot like Casey, with bleached-white hair shaved close on one side, longer on the other.

When they got to the truck, Casey pulled open the door and said breathlessly, "This is Liza, can she come over?"

Liza smiled. She had on dark eye makeup and a black T-shirt with a red scorpion on the front.

Steve hesitated. It was the same short pause he took every time they asked him something they might normally ask Mom, if she were there. Like he wasn't sure how much of a parent he was supposed to be.

"There's not really room in the truck cab . . ." he began. The second row seats were still out from the move.

Liza said, "That's okay, we can ride in the back."

"I don't think—"

"Please, Steve." Casey leaned as far into the truck as she could, away from Liza. "I told her she could. Just for like an hour. Then her brother can come get her."

Steve glanced over his shoulder. Cars waited in the line for them to move along. He gestured to the back of the truck with his thumb.

"Thank you," Casey said in a rush of breath. She closed the door and she and Liza ran around to the back to climb into the truck bed.

Steve drove a little below the speed limit all the way home. "It makes me nervous, having them back there," he said. "When I was in high school, these kids I knew bounced out of a truck bed going too fast. Cracked their heads open on the street."

"Did they die?" Lu asked. She cast a worried glance behind her.

"No. But I doubt they got too much smarter after that."

At home, Casey and Liza took a bag of chips and some sodas into Casey's room. Lu made a piece of peanut butter toast and poured a glass of root beer over ice from the ice maker in the refrigerator door. The ice maker was one of her favorite little things about the house.

"I'm going to do some yard work," Steve said. "I've got lots to do before the block party, if you want to sit out there with your snack and keep me company."

She wanted to practice before her guitar lesson tonight, but she couldn't do that at the same time as eating peanut butter toast anyway. So she settled into a lawn chair and watched Steve pull weeds and turn the compost barrel and sweep the patio.

"My mom and I kind of started the block party tradition together," he said as he scooped up a pile of leaves to add to the compost. "She always said people knew their neighbors better when she was a kid, and that was a good thing. When she wasn't able to do much for it anymore, I ran with it, big time." He scooped another pile. "It's a lot of work, but the more tense and political everything in the world gets, the more I want to go all-out to have this one thing where everyone is invited and welcome and they don't have to do anything but show up. And it's not about buying or selling or who you are or who you're not . . . any of that. Just a big, free party. Which is I guess how I picture heaven."

It might have been the most he'd ever said to her at once. Lu let the root beer wash peanut butter off her teeth. "Do you want help?"

He brushed his hands off on his jeans and looked around. "Are you grossed out by snails?"

"Not really."

"Finish your snack and you can help me pluck and toss. I find snails down here in the yard and throw them up the hill and hope it takes them a few weeks to make it back before I do it again." He turned the compost barrel a few times. "I could never bring myself to use poison."

She took another bite of toast, another sip of root beer. "Do you miss your mom?"

"Yes and no. She had a long life. A good one." He looked at her. "You miss your dad?"

She thought. She missed the version of him that had only existed in moments, in short periods of days, longer ones of weeks. She missed the idea of a dad who would be there and tuck her in at night and be in pictures you could put on the fridge. But him, her actual dad, the way he really was? Mostly she wanted him to miss her.

"Yes and no," she answered.

Steve smiled. "That's fair."

"Right now, I don't even know where he is."

He leaned against the stack of railroad ties he'd put in the yard to shore up the hill. "I think he's still in the city, right? He hasn't moved or anything, as far as I know."

"But where in the city?"

"That I don't know, Lu. I guess he could park his van just about anywhere."

So he did know *something*. He knew about the van. "Don't you think our dad should know where we are?"

"Well, I think he does."

"I mean our address."

Steve nodded. "He knows."

Lu blinked. "How? Mom said we weren't going to tell him."

"That was the plan at first, but then she did give him the address. It seemed like the right thing, given we weren't sure how to find him once he moved into the van."

Lu went over this information in her mind. "She called him?"

"She emailed him, then texted to say she'd emailed."

So Dad knew. But Lu and Casey didn't know he knew. Or maybe Casey knew? Anyway, Dad knew, was the main thing, but he hadn't tried to contact them since they moved, not once. "Oh" was all she could think to say.

Then a thing started happening that she didn't want to happen. Talking to Steve about Dad, about missing him and not missing him, about where he was and where he wasn't, something in her came loose. She couldn't take a deep breath without her shoulders shaking. Then her nose filled, and her chest hurt, and she couldn't control the shape of her mouth.

In other words: she was crying.

She put her face in her hands so Steve wouldn't see it, even though he'd been looking right at her when it started.

Don't cry. Don't cry, Lula.

Her dad's voice, still in her head. Even though he hadn't even cared enough to write a letter or call them on Casey's phone or even write a text. Not one sentence.

Why should she let that voice tell her how to be, when it belonged to someone who wasn't any good at being what *he* was supposed to be?

She felt an arm around her shoulder and heard a different voice. One that said, "It's okay, Lu. I know, it's hard. My dad left, too. I know it hurts. You'll be okay. You're doing really great."

She leaned against the person that the arm and the voice belonged to.

41

Lu ACCEPTED THE FACT THAT Casey walking her to her guitar lessons was all about Casey getting to talk to Shannon. Casey even started calling her "Aunt Shannon" in a way that had a joking tone but real feelings. They would get to the house, and talk to the kids a little if they were downstairs, eat a cookie or piece of cake or—hopefully not—some pie. Then Casey would go off to tell Shannon everything she wasn't talking about at home, and Lu and Marcus would get out their guitars.

"Let's hear how your talent show song is coming along," Marcus said, while they stretched out their hands by making fists and then releasing them, wiggling their fingers all around, rolling their wrists.

Lu bent her neck forward and backward, then side to

side, which was the next part of warming up. Her neck cracked loudly when she bent it to the left. "Whoa."

Marcus laughed. "Everything okay in there?"

"Yeah."

And she did feel pretty good. She had always worried that crying would make her hurt *more* because if you let yourself cry it was like admitting something was bad. Something in your real life, not just something in a book. But after crying in the yard and Steve saying it was okay, she actually felt less sad.

She settled her hands into position on her guitar, and tapped out the beat with her foot.

She hit most of the chords. Marcus had shown her simplified versions of ones that were too hard, and also how to skip over ones she couldn't do at all by tapping the guitar with her hand. The C sounded dull, like always, but someday her hand would be big enough and strong enough to make it sound better. She kept her right hand as loose as she could for strumming, without being so loose that the pick flew across the room like it had a few weeks ago.

When she'd gone through it once, Marcus nodded and said, "That was awesome. Your chord changes get better every time. Your count was super steady. How did you feel?"

"Good."

"Just good?"

"Well, it doesn't sound anything like how it sounds in the video."

He rested his chin on his guitar. "What do you think is missing?"

"Um . . . talent? Puppets?"

He grinned. "Nooo. Practice, maybe. Experience, definitely. What about . . . expression? The song is kind of fun, right?" He played it on his guitar and bobbed his head up and down. "Do I look like a big dork?"

"Kind of."

They laughed.

"Sometimes putting the feeling into a song or a performance means forgetting what you look like. Maybe you look silly or feel silly, but if it helps you get in touch with the feeling of the song, it's worth it."

"How do you express the feelings when you're trying to do the chord changes?"

"Great question." He strummed a chord. "The first step is practicing the chords so much that you don't really think about them anymore. Your fingers just know where they should be. After that . . . I guess the bottom line is about letting go. You're not going to gain *that* much more skill between now and the talent show. So why don't you let go and express with whatever you've got?"

"Kyra's the one singing. She'll do a lot of expressing."

"You're not gonna sing, too?" Marcus drummed his fingers on the top of his guitar. "You have a nice voice. I can teach you a little easy harmony part on the chorus if you want."

"Well, we're doing sort of a skit. Like, I have lines. And I'm doing the 'dooga-doons.'"

He took his guitar off and set it on the floor. "This sounds amazing, I can't wait."

"You're coming to the show?"

"Heck yeah, I'm coming, what do you think?"

"I didn't know."

"Do you not want me to?" He cracked his knuckles. "If it would freak you out, I don't have to."

She shook her head. "No. I want you to."

On the walk home, the guitar case kept bumping into Lu's knees. She switched from sore hand to sore hand and asked Casey, "What did you and Shannon talk about?"

"Stuff."

"What kind of stuff?"

"You know. A little bit of 'none of.' And also some 'your business.'"

"Ha-ha." She looked at Casey. "Can I send Dad a text from your phone?"

"You can try." Casey took a deep breath of the night air. "Honestly, Lulu? What's the point? He never answers."

"Did you know . . . Well, Steve said his dad left, too."

Casey stopped walking. "Really? Why?"

"I don't know. He didn't say that part."

"Here, give me that," Casey said, taking the guitar case from Lu's hand. "I can't stand to watch you tripping all over this thing."

They stopped at the crest of the hill. The night was unusually clear; the moon almost full. The stars looked bright and cold. Casey seemed happier, too. Maybe it was the time she got to spend with Shannon. Maybe it was having a friend over today.

She looked at Lu. "I might try that Alateen thing again. There's one that meets at the library here. They have a flyer at school."

"They do?"

"If I go, I promise to tell you all about it." She switched the guitar case from one hand to the other and got her phone out of her back pocket. "What do you want to text Dad?"

"I want to invite him to the talent show. Then he can see, like, how I learned to play the guitar he gave me and all that." Now that she'd said it out loud, it didn't sound like a silly fantasy or a wish for a miracle. It would remind him they were still there. Remind him he had daughters. Casey was strong and smart. Lu already learned enough guitar to perform.

Casey handed her the phone. "As long as you know he probably won't show up. He might not even be *getting* these texts."

"I know."

She stared down at the phone. They were still standing

in the street. In this town, you could walk down the middle of a street and a car might *never* come. She typed in the message. *It's Lulu. I'm playing the guitar in the school talent show. Do you want to come?* She put in the day and time and place and looked up at Casey, who was beautiful as ever in the moonlight.

"You didn't hit send yet," Casey said.

"I will."

She heard Steve's voice in her mind.

My dad left, too.

She didn't know when it happened to Steve, but she imagined him at her age. Maybe he'd watched out the window of the house, maybe even the same window in Lu's room, wondering if his dad would come back.

Maybe he wondered what he'd done that made him leave.

Maybe, when he was a kid, every time the phone rang, he wondered if it would be his dad. Calling to say happy birthday. Calling to say hi. Calling to say I love you. And then maybe it never was him.

If Lu didn't send the text, then it couldn't hurt if he didn't come.

Mom and Steve will be there, she told herself. And Casey. And even Marcus.

Dad could be there or not, but she wouldn't be alone.

"Do you want me to do it?" Casey asked, holding her hand out for the phone.

Lu shook her head. "No. I can." She sent the text and watched it turn from gray to green.

Now, she'd have to do what Marcus said to do about the song: let go.

42

STEVE WAS GOING TO TAKE them all camping for two nights during the spring recess. He said it was his "last hurrah" before every free minute would be for getting ready for the block party. He couldn't believe Lu and Casey had never camped out. They'd been on two church retreats in the Santa Cruz mountains where they stayed in cabins, and Casey slept in a tent one night for Outdoor Education when she was in sixth grade, but that was it.

Steve had all the equipment: a tent, some blowup mattresses, a camp stove, flashlights and lanterns, folding camp chairs, sleeping bags. "My gear is old," he told Lu when she helped him load the truck. "But it works."

Casey didn't want to go, of course. The morning they were supposed to leave, Lu found her sitting on her bed, peeling a boiled egg, still not packed.

"You just don't like anything that's Steve's idea," Lu said.

"No, I don't like anything that's dirty and boring and stupid."

Mom leaned into the room. "Case. Finish packing. Now. We're leaving in fifteen minutes."

"I bet Marcus and Shannon would let me stay over there," Casey said, close to whining.

"Casey. Enough. Don't forget flip-flops."

They drove a couple of hours to a campground right on the Russian River. After they passed the main gate, Steve pointed out the general store and showers and bathrooms. "See, Casey? It's not exactly the wilderness."

"I know," she replied quickly, as if she hadn't been complaining for days leading up to the trip.

The four of them worked together to unload the truck, and Steve gave them each jobs to do to help set up camp. Lu plugged an air pump into the outlet on a little metal pole at the corner of the site, and filled all the mattresses. When Steve asked Casey to help him with the tent, she said, "I don't know how. Why can't Mom do it?"

"*I* don't know how, either, Case," Mom said, "and your knees are younger than mine."

As far as Lu could remember, Casey had never said she didn't want to do something just because she didn't know *how*. No one knew how to do anything until they learned it.

Then when Steve explained how Lu and Casey would

set up their beds in the back of the truck and Mom and Steve would be in the tent, Casey said, "What if we get attacked by bears or bats or . . ."

Mom laughed. But Lu could tell Casey really was worried. Steve seemed to understand it, too.

"There *are* bears in this county," he said, "but they don't come around here. And we're not going to see any bats. It's not even really mosquito season yet, so it should just be a nice night under the stars. You see so many more out here than at home."

Casey didn't look reassured.

Later, they swam in the river, and Casey screamed when she thought she felt a fish or a snake or something brush against her legs. Mom laughed again. And again, Lu saw Casey was actually scared. Steve said, "Don't worry, it's probably a bluegill. They're harmless, I promise. We can go fishing later, if you want, and you can get your revenge."

Casey laughed a little at that.

That night in the back of the truck, Lu and Casey lay close to keep warm. Steve had built a fire and they had hot dogs for dinner, and made s'mores. Lu was full and a little sunburned, and the air mattress was pretty comfortable.

Steve had been right—without the light from cars and buildings and streets, the stars seemed to almost cover the night sky.

"Those stars are there all the time and we don't even see them," Lu said quietly.

"Yeah."

Lu asked what she asked every day but hadn't asked *yet* on this day: "Did Dad text you back?"

"No, Lulu. I'll *tell* you if he does, I swear. There's not even a signal here."

Lu, sleepy, couldn't help but have one more fantasy about how the talent show night could go. She pictured it in her mind like she was directing a movie. After the show, Dad would find Lu and say how good she did. Then Marcus would appear. He'd put his arm around Lu and say, *She's pretty great! My favorite guitar student.*

Dad would remember him from the wedding. *By the way, thanks for looking out for my girls at the wedding. I was out of line.*

They'd shake hands.

Steve and Mom would be watching and Lu would say, *Well, Steve is taking us out for ice cream now so I have to go, but you can come over in the morning and we'll get doughnuts.*

She started to hear music and felt her fingers twitch, and sank down into the fuzzy comfort of this little movie, until Casey suddenly jerked and shrieked beside her.

Lu sat up. Mom called from inside the tent, "Everything okay out there?"

Casey was thrashing at her neck and swearing under her breath. "A freaking spider or something crawled on me."

In the dark, Lu could just make out the string of Casey's hoodie resting on her neck. She reached over and pulled it away from her skin.

"Was it this?"

Casey held the string out and stared at it. "Maybe," she muttered, before flopping back down onto the mattress. After a minute, Lu heard Casey sniffle.

"Are you okay?" Lu whispered.

After a few seconds of silence, Casey added: "Nature scares me. I like the city."

Bats and bears, imaginary snakes in the river, hoodie strings that turned into spiders.

Moving. Changing. Starting a new school.

Lu looked at her sister. All those things from the past few months that seemed to make Casey difficult and moody and full of complaints . . . maybe that whole time, she'd just been afraid.

Casey wiped her nose. "Stop staring at me."

"Okay," Lu said. When she snuggled tight to Casey, Casey didn't move away.

The day they left the campground, Casey turned her phone back on as soon as they were on the highway. A bunch of notifications buzzed, all in a row. After a few seconds, Casey handed Lu the phone with the screen open to a message from Dad:

Sounds good. I'll try to be there.

She read it at least ten times. It sounded so . . . normal. Two short sentences. Seven words. All of her thoughts and dreams and worries, the weeks and weeks of not hearing from him, the indecision about the talent show—and now this.

Casey took the phone back and put her mouth to Lu's ear so Mom and Steve wouldn't hear them. "Do you want me to answer?"

Traffic zoomed around them. Mom's hand was on Steve's leg. They were passing around a bag of leftover marshmallows they'd brought for the s'mores.

As bad as it felt when Dad wasn't answering and didn't seem to care, this felt hard, too.

She shook her head and said, "Not now."

43

WHEN LU TOLD KYRA THAT her dad might come to the talent show, Kyra got a blank look on her face and only said, "Oh," before going through her choreography again.

They were in Lu's room after school, practicing the song. Kyra was improvising some arm moves and simple dance steps. Lu couldn't tell if it looked good or bad or embarrassing or fine.

She didn't want to make Kyra more nervous than she already was, but she also wanted her to understand how important it was to perform well.

"I haven't seen my dad since Mom and Steve's wedding," she explained.

Kyra watched herself in the mirror and adjusted the angle of her right elbow. "I haven't seen my dad since I was six."

Lu strummed the guitar. "So if he *was* going to come to the talent show, you'd want to be extra good."

"Well, he's *not*, because he's not even in California anymore, so it doesn't matter."

"It matters for me, though."

"If he shows up."

Frustrated, Lu pushed her guitar off her lap and stood up. "I'm going to get some water."

At the kitchen sink, she took deep breaths. She had learned that Kyra was not as predictable as Beth in terms of her moods and reactions. She sometimes didn't think about her words before saying them, it seemed like.

When she got back to her room, Kyra said in a rush, "I'm sorry. I'm just jealous. I don't think I'll ever see my dad again, and yours might come to the talent show. We'll make it good."

That was another thing she'd learned about Kyra: her apologies came as fast and easy as her bad moods, and she didn't hold grudges.

"It's okay," Lu said. "You're right. He might not show up. We'll just do the best we can."

"I feel like we need to practice it in front of someone. Would Casey watch us and tell us if it's good or not?"

"Ummm . . ." Lu wasn't sure she wanted Casey to see yet.

"What about Steve?"

"He had to go to Costco for more block party stuff."

The famous block party was coming up this weekend and all Steve's time since the camping trip had been taken up with his planning and preparations. Which was what he'd said would happen but Lu didn't know how serious it would be. He was always in the kitchen making sauces and marinades, homemade pickles, even his own special ketchup.

"We have to do it in front of someone! We can't have the talent show be the very first time we have an audience."

Lu agreed they could ask Casey, and they went and knocked on her door.

"What?" Casey called from inside.

"Can you watch us do the song?"

"I've been hearing it for an hour."

"Is it good?" Kyra asked, way louder than necessary.

In a few seconds, Casey opened the door. "Kyra, you don't have to *shout*."

"Sorry."

"I'm trying to do geometry. If I watch you do your song *once*, will you guys stop practicing?" She held up one finger. "*Once*."

They nodded, and made Casey sit on the edge of her bed while Lu got her guitar. Lu sat cross-legged on the floor with it in her lap. "Wait," Casey said, "are you going to be sitting on the floor for this?"

"On a chair. I can't play standing up. Yet."

"Hm. Okay." Casey held her phone up.

"What are you doing?" Kyra asked.

"Recording. Then you guys can watch yourselves and you won't need me to tell you how it looks."

It was a good idea, but Kyra said, "I don't want to be recorded."

"Why not?" Lu asked.

"I just don't."

"I'm not going to, like, send it to your enemies or anything," Casey said, laughing.

"I know. I just don't like it." She looked at Lu, and Lu said to Casey, "Don't record."

"Whatever you say." Casey put the phone down.

Lu got her hands into position and started playing. Even only Casey watching made her nervous and she messed up a little. What would it be like with so many other people watching, maybe including Dad?

Casey watched, expressionless, until she laughed when Lu did the "dooga-doon dooga-doon" part, then watched the rest with a little smile. At the end, she clapped.

"That was cute," she said.

"Cute?" Kyra asked.

"Yeah. Can I make a suggestion?"

"What?" Lu asked.

"I think maybe with the choreography, less is more." Casey stood up and went to Kyra. "You're pretty tall, right, and I think you'll have a lot of natural presence onstage. You don't need to move around so much. And your voice sounds better when you aren't trying to dance, too."

"I like the dancing," Kyra said.

"You can still do a little. But smaller moves. Like this." Casey demonstrated a version of what Kyra was doing.

"Are you sure that's not boring?" Kyra asked.

"I think she's right," Lu said. "And your voice does sound better without it."

"Maybe."

"Also, you know what would look cute on you?" Casey asked Kyra, and reached for her hair.

Kyra drew back. "Don't."

"Sorry! Can I just show you something?"

"Show me without touching my hair."

"I was just going to say I think kind of wrapping your braids around your head and pinning them in place would look cute for the show. And it would keep your braids out of your way while you move."

Kyra picked up her braids and held them against her head. "Like this?"

"More to the front. Yeah. There."

Lu watched Casey and Kyra. Because Beth didn't come over to their apartment, Casey never really got a chance to know Beth and Beth didn't really know Casey. It made Lu feel good to see her sister helping her friend. Like they were part of some bigger family that could include a lot more people than only the two of them.

"*Now* can I do my homework in peace?" Casey asked.

After Kyra had gone home, after dinner, after homework, Mom came and stood in Lu's doorway. "Can I come in?"

"Mm-hmm."

Mom stretched out on Lu's bed and sighed. "Oh boy, I'm tired. I'm looking forward to the party this weekend, but I'll be glad when it's over. Just watching Steve do all this running around wears me out." She patted the blanket. "Come here. Two things."

Lu sat next to her. "One is Casey helped me and Kyra today."

"Oh yeah? Good."

She let Mom pull her down next to her.

"Two is . . . Dad said he might come to the talent show."

"Case told me," Mom said softly.

"Is that okay?"

"I think it's really nice that you invited him, Belle, whether or not he comes." Mom paused, then said, "How much you do or don't want him in your life, I want that to be up to you. He hasn't asked for any custody or visitation rights, so he doesn't get to decide. You do. Unless something is going on that I think isn't safe for you, I want it to be your choice."

"What about Casey?"

"Hers, too. And she might want different things from you, and that's okay."

Lu put her cheek against Mom's fuzzy sweater. "What

if I don't know what to do?"

"Then you don't have to do anything." Mom kissed her head. "You can wait until you do know, and you can take as much time as you want to figure it out."

44

THE MORNING OF THE BLOCK party, a thin blanket of fog crept over their street. It didn't mean they weren't going to have any sun. Fog was often there when she woke up and then gone by midmorning. Lu opened her bedroom window a few inches to feel the dampness on her face.

Parties were complicated. She liked people but not a *lot* of people at once, especially a lot of people that she didn't know very well or at all.

So she would know Kyra and Meg. The Merritt-Mendozas. Maybe Beth and her parents, if they came. Mom had called last week to invite them.

Steve was already up—she could hear him rattling dishes in the kitchen. Even Casey had to be impressed by all the work he'd done to get ready for the party. All on his own, too, without asking Mom or any of them for help. Mom kept offering but Steve repeated that he'd been doing it on his own for twenty years and he had it down to a science.

All week he'd been marinating chicken and making big bowls of potato salad, packing it into plastic containers, and then disappearing into the garage to put them in the extra fridge.

Lu got dressed in jean shorts and her favorite soft gray hoodie, and brushed out her hair, which was getting long again. She slipped on the green sneakers that Casey had passed down to her, and went to the kitchen.

Steve looked deep in concentration with his hands in a huge bowl of a beige-and-brown mixture, squishing and mixing it.

"What's that?" she asked.

"It's going to be veggie burgers."

"You could've got frozen ones."

He laughed. "No way! People who love my special recipe really *love* it. It would be a huge betrayal to buy frozen. I was supposed to have made these ahead of time, though. I can't believe I forgot." He glanced at her. "You want to help?"

Lu shrugged. "Sure."

"Great. Roll up your sleeves and wash your hands."

When she'd done that, he showed her the size of patty to make and how to stack them with wax paper in between. "What's in here?" she asked.

"Beans. Oats. Spices. My special barbecue sauce. Some ground-up walnuts."

"You like meat, though."

"I do. But part of hospitality, especially for a big event like this, is trying to think of everyone and everything, and having options for them so they can relax and enjoy the party, too."

Hospitality. Lu liked that word.

When they had several stacks of patties lined up on a tray, Steve said, "Could you carry these to the garage freezer while I clean up? I'm out of room in here. It's better if they can set a little before they go on the grill."

There was no inside entrance into the garage, so Lu carried the tray carefully down the outside steps, and balanced it in one hand as she entered the code for the door. After it lifted, she checked—as always—the side of the garage that still had some of their stuff from the apartment. Just to make sure he hadn't given anything else away.

Then her eyes went to the other side. And her heart began to race.

Along with the bags of chips and burger buns and the fridge full of chicken and salads, there was now beer. Lots of beer. Cases of it, stacked all around. There were also bottles of liquor, all kinds. Bags of lemons and limes leaned against the bottles. Steve had been collecting coolers from various neighbors "to keep the drinks cold." These were the drinks he was talking about?

She opened the chest freezer to put the veggie patties in. There were two big bottles of vodka in there. That was Dad's drink. Vodka and orange juice. Or vodka and nothing. He'd kept his in the freezer, too. And under his bed, and in the cupboard behind the cereal, and in the hall closet under the towels.

Little pinprick zaps stung and tingled in her arms and hands.

Mom didn't drink, Steve didn't drink—she *thought*. Beth's parents didn't drink and she'd never seen Marcus or Shannon drink. People at their church didn't drink, that she knew of. The only person she knew for sure who drank was Dad.

She left the garage and pressed the button to lower the garage door.

Mom was in the kitchen now, too, drinking her coffee while Steve did dishes at the sink. She had on jeans and a pretty embroidered top, and new flat strappy sandals.

"Look at you," Mom said. "All up and dressed."

"Yeah." Did Mom know about what was in the garage?

"I suppose I should try to get Casey going. I need more caffeine first."

"Hey, El," Steve said, "you want to run up to the Merritt-Mendozas' and pick up the cooler they're lending? It's big but it's on wheels. Marcus said he'd put it out on his porch this morning."

She listened for the tone in the kitchen, the way Marcus

had taught her to listen to her guitar strings and compare them to the tone on the guitar tuner. It sounded normal. Mom's voice was the same. Steve's as friendly as always.

It didn't matter. She was on alert now.

Marcus was outside with Tala and Bossy. As Lu got closer she could see he was picking up dog doo with a shovel and putting it into a bucket. Bossy ran up to her and slobbered on her shorts.

"Hiya," Marcus said. "How's the prep going? Just trying to do my part here," he said as he dumped another scoop of poop. Tala was picking dandelions.

"Steve said you have a cooler . . . ?"

"Oh right, I was supposed to put it out. Totally forgot. Let me just finish this and I'll get it for you." Lu sat on one of the big rocks in the yard and hugged her knees. Marcus glanced at her. "You all right?"

She nodded.

"No, you're not," he said with a laugh. "I've seen that face. What's up?" He scanned the ground for more poop.

"There's going to be a lot of people today. People I don't know."

"That's true."

"The only big, like, adult parties I've been to are church ones."

"Where you already know everyone," Marcus said.

"Sort of. But also . . . it's church. We pray over the food

and stuff." She rubbed a smudge off the green toe of one sneaker and added, "People drink coffee and water and soda."

"Steve actually does say a prayer before we eat. It might be more like a church potluck than you think."

He wasn't getting it. Probably she was being a baby about the alcohol. "Yeah," she said. "It'll be okay."

"Let me go grab that cooler for you. Keep an eye on Tala real quick?"

She got up off the rock and crouched down to help Tala, who had two fistfuls of dandelions and was still trying to pick more. "You have to put some down," Lu said, "if you want to pick more."

She tilted her chubby face to Lu and held out one handful of crunched-up dandelion stems. When Lu tried to take it, Tala screamed and yanked her fist back.

"I thought you were trying to give them to me!" Lu snapped.

Tala said, "No!"

The pinpricks Lu had felt in her skin since seeing what was in the garage grew sharper and hotter. She heard plastic wheels on cement and stood up to face Marcus, who was dragging a big blue cooler behind him.

"Did you know that I never said you could have our bunk bed?"

He cocked his head, half smiling. "What?"

"The bunk bed in Rosie's room. That was mine. And

~320~

Casey's." With him looking at her now, puzzled, the hot prickles turned cold. Marcus had only ever been nice to her. The nicest. "Never mind," she muttered to the ground.

He passed the handle of the cooler to her. "I didn't know. Steve asked if we could use a bunk bed and we said sure. That's it."

"I know." Her voice came out croaky.

Tala had waddled over and wrapped her arms around Marcus's legs. He put his hand so softly on her head. That only made everything hurt more.

"I'm sorry, Lu," Marcus said. "I wouldn't take anything that was yours, not on purpose. Do you want it back?"

"No." Barely a whisper.

She turned to drag the cooler to Steve's house.

"Okay. . . . Tell Steve to let me know if he needs anything else. I can do an ice run or pick up charcoal or whatever."

The fog was already burning off, and Lu's gray hoodie felt too hot on the walk back to the house. She left the cooler in front of the garage door with some other ones of all different sizes that neighbors had dropped off.

By ten thirty, Steve had been to the store twice already, bringing back ice and more rolls for the hot dogs and burgers; big disposable aluminum trays to serve meat and beans and salad in; red plastic cups.

Steve said to Casey, "Next year you'll have your driver's license, and you can be my runner."

Lu thought he'd get an eye roll for that, but Casey

actually smiled and said, "You'll let me drive the truck?"

"As long as you don't try to go off-roading or anything," he said with a laugh.

If Casey had seen the alcohol and had any worries, she didn't say anything. Lu tried to give her meaningful glances as they ran around helping Steve. Maybe today was the day Casey had predicted—the day the *real* Steve would come out.

By eleven, Steve had filled all the coolers with beer and ice and lined them up on the driveway. The wine and liquor sat on top of the deep freezer with a stack of the red cups and more ice. He'd emptied some bags of chips and peanuts and pretzels into plastic bowls and put those on the freezer, too, then left one garage door open. He taped a hand-written sign on the other garage door that said *BAR* with an arrow pointing right to it.

"This is the signal," Steve said as he put another piece of silver tape on the sign to keep it up. "The party has officially started."

Mom stood in the driveway, watching. Lou tried to catch her eye and read her face, but there was nothing to see. Just blank smiling.

Then Steve opened a beer and handed it to Mom. And she took it.

Neighbors started showing up, drifting in and out of the garage with drinks and snacks. Steve set up his grill in the driveway and two other people brought grills, too.

Lu had settled on a step out front where she could keep an eye on things, but couldn't be seen from most angles. This wasn't a time to go into her bubble. This was a time to keep watch.

Everyone was friendly and happy now, but it was still early. And where was Casey?

She got up and went into the house. Casey wasn't in her room or in the TV room or the kitchen or anywhere. Lu couldn't help remembering how Kyra's mom had started drinking in high school and then didn't really stop until four years ago. The more she looked around the house, the more panicked she felt.

One part of her brain told her it was okay, she could trust Mom and Mom trusted Steve and there were Marcus and Shannon and Meg, and all these months had gone by and none of them had ever acted like Dad.

Another part of her brain told her to be ready for anything.

She went to her room where she couldn't see that much from her window, but she could listen. Soon, she heard Kyra's loud and happy voice.

Lu got on her knees on her bed and shouted, "Kyra!"

When Kyra looked up, Lu waved at her to come inside. A minute later, Kyra opened the bedroom door. She had on jeans that had the kinds of holes in the knees that were supposed to be there and a flowered T-shirt and fresh braids. "What are you doing?"

"Hiding."

Kyra closed the door behind her. "Why?"

"Can I ask you a question?" Lu said. "About your mom?"

Kyra nodded and came closer.

"When she's at a party like this one. A party like this. Do you worry, like . . ." Lu touched her callused left hand with her softer right one. "With so much beer and vodka and stuff around?" Her voice had become so small. She didn't know how to talk about this stuff. Mom barely did. Dad never did. How was she supposed to know what to ask? "How does she not drink?" Lu finally said. "Is that a stupid thing to ask?"

Kyra shook her head. "No."

"Do you worry?"

"Sometimes." She pulled the tips of both braids together under her chin. "Do you want to ask my mom?"

Lu's stomach dropped. "Won't she be mad? Or . . ." "Mad" wasn't the right word. "Will she answer?"

"We talk about this stuff a lot."

"You do?"

"Mom says you're only as sick as your secrets."

Lu wasn't sure what *that* meant, but when Kyra said "Come on" and took her hand, she let herself be pulled out of hiding.

45

MEG AND MOM WERE CHATTING in the driveway. Mom still held the bottle of beer. Meg was drinking a bubbly water.

"Hey, girls," Mom said with her usual smile.

"Mom, can we talk to you for a minute?" Kyra asked Meg.

"Go ahead," Mom said. "I have to circulate."

They went around the side of the house into the backyard and sat at the picnic table. Meg had on a sundress. Her arms were strong and tan, her bright blond hair loose. Lu wasn't sure how to start but before she could think it through, Kyra said, "Lu wants to know how you don't drink when there's all this booze around. Like at a party."

For a second, Meg *did* look mad, and Lu was sure they'd done something wrong, asking something like that.

"I didn't mean, like, *you* you," Lu said. "My dad . . ." Her face twitched. Heat burned behind her eyes. What was she trying to say? "Drinking ruined my dad's life. If it's so bad, why did Steve get all this alcohol? Why does my mom have a beer?"

While Lu had been talking, Meg's face had softened. "Well," she said, "not everyone has the kind of problems with alcohol that I have."

"Or your dad," Kyra added.

"Some people have a drink and they enjoy it and then they don't feel like they need to have five more or ten more or a million more. Some people have a couple of drinks at a party like this. Some people even get intoxicated, but they don't go stick their head under a chocolate fountain or fall off their kid's skateboard and break their arm."

"She did both of those things," Kyra said, pointing at Meg.

"At the same party!"

Then, they both laughed. They *laughed*.

"Now, Steve *does* always go overboard with the booze at this party . . ." Meg said.

Lu flinched.

"Oh no, no, I don't mean that he drinks it. I've never seen Steve drink too much. I mean buying it. When he throws a party, he wants everyone to have a great time and have every single thing they want. It makes him happy."

Lu thought about the veggie burgers. "Hospitality," she said.

"Right. In his mind, he's not a good host if he doesn't have about gallon of tequila per person." Meg smiled. "I happen to think that if people want to drink, they can and should bring their own booze, but it's not my party."

"I used to worry, too," Kyra said to Lu, "when she first got sober."

"Oh yeah. Back to your question," Meg said. "How do I not drink. It's complicated and it's also simple. The simple version is: by not drinking. I just don't pick it up. I don't touch it, I don't put it in my body, one day at a time. The end."

One day at a time. Like the magnet on the fridge at Kyra's house.

"Why can't my dad do that?"

"That's the complicated part, honey. And I can't answer that for anyone but myself. Why didn't I stop sooner? Why didn't the first few times I tried stick? Those reasons are personal, and they're specific to each person with a problem." She tipped her head forward. "Does that make sense?"

It did, even though it wasn't an answer. Lu might not ever know what Dad's answers were. Maybe he didn't even know them himself.

Meg took a deep breath and clapped her hands down on her legs. "One last thing, okay? You don't have the power to make your dad drink, or to stop him from drinking. You know that, right?"

"I used to think I could stop her," Kyra said. "Or that it was my fault she did it in the first place. Or . . ." Her eyes flicked to Meg for a second and then back to Lu. "Or that it was my fault my dad left."

Meg put her arm around Kyra's shoulders and pulled her close.

"Did I answer your questions?" Meg asked Lu. "Is there anything else you want to know?"

Lu shook her head and noticed the skin prickles and zaps had stopped. Meg hadn't promised anything, or even really given her anything to hold on to about her dad, but she felt lighter anyway.

"If you think of anything else you want to ask," Meg said, "I'm here. And I'm glad you turned up in Kyra's life. It's good to have buddies to talk about all this stuff with. That's why I go to my meetings. One reason, anyway." She stood up. "Keek, let's me and you go get some food, okay? Lu, you can join us, if you'd like, or take a minute if you need."

They left the yard and Lu got up to go in and use the bathroom. As she did, she realized there was someone in the plastic chaise in the corner of the yard. The sun umbrella was angled so Lu could only see feet. Feet that were in Casey's black boots.

Lu pushed the umbrella back a little. "Were you sitting there this whole time?"

"I didn't mean to eavesdrop. Not on purpose." Casey

raked her fingers through her hair. "What Kyra's mom said was . . . good. I'm glad I heard it because honestly I was kind of freaked out, too, about all the booze."

"You were? I thought you didn't even notice."

She snorted. "How could I not notice? I mean, Steve bought *so much*. And he and Mom never mentioned it to us? Hello? A little heads-up would have been good. I think Mom sometimes forgets what we've been through. She's just glad everything with Dad is basically over and would rather focus on happy stuff."

"Sometimes she thinks about it, though." Lu thought of their bedtime conversation last night.

"True." Casey sighed. "I don't even like smelling alcohol on anyone's breath. Even a little. It just, like, triggers me. Even more than seeing people drinking. It's that smell."

Mom appeared at the sliding door just then, and stepped out of the family room into the yard. "There you are! I've been looking all over for you two. Everything okay?"

"Yep," Casey said.

"Belle, honey, Beth is here. Why don't you come join the party?"

Lu gave Beth a tour: family room, kitchen and dining area, living room. She pointed out the stairs to Mom and Steve's room, and then down the hall to Casey's. Finally, in her own room, she closed the door.

"Here it is. This is the smallest room in the house."

Beth sat on the edge of the bed. "It's so cute, though."

"At first I missed sharing with Casey. Now I like having a room all to myself. When you sleep over I can use this air mattress we used when we went camping, and you can have the bed. Oh yeah, we went camping! I swam in a river. Steve taught me how to build a fire. The main thing is to use enough kindling and make sure there's airflow between the logs. I'm learning a lot more guitar chords. I have calluses and everything so it doesn't hurt when I play. See?"

Lu held out her hands to Beth, palms up. Beth stared at them.

"You can feel the tough part at the tips of my fingers."

Beth silently touched her fingers; Lu suddenly realized how much she'd been talking. She sat next to Beth on the bed. "How about you?" she asked.

"I miss you at school. I wrote my own report about sad books but it wasn't very well organized, Ms. Tom said. I got a B-minus. I know if we did it together we would have at least got a B-*plus*."

"At least."

"You actually live pretty far away. It's not how I imagined when you first told me you were moving."

"I know. For me, either." Even for Casey, who had a phone and friends with cars, it hadn't turned out the way she thought.

They sat quietly on the bed for a minute, then Lu

said, "I'm hungry. Are you hungry?"

Beth nodded vigorously.

The party turned out to be a lot about the food. Everyone crowding around for seconds, thirds, fourths, however many servings they wanted.

Alan and Mr. Tsai hadn't come, but Beth's mom enjoyed Steve's food and chatted with him about the spices in his chicken marinade. And she drank a glass of wine.

Marcus had a beer in his hand every time Lu saw him.

She heard Shannon talking about her pear margarita recipe.

Meg only ever had bubbly water, and a few other adults also drank that or root beer or Cokes or whatever. It was a mix of people drinking all different things. No one was falling down or yelling or crying, the way Dad did when he drank.

Kyra and Beth tried talking to each other. It was nice, but Lu could tell they were both being nervous and polite, and after an hour or so Beth and her mom said goodbye.

"Now that I know where you are," Mrs. Tsai said, "maybe Beth can come down here and sleep over." Beth grinned and bounced up and down. Mrs. Tsai put her hand on the top of Beth's head and said, "We'll ask Daddy."

The party got quieter, and more of the people who'd come from places other than their block left, except for Kyra and Meg. The fog began to tumble down from the hillside and mostly who was left were neighbors like the Merritt-Mendozas and the people who lived right next door, and also an old friend of Steve's mom's who'd known Steve since he was little and lived around the corner.

"This is the lady who taught me how to cook, right here," Steve said with his arm around the lady, Mrs. Chandler. She was whitehaired and short, with a round face and pretty blue eyes.

"Not your mom?" Lu asked.

Mrs. Chandler and Steve both laughed. "Loreen hated to cook. Stevie would loiter around my yard with my own son after school when he smelled the bread baking."

Soon after that, Meg and Kyra left. "Remember," Kyra shouted, "only one week until the talent show!"

Marcus had Noodle in the baby carrier on his chest, and Shannon was herding Tala and Rosie toward their house. Before he left, too, Marcus came over to Lu. "Listen, about the bunk bed . . ."

"It's okay. It's just . . . well, my dad built it."

"Ah," Marcus said quietly, patting the baby. "I didn't know."

"We don't really have, like, pictures of us together. Me and my dad and Casey and everything." Lu swallowed, afraid she might cry. "Or a lot of good memories," she added carefully.

"But you had the bed."

He understood. She swallowed back more tears, but one

got out. She brushed it off her cheek.

"And you have the guitar," Marcus said. "Right?"

"Right." She managed a trembly smile.

Noodle cried a little in his carrier. Marcus said, "Shhh. Shhh." Then to Lu: "I'll see you Wednesday for one more practice before the talent show?"

They said goodbye, and fog continued to settle over the block, bringing a peaceful feeling to where there'd been noise and people.

When the house was dark and quiet that night, there was a knock at Lu's door. Casey came in wearing her pj's. She lay down on Lu's bed with her feet near Lu's head and her head at Lu's feet.

"That party was . . . *a lot*," she said. "I liked it, though."

"Me too."

"Dad texted to get the time and place for your talent show."

"We already told him."

"I know. I told him again." She lifted her head to look at Lu. "I can tell him not to come if you want. If you've changed your mind."

She was too tired to know if she'd changed her mind or not. "Don't you want to see him?" she asked Casey.

"I don't know. Sometimes I think I do, but then he's never what I want him to be."

Lu wrapped her arms around Casey's calves.

"Don't tickle my feet," Casey said drowsily.

It was tempting. Casey's feet were very ticklish, and tickling them would make her scream and jump up and run around the room.

She decided she'd rather keep her sister right here.

46

FOR DAYS LEADING UP TO the talent show, Mrs. Kemp, the principal, kept reminding everyone that it was supposed to be *fun*.

"Remember folks: *F-U-N*. Fun!" Mrs. Kemp said as she looked around at the cafeteria full of students on Friday. "This isn't a competition or Broadway or TV or YouTube, okay? This is just our little school and having fun with our creativity."

She reminded everyone there was no booing or other inappropriate behavior. It had never even crossed Lu's mind that someone might *boo*.

All she could think about was Dad maybe being there. It seemed like he was really going to come, double- and triple-checking the time and place. At bedtime last night,

Mom had asked Lu how she was feeling about him maybe coming, and if she wanted to uninvite him.

"Because you can," Mom had said. "You can ask him not to come or I can do it for you, if you've changed your mind."

"I want him to come." She was sure of it.

Mom, lying next to her, shifted her weight on the bed. "Even if he's like he was at the wedding?"

"He wouldn't be able to drive here and also be like that. Right?"

"Probably not. I can't be sure."

Lu sat up and scooted back to lean against the wall. Mom was still lying down. Her eyes were closed.

"I want to show him I learned to play the guitar he got me. I think that's what he wanted, and if I do a good job . . ." Then what? She thought about what Meg said, how there was nothing she could do to make him drink or not drink. "If I do a good job, he'll see. He'll see me."

"Oh, Belle." Mom opened her eyes and reached to put her hand on Lu's cheek. "I hope he does see you. You are a wonderful sight."

Part of her still wanted to ask: Then why did he leave? Why did he drink? Part of her wanted to play those questions over and over in her mind until she got calluses, until it didn't hurt to ask.

"But if he doesn't," Mom continued, "that's because of him, not because of you."

Lu nodded. She would have to play that thought over

and over, too. Practice it so much that she didn't really have to think it anymore, she would just know it.

Kyra and Lu had gotten as good as they could get. Alone, together, Lu with Marcus, and then in the run-through after school. Their song came in the second half, right after Chris Alcantara's trumpet solo. The run-through was okay until the middle of the song, when Lu played the wrong chord and then lost her place completely for the whole rest of it. Kyra kept singing but Lu never really got back in rhythm, so it didn't *sound* right.

"This is why we have run-through!" Mrs. Kemp said. "Get your nerves out so tomorrow it's perfect. I mean not perfect, but *fun*! And remember, folks, *please*, I *beg* of you, start walking onstage when the audience is applauding the previous act. Transitions are so important!"

"You're not going to mess up tomorrow, right?" Kyra asked when they were backstage after. "Because that was *bad*."

"I'll try not to."

"You have to do more than try!"

"I said I'll try!" Lu snapped.

Then they didn't talk to each other until they got there on Saturday for the performance.

They'd planned their outfits: jeans and black T-shirts. They had been talking with Meg about getting or making matching dresses with some sequins or something, but when Casey heard that, she said, "No no no. Keep it simple. That's how you look cool. Trust me."

Lu did trust Casey but she'd also double-checked with Marcus when they had their lesson on Wednesday. "Casey is one hundred percent right. One *hundred*." He held up a finger and added, "Also, you need a super-awesome guitar strap." He reached into his guitar case. "Like this one."

It was a black strap embroidered with neon-thread stars.

"Where'd you get that?" Lu had asked.

"I made it."

"*You* made it?"

"Yeah. My mom taught me how to sew when I was in high school. She's a seamstress."

Now the black strap with stars was attached to her guitar. And they had their black T-shirts and their jeans and sneakers. Kyra's braids wrapped around her head like Casey had shown her, and Lu's hair was pinned back so it wouldn't get in her face when she played.

Backstage, Lu tuned her guitar while Kyra watched. "You practiced since yesterday?" Kyra asked.

"Yes."

"How was it?"

"Fine. It's always fine when I'm alone in my room."

"I know, but—"

"Kyra, can you please stop talking about it? You're making me more nervous."

"Sorry. Is your dad here?"

"I don't *know*."

In the audience were Meg, Mom, Steve, Casey, Marcus, Shannon, and Rosie. Tala and Noodle were home with Marcus's mom. Lu hoped Rosie could stay quiet enough for the whole thing.

She'd worked out a system with Casey. If when Lu went out onstage, Casey's blue scarf was on, it meant Dad wasn't there. If he *was* there, she'd take her scarf off. That way Lu wouldn't be distracted scanning the audience for him while she was supposed to be remembering and playing chords.

The show started. They could hear kids doing jokes, kids tap-dancing, kids playing piano, kids singing. When it was very quiet, they knew it was a boy from fourth grade doing a monologue in sign language. Next would be Chris and his trumpet. Then them.

Kyra was hopping from foot to foot and shaking her hands out.

Lu took deep breaths and went through the chord progression in her head.

She repeated what Meg had said to her in her mind, and also what Mom said last night. She couldn't make Dad drink or not drink. She couldn't make him leave or not leave. Love her or not love her. *See* her, or not. And she couldn't make him be here, or go away. Whatever he did, it was up to him.

Chris was in the loudest part of his solo, which meant it was almost over.

Kyra turned to Lu and said in a rush, "No matter what, it will be good. It will be fun! I'm not worried, okay? We'll just do our best."

Lu smiled and nodded. She was still nervous, and she didn't know what was going to happen, but standing there with Kyra next to her and people who loved her in the audience, she was glad she'd decided to do this.

Chris played the last note, and everyone clapped. Mrs. Kemp waved them out and whispered, "Go now! Go!"

Kyra adjusted the mic she was going to sing into while Lu positioned her chair and set the other mic up so it was pointing toward the hole in the guitar, just like Marcus had shown her. She looked at the spot in the audience where Casey should be sitting—on the aisle halfway up. She was there.

And she wasn't wearing her scarf.

Lu thought she would be happy—and she was—but as Kyra nodded to indicate she was ready, Lu's eyes didn't go to the crowd to find where Dad might be. They went to Steve and Mom. Steve's arm was around Mom's shoulders and her hand was on his leg. Steve saw Lu look, and grinned.

For confidence, she found Marcus next to Steve. He gave her a thumbs-up.

Her eyes went to Meg, beaming. And then back to Casey, where she'd started, who now had her phone up to take a picture.

Lu played the first chord.

"Well, it wasn't the *best* we've done, but it wasn't the *worst*, either," Kyra said as soon as they got offstage.

Lu's head was buzzing from what just happened. They did the song and she only messed up once, at the beginning, and it was over in a flash. The rest was almost perfect.

"He's here," she told Kyra, and suddenly wanted to burst into tears. She held it in.

"You saw him?"

She pressed her lips together and shook her head. "Not yet."

"Girls!" Mrs. Kemp had her finger up to her lips.

After all the performances, the kids in the talent show went out to find their families and friends in the audience. Lu hunted for Dad but couldn't see him, or Casey. But Mom and Steve were waiting for her.

Mom hugged Lu and said what a good job she'd done. Steve said, "Can I give you a hug, too?" And she said yes.

Marcus arrived next, and gave her a high five. Shannon said, "You guys looked very chill up there!"

"Thanks," Lu said, craning her neck to see through the crowd. "Where's Casey?"

Shannon pointed toward the main entrance. "She's out there. With your dad."

Lu maneuvered her guitar case through the crowd of kids and parents and out into the schoolyard where people were having punch and cookies.

Dad and Casey were standing a little ways from the door.

Dad didn't look drunk. She wasn't sure he was sober, but he was sober enough to not look drunk. When he saw her, he smiled, and opened his arms.

Lu went to him and hugged him. He felt both thinner and softer. Older. His face looked tired and his clothes didn't smell too fresh. She felt a surge of love and sadness at the same time. She didn't want to let go. Tears pushed at her eyes. He let go first.

"Hey, don't cry, Lula." It came out sweeter, kinder than the version she always heard him saying in her head, and she wondered if she'd remembered it wrong all this time. He held her back from him. "You were great. I forgot you had such a nice voice."

"You heard me on the 'dooga-doon's?" She looked up into his face. His eyes weren't quite finding hers.

"Sure did."

"Yeah," Casey said. "It came through."

Dad asked about school, and she said it was fine, and he said, "I'm working on getting a place again. We'll see. I might have to move over to the East Bay, or I was even thinking about Sacramento or Redding . . ."

Sacramento. That was far. Farther than they'd ever been from each other.

He kept talking, and she waited for him to say something about the guitar, but he never did, and when their talking dwindled down, and Casey started biting her thumb, Lu said, "I've really been working on learning this." She patted the case.

"Yeah! I'm impressed."

"I have some of your old records, too. I've been listening to those. I'm going to try to learn a song from one of them next."

"Oh, good." He nodded, as if to himself. "Yeah I miss those records. I miss a lot of my stuff, but there's not much room in the van."

Lu glanced at Casey. "The guitar . . . it's kind of big for me now, but I'll grow into it and be able to do more chords."

"You will." He touched the case. "Yeah, that's maybe a full dreadnought. A lot of guitar for a little girl. Where'd you get that?"

Casey looked at him.

"It's . . ." Lu stopped, started again. "It's the one you gave me."

"*I* gave you?"

Maybe he'd forgotten. It wouldn't be the first time he'd forgotten things, blacked out, lost his sense of time and memory.

"For my birthday," she said. "Back in February."

"You left it by the front door of the apartment," Casey added. "Or you got someone else to? Remember?"

He shook his head. "I was in the drunk tank on your birthday, kiddo. I got picked up for disorderly conduct and

~343~

I remember because I told the officer it was my daughter's birthday and I'll never forget what he said. 'I hope you got her a better present than this,' he said. And I realized I hadn't. I hadn't gotten you anything."

"Dad," Casey said. "Are you sure?"

Lu watched his face. He didn't seem confused at all.

"I don't know what to say, Lula, but I didn't get you that guitar."

47

Lu watched more of the post-show commotion, hugging her guitar case against her and watching as Mom went over to Dad without Steve, and then Dad leaving barely a minute after that. She felt she had one foot in her bubble and one in the real world as Dad glanced back and waved goodbye. Casey stayed near, and Kyra and Meg hugged Lu.

Then they were in Steve's truck, driving home.

When they got there, they made ice cream sundaes the way Mrs. Chandler had taught him when he was a kid: Vanilla ice cream. Hershey's syrup. Dry-roasted peanuts. Whipped cream from a can.

"No cherries because I hated cherries," Steve said. "Still do."

Lu began to feel more anchored, closer instead of far

away. Steve and Mom talked about the different performances in the show, and Casey gave them all her reviews.
She showed Lu the pictures and videos she'd taken. "I was
right about the jeans and T-shirts. You guys were the coolest."

After they'd had their dessert, Lu started to help clean
up but Steve said, "Hey, El, can I talk to you in the yard for
a minute? You can leave the dishes, it's okay."

She followed him out to the back. There hadn't been
any fog that night, so the yard furniture was dry enough to
sit on. Lu took the chaise and Steve perched on one of the
picnic benches. A light breeze rustled the trees.

"I have to confess something," he said. "And I'll understand if you're upset."

Lu swallowed. She realized then how exhausted she
was. "What?"

"I'm the one who gave you that guitar."

Lu froze. *Steve?*

"Your birthday was coming up, and well, I knew you
weren't exactly the biggest fan of me." He sliced the air
with his hand and chuckled. "Probably an understatement."

That felt like such a long time ago now. "Sorry," she said.

"No, no, that was your right. You don't have to apologize.
Anyway, a guy at work asked me about the cargo box I used
to have on my truck. I wasn't really using it much, so I
asked him if he maybe wanted to trade." Steve held up one
finger. "He had a mountain bike." Held up another finger.
"A brand-new chain saw." He held up a third finger and
wiggled it. "And a guitar."

"But . . ."

"I know." He held up his hands. "It seems kind of random. But I don't bike. I heard him say 'guitar' and thought, 'Sure, I'll take that.' Maybe one of you girls would like it, I thought. And then it was your birthday. We'd already gotten you the jacket, but I'd seen you packing up your dad's old records even though your mom had set them aside to be thrown out. And I thought you might be interested in . . . Well, I didn't want to overdo it and make some dumb Steve move, trying to look like I wanted win you over. Which . . ." He chuckled again. "It pretty much was."

"It wasn't dumb." Lu was still trying to catch up, still thinking—*Steve?* But she knew what he did wasn't dumb.

"I don't know. I guess I thought a mysterious, anonymous gift would be fun. Something sort of magical during a time that was obviously hard for you. I didn't even tell your mom. I probably should have." He ran his fingers through the fluffy part of his hair on the back of his head, then patted it down. "I didn't know you'd tie it in to your dad and all. I didn't mean to make a hard thing harder."

"You didn't." At first she said it to make sure he didn't feel bad. But when she heard those words they felt true, too. "You didn't," she said again.

Steve had a funny smile on his face, like he could either laugh or cry in an instant. "I know, um . . ." He cleared his throat. "I know you've been working hard at it, maybe to prove something to your dad. Thinking it was from him. And now that you know it wasn't, it's okay if you don't

347

want to play anymore. You don't have to like it."

"I do like it," she said. In fact, she couldn't picture the last few months without it. Without lessons with Marcus and practicing with Kyra and having something of her own.

"Well, you can change your mind down the line, if you want. You don't have to prove anything to me. You know?"

She nodded. "I know."

"Good. Well."

He stood up and she stood up and they both headed for the sliding door, and when they were right next to each other, she put her arms around his waist and held on tight.

That night in bed, a heaviness in her chest pressed harder and harder as she thought about the whole evening. She wasn't mad at Steve. Not at all.

But she missed the idea that Dad had given her the guitar. In the end, there'd been no secret message from him, no hidden sign of his love or her specialness to him.

Maybe, she thought, those things shouldn't be secret or hidden.

He *had* come to see her. That was real.

And she did miss him; that was real, too.

The pressure in her chest moved up to her throat, her nose, her eyes. What she needed to do was cry.

Don't cry, Lu, Dad's voice said. It was the softer, kinder voice, like he'd used tonight. But still: *Lula, don't cry.*

Then Steve's voice in her memory interrupted. *It's okay, Lu. I know it hurts.*

She rolled over to push her face into the pillow, and stopped trying to hold everything back.

You'll be okay, Steve's voice continued. *You're doing really great. You'll be okay.*

PART VI

We, Again

48

DURING THE NIGHT, THE FOG stole in and brought its chill all the way to the ground. Lu would need both her fleece vest and her jean jacket for the ride to church.

The fleece felt heavier than she expected. After she put it on, she remembered: the secret pocket. It was still full of the stolen things. She hadn't stolen since . . . the Jolly Rancher stick, the day she'd found Daisy Dobrov over at Beth's. Half of it was still carefully wrapped up in the pocket.

She took it out and put it on her desk. It wasn't exactly in any condition to be returned to the store, and she still might want to eat it later.

Casey had been in the shower for ages and it would take her another eon to do her hair and makeup. Lu went into her room and laid the eyeliner pencil on the geometry book that was open on her bed.

Steve was in the kitchen, on coffee duty as always. Lu told him she had to run up to the Merritt-Mendozas' for a minute. "I'll be right back."

"Okey-doke."

She ran up the block and looked around the front yard. She took Rosie's troll doll from her pocket and left it standing up on the big rock she liked to sit on. Its green hair stood straight up.

Back at home, when Steve had taken Mom's coffee upstairs, Lu put his marker in the kitchen drawer where he kept scissors and rubber bands and more markers. The carved wooden acorn was harder to let go of. It fit so neatly in her palm, the little cap and stem made with such detail. She'd let go of a lot of stuff this year that *did* belong to her and she wished she could keep this. But she placed it carefully on the same shelf she'd gotten it from, only a few inches over, and hoped Steve wouldn't ask any questions.

That left the red envelope and the rest of Alan's money. If the acorn was hard to let go of, the money she wanted to burn. It was a reminder of being a bad friend to Beth and of the moment Beth had discovered it.

She reminded herself that Beth had forgiven her.

It wasn't the same as making it up to Alan, but she couldn't think how to do that. For now, she decided she'd put the leftover money in the offering plate at church and let God sort it out.

Even though everyone had gotten up on time, there was a sudden rush in the last ten minutes before leaving for the city. Mom spilled coffee on her shirt and Casey couldn't find her last boiled egg.

"It's not as if there's a food shortage, Case." Mom dabbed a wet towel at her blouse. "There's still enough party leftovers to throw another party. Find something else and let's go."

"I'm having chicken and potato salad for breakfast," Lu said, showing Casey her plate.

"But I always have boiled eggs!"

"Yes, Casey," Steve said with a laugh, "we all know about your boiled eggs."

We.

Lu smiled.

"I'm going to have to change my shirt," Mom said, and threw the towel on the rim of the sink.

"We'll wait," Steve said.

There it was again. *We.*

Mom ran up the stairs, her footfalls clomping on the wooden boards. Steve gently moved Casey away from the fridge door and dug through shelves of leftovers. In a minute, he straightened up and said, "Is this what you're looking for?"

He held out a boiled brown egg.

Casey squealed and grabbed it. She gave Steve a fast little hug. "Thanks."

The real Steve *had* come out after the honeymoon, and this was him.

Lu wanted to try out the *we*, too. "We might all need a nap after church."

"Yes," Steve said, "I think we might."

Casey cracked her egg against the edge of the kitchen counter and started to peel it. Lu caught her eye. "Don't you think we'll be tired?" she asked Casey. "After yesterday?"

"Um, probably."

"Or we could go to bed early," Lu tried.

"Also an option." Casey shook salt onto her peeled egg.

Mom's footsteps clomped back down and she came into the kitchen while pulling back her hair. "We're all ready?"

Casey rolled her eyes. "*Yes*, Mom. We've *been* ready."

Lu took her last bite of breakfast and laughed.

"What's so funny?" Casey asked. "Are you laughing at me?"

"No. Just that I got you to say it."

"Say what?"

"Girls, we do not have time for whatever this is," Mom said. She swung her arms as if scooting them out of the kitchen. "Figure it out in the car."

Lu couldn't help herself.

"We will."